Grant Hill

Grant Hill was born in Dundee in 1979. He has worked in journalism, public relations, call centres, pubs and a pea factory. A DJ of extremely limited technical ability, he founded the now infamous Teckle Collective and counts Shaun Ryder, Eric Cartman and Tommy Coyne among his heroes.

Clubbed to Death is his first book.

D0321439

CLUBBED
TO DEATH

by
GRANT
HILL

CLUBBED TO DEATH

Published by Teckle Books Ltd

286 Blackness Road
Dundee DD2 1RZ

For more copies of this book, please email:
frank@tecklebooks.co.uk

Designed and set by Chris Collins

Printed in Great Britain by Bell & Bain Ltd, Glasgow

For Vicki, who makes my life better in every way,
and the bump, who will change it in every way.

ONE

As she glanced over her shoulder, Emma Morgan was being assured that the cavernous church had been built during less secular times, so the sparsely-populated pews were no reflection on the popularity of her recently deceased father.

The comforting voice belonged to her husband, Cornelius, who added, 'unlike the big stand at Kenilworth Road' before chuckling, oblivious to both accepted standards of funeral etiquette and not everyone being conversant with the Luton-Watford rivalry.

Emma's murderous stares were not reserved for Cornelius. The bulk of her ire was directed at Andy. Her brother had insisted that funeral arrangements weren't something a six-months pregnant woman should have to deal with. This selflessness was exposed as a sham when Father Kevin announced that the organist had been replaced by an indie-dance mix tape supposedly compiled in honour of the late Dave Brennan. Emma confidently predicted that the staunch Elvis fan would be denouncing his funeral soundtrack as 'tuneless pish' should he happen to be listening in from the next world.

Upon arriving at the church, Emma learned her younger sibling had also insisted on delivering a eulogy, which she felt sure would be little more than another shameless exercise in self-promotion. She and her husband sat on the other side of the church from Andy, such was the very real risk she would assault him at the most inappropriate moment possible. To Emma's further consternation, Cornelius complained about this arrangement, telling her, 'I need to be there for Andy, baby'.

In contrast to the sober funeral attire worn by other mourners, Cornelius was sporting an electric blue tuxedo and a pencil-thin moustache he was growing in an attempt to look like Otis Redding. He tapped his foot to Blue Monday, the

7

famous synth bass line incongruous as it echoed around the stone walls, and Emma wished she was as promiscuous as she had been in her younger days so the baby she was carrying might not be his.

The song faded out and Emma found herself praying the whole shambolic prelude had finished, only for her hopes to be shattered as the intro to Ebeneezer Goode kicked in from somewhere behind the pulpit. Cornelius leant into his wife and whispered, 'You've got to hand it to Andy, that's a cracking compilation, eh?' in her ear.

Whether through grief or awareness that she was pregnant by an utter buffoon, Emma burst into loud, uncontrollable sobbing. This continued as Father Kevin ran through all the usual guff about God and the Bible, even though the dead man was nominally Catholic at best. He then outlined a few biographical details, mainly erroneous, before Andy was invited up to the pulpit to pay tribute. His fiancée Michelle squeezed his hand and whispered something supportive in his ear before he grunted and staggered to the front of the church. Ashen-faced and startled, Andy looked up, coughed and started to speak.

'First of all, I'd like to thank youse for comin, I know my old man would...I know my old man'd be happy to see so many people here. Although if he were still alive youse wouldn't be here so really he wouldn't erm...' Emma's wails subsided and her heart raced in dread.

'Ummm. There's a Jane's Addiction song called Had A Dad,' he continued. 'An it ended with the words "God is Dead"!'

Father Kevin looked concerned, offended and angry, though not as much as Emma.

'An that's pretty insightful for Perry Farrell. But I'm no here to talk about how the alternative crossed over to the mainstream in the early 90s...'

'Awww,' moaned one visibly distressed mourner only to be silenced by the angry grinding of his wife's teeth.

'But what Dad meant to us. He did everythin for me an Emma. He raised us on his own. He'd come home exhausted every day from a job he hated, an that got me thinkin about work an love an family an what it means to live your life.'

Wiping away a tear, Cornelius leant over to his wife and whispered, 'Lollapalooza' in her ear as if explaining the world's greatest mystery.

Andy went on. 'An Dad gave everythin to us. An I know he'd want us to live the lives we want, no be stuck in jobs we hate. Errm, the point is my Dad worked to give us hope, to support us an nurture us. An now he won't even see his first grandchild born.'

Andy paused at this point to let the full tragedy of his father's untimely passing sink in. Looking around to ensure the last line had had its desired effect and satisfied to see tissues be proffered around, he drew himself up to his full height and changed gear as he approached the speech's life-altering climax.

'An that's why I've decided to do somethin to honour him. So I've quit my job.'

Gasps could be heard around the church. Michelle looked stunned. Emma looked as if she might go into premature labour. The smattering of mourners began muttering to each other before Andy hushed them with a raised hand.

'I've decided to invest in somethin, my own business, a family business. I'd like to invite youse all, my family, my father's friends, even though there aren't that many of you, to the grand openin of Dundee's newest nightclub!'

The muttering ceased. Everyone sat open-mouthed and confused at Andy's stupidity, except for one renegade funeral-goer who clambered onto his pew and began applauding.

*   *   *

Emma eventually succeeded in pulling Cornelius back into his seat by grabbing his tuxedo, and continued to take her anger out on her husband's favourite fashion item during the short journey to the crematorium, wrenching the sleeve until the stitches surrendered. As the body of a man he loved and respected was reduced to ash, Cornelius watched his wife transfer a considerable volume of tears and snot on to an oversize, electric blue handkerchief. He wondered how anyone could do something so violent to such a beautiful piece of tailoring. The awesome power of grief, he reasoned with a shudder.

A quarter of an hour later, Andy had finally shaken hands with the last of the mourners, most of whom had advised him not to make any rash financial decisions and reminded him of the Bank of England's gloomy economic forecast. Michelle rubbed his arm and looked concerned, not least because her future sister-in-law was making a mockery of her condition by pacing towards them wielding a shovel stolen from the nearby garden of remembrance. Pushing assorted relatives, family friends and hangers-on aside she broke into a sprint as she neared Andy, with Cornelius, hampered by the tightness of his tuxedo trousers, lagging some way behind. Emma grabbed her brother, pinned him against the wall and held the shovel to his throat.

'Did you just ruin your own father's fuckin funeral to talk about fuckin Wayne's Addiction an a fuckin nightclub?'

'Jane's, baby, come on."

'Shut up, Cornelius. Did you Andy? Did you just do that?'

'I didn't ruin anythin.'

'Andy, what've you done?' Michelle asked whilst attempting to wrest control of the potentially lethal digging implement from Emma, who refused to surrender her grip on either it or Andy.

Several minutes of undignified grappling followed before the combination of Cornelius and Michelle managed to prise Emma away from a life sentence in Cornton Vale as she swore there was literally nothing in her brother's stupid, massive head.

'Metaphorically nothin, you mean,' he said, after regaining his composure and adjusting the collar of his shirt to restore blood flow to a dome that would, by any objective standard, indeed be described as substantial. 'An I've done somethin brilliant. We've got it all worked out.'

Bitter experience made Emma all too aware of the last

sentence's significance. 'We?' She turned to her husband. 'Cornelius? What d'you know about this shite?'

'Well, Andy mentioned it and I mentioned I know this DJ who'd be perfect. I mean, I can't be the DJ, even though Andy asked me to...'

'I didn't.'

'...when you're in such a delicate condition.' He attempted to pat Emma's belly only for his hand to be slapped away.

'Andy, we need to talk about this,' pleaded Michelle, her eyes fixed on the shovel Emma retained possession of whilst making it explicitly clear why it was unacceptable for him to blow half the money their father had worked his whole life for the minute he died.

'It's what he would've wanted,' he protested, looking sky-wards. 'I'll make him proud of me. An besides, I can't fail. The Quantum's already locked in.'

'Oh? An what the fuck's the quantum?'

'It's not an it,' interjected Cornelius. 'He's a he. The DJ.'

Andy nodded enthusiastically. 'DJ Quantum. You know quantum theory? That for every decision you make, there's a parallel dimension where you made the other decision, went left instead of right.'

'Where your Dad listened to the doctor about all that red meat,' added Cornelius sagely.

'Well, that's DJ Quantum. He's got every possible song in his head, every possible mix, so he always knows what the best song to play next is.'

Cornelius manoeuvred his sleeveless arm around as if work-ing a turntable. 'Every song. Is the best song. Ever. He's even better than me when I had that residency in Ibiza. If he DJ'd a wake your Dad would get up and dance.' He considered this for a moment. 'Maybe not after being cremated right enough.'

Emma pointed at Andy. 'You're a prick. You,' she pointed to Cornelius, 'don't get any ideas. Let's go before I kill him. Michelle, you really can do a million times better than that big-headed cunt.'

Emma turned on her heels and marched off in the direction of the street. Cornelius watched her go before turning to Andy and Michelle.

'Remember, if DJ Q needs a night off I'm your man. Residency in Ibiza.' He gave them the thumbs up before waddling off after his wife.

Andy watched them disappear into the distance and put his arm round Michelle. 'What a bitch, eh? Imagine actin like that at your own Dad's funeral.'

TWO

Prior to rashly blowing his inheritance on a failing nightclub, Andy had not been a man for extravagant purchases. His previous biggest investments had been Michelle's engagement ring and a red vinyl copy of Screamadelica, the price differential between alleged precious minerals and coloured plastic not being as great as one might imagine. Money well spent, he reasoned, as he paced around the living room displaying more excitement than a man who'd just returned from his father's funeral rightfully should. The cover sleeve was waved at Michelle for emphasis as he shared his plans for an after-dark emporium with her.

'I mean, can you imagine it?' Andy asked. 'It's half two in the mornin. You're out your box. You've just had three hours of beautiful, seamlessly mixed tunes an then, "Just what is it you want to do?" Thousands of fellow ravers...well capacity is about 200...point is youse all raise your arms in the air an answer as one, "We want to be free, we want to be free to do what we want to do". How can that fail? Know where I was when I first heard this? The church under-18s disco. Then the DJ took it off an played I Am The One An Only. From that moment onwards it was my mission to never let Primal Scream play second fiddle to Chesney Hawkes again.'

Michelle had heard many versions of Andy's 'I had a dream' speech over the years, normally focusing on how under-appreciated his numerous indie-dance bands had been, particularly The Go-Ahead Seagulls, whose implosion he remained acutely bitter about. The awkward minutes of silence that characterised Cornelius' pitiful attempts to mix records had briefly inspired him to attempt DJing before quitting due to the industry becoming 'too political'. Never had he expressed a burning desire to become an impresario though.

She handed Andy the umpteenth cup of tea she'd made since returning from the wake some hours earlier, smiled sadly and stroked his arm before clearing her throat.

'Aye, but that's no reason to blow everythin your Dad worked for..."

'Half.'

'...half of everythin he worked for when you're no thinkin straight.'

'Dad wouldn't want me to waste my life sellin insurance in a call centre.'

'But he always said you were lucky to have that job.'

'Know what his dream was?' asked Andy, ignoring Michelle. 'To eat the legendary 72oz steak at the Big Texan diner in Amarillo. Said he'd do it when he retired. He'd been in trainin for months. Then, two weeks before retirement, he drops dead of a heart attack. What does that tell you?'

'That high cholesterol really is a killer?'

Andy kissed his fiancée and put his arm round her before returning to his discourse on the matter of unrealised ambition. 'Cornelius's dream is to own the world's rarest collectable record. Twenty year he's been savin up for Frank Wilson's Do I Love You? He's got thousands stashed away for the next time it comes on the market. He says the club's a definite goer.'

Michelle was neither reassured nor surprised to hear that what amounted to due diligence on the deal was a thumbs-up from Andy's brother-in-law, an accountant unable to tell the difference between odd and even numbers.

'Carpe diem,' said Andy, looking into the middle distance. 'This's my diem.'

'But...'

'Look, you seen the state of me when I heard about my old man. Then the very next day we were round at Emma's sortin stuff out an Cornelius mentioned that it was the second piece of bad news that week after Storm was put up for sale. It was a sign, Michelle.'

Michelle, impatient for the point of this "How I Came to

Have an Epiphany" anecdote to be reached, protested that she didn't even know what or where Storm was.

'Storm,' explained Andy, 'is the best nightclub in Dundee. The only one to play proper music. Well, it was great a few year ago when it was the Boogie Room. Mind, we used to go all the time. Before that it was Babylon. An Empire. Le Storm, the Perfect Storm. It keeps shuttin down an re-openin with a new name.'

She shook her head, long brown curls bouncing from side to side as she did so. 'Does that no tell you somethin?'

'It tells me there's a great business opportunity to be had.' Andy kissed Michelle's head and pulled her closer to his chest. 'Look, I know you're worried, but this place is totally goin to blow you away.'

*   *   *

Storm was a run-down nightclub in a run-down former industrial unit in a run-down part of Dundee city centre, sandwiched between the bus station and a homeless shelter. As she approached it the day after the funeral, Michelle winced at the memory of previous visits. Empty dancefloors. Weird music. Unsuccessful attempts to copulate in disgusting toilets. If anything, the place looked even more dilapidated now. Rain lashed down as they stood across the road looking at the heavily bolted steel door and the sign (minus the 'M') above it that picked out the club's name. Andy's enthusiasm was irrepressible, if not infectious, as he led Michelle by the hand to the entrance.

'Impressive, eh?'

'It's like somethin from a horror film.'

Missing that the observation was not intended as a compliment, Andy nodded, bashed on the door and shouted at no one in particular, 'HELLOOO?'

'Does anyone even go clubbin these days? I thought you said they all just sat in gettin out their face, watching X Factor an doin bad karaoke on the PlayStation?'

Andy's smile colonised new areas of his not inconsiderably

dimensioned face as he rubbed dirt from the door on to jeans that remained baggy in defiance of post-90s style. 'Ah! But that's where I come in, Michelle. Technology is killin music so someone needs to take a stand.'

'But why does that someone have to be you?'

'Cos I happened to be the one who got lucky with their Dad dying. It was a sign. No thon one though,' he said nodding upwards to the M-less neon. 'Pop Factor. Downloadin. MPfrees. Pish. I want to read sleeve notes, admire the cover artwork, feel a smooth 12 inches in my hand.'

'Well, we'd all like that...'

The sound of a bolt being undone from inside made them jump. Then another. And another. In all, 17 heavy security devices were unlatched before the door swung inwards. A slim man in his mid-20s sporting a Fairisle jumper, skinny chinos that stopped above sockless ankles and a hipster quiff stood before them as a smell of pure evil invaded their nasal cavities.

'Oh my god,' said Michelle, recoiling. 'What's that smell?'

Their host held his hands up. 'Apologies. Bit of a rough night to be honest. Toilet's a bit backed up but the smell won't last.' He appraised his visitors. 'You must be Andy, aye?' He offered his hand, re-thought the gesture, and wiped it on his shirt before holding it out to Andy, who dubiously accepted the shake.

'Errr, yeah. An this is Michelle.'

Appraising her with Carry On-subtlety, he turned back to Andy. 'Here, you've done alright for yoursel, chief. Must be true what they say about a man with a big head.'

Pointedly declining the stranger's hand, Michelle asked who he might be.

'I'm Gibby. Gibby Wisdom. I manage...' he said, glancing up. 'Stor. You might want to fix that.'

'We're thinkin about changin the name.'

'Good idea. This place hasn't had a great reputation since the drownins.'

Michelle had tried to learn as much as possible about grief in the past fortnight, but nowhere had any of the literature on the

Kubler-Ross Model mentioned obliviousness to a nightclub's shortcomings. With each health hazard Gibby pointed out on the subsequent tour, Andy seemed to grow more positive, meeting each troubling revelation with an effusive nod.

Following on from a cellar Gibby described as 'wetter than the front row on the Take That reunion tour', toilets unfit for human use, numerous shattered windows and a stairwell with more broken than functioning steps, Michelle and Andy were led through a set of double doors towards the main body of the club. A bleak dancefloor was set in the middle of upholstered bench seating that was pockmarked by slash marks and cigarette burns, yet still appeared grander than the standard issue school-plastic chairs, rickety wooden stools and garden tables that complemented it. Peeling wallpaper exposed cracked plaster. A bar that appeared to have been transported from the 1850s, complete with spitting trough, stood – just – at one end of the room, a beat-up booth bearing the grafitti 'THIS DJ DOESNT DOO REQESTS" at the other.

Flipping a switch which failed to provide any light, Gibby turned to the tour party. 'An this is where the magic happens, chief.'

While the new boss was almost beside himself with excitement, his fiancée had spent the visit calculating the cost of bringing the place up to a level that concentration camp inmates would not baulk at.

'I say this whilst tryin to be positive an supportive, you know that, but I can't...I just can't escape the feelin that Stor is a bit of a shithole.'

'A what?' spluttered Gibby. 'I'll have you know I clean this place thoroughly whenever I get tipped off about a visit from Health & Safety. Our regular works for them.'

'This place has regulars?'

'Aye, Brian. Good lad.

'There is an overpowerin smell of damp though.'

'Like I said, there was the flood. Tragic like, but Brian fixed it. Coroner eventually ruled death by misadventure. No our fault.' He winked at Andy, whose thoughts were racing ahead.

'So, the future. No one knows a club like its staff so I want to hear your ideas.'

'For this place?'

'Yes.'

'My honest opinion?'

'Absolutely.'

'Fanny.'

Gibby's suggestion was delivered with enough force and conviction to divert Michelle's attention from the rodent-like movement across the bar top and ask him to expand upon his theory.

'We need decent fanny. This place is like the Ministry of Hound most weekends. Get fit birds in an then the lads will follow an buy beer.'

'Right, I'm thinkin more along the lines of phat beats an that...'

'Base desires, chief. Satisfyin them lies at the heart of every successful business. We're naked apes that need to pass on our selfish genes. Sex drove millions of years of evolution, no the Oakenfold remix of Wrote for Luck.'

'But that's cos the Vince Clark version's better.'

'Look, I've got two left feet but I've still made more women scream than Peter Sutcliffe. All the indie kids lookin to meet someone who really loves them but who go an stand on their own etc etc, well all they really want is their hole. But they're gloomy an spotty an shy so they pretend they're just all about the music, an hope some lassie who looks like that burd from Sleeper will think they're really deep an go back to their fetid bedsit with them.'

'Well, we're no playin any of that cheesy chart shite that fit lassies like,' said Andy, keen to steer the conversation away from Louise Wener, the very mention of whose name brought back painful teenage memories.

Gibby moved closer to Andy and lowered his voice. 'I know some people who know some people who know some lassies with debts an compromised morals. A few handjobs in the darkened corners an word will soon get around about a happenin joint with two types of easy skankin. Course, you'll need to settle the lassies' debts with some pretty shady characters but after a few weeks you'll be slappin me on the back sayin, "Gibby, they're queuin round the block. You are a genius."'

'Yeah, I'll keep that in mind but at the moment I'd say the nuclear option would be to bring in sex workers.'

Stor's manager shook his head and adopted a look of hurt. 'You make it sound altogether seedy. It's the simple business of supply an demand.'

Michelle turned to Gibby and placed a hand on his shoulder. 'I'm sure this is a conversation that can wait til later. Would you mind givin the two of us a chance to talk things over?'

Gibby gently picked up Michelle's hand and kissed it before bowing to her. 'Sure thing, sweetheart. If you've ever got any questions about this place give me a shout, aye. Gibby'll sort you out.' He winked again and departed.

While Andy remained lost in the wonder of his new kingdom, Michelle produced a pile of documents from her handbag.

'You know, Andy. I had a look over the accounts last night when you went to bed. You know, the ones you didn't bother to look at. I think you should see them.'

Andy began swaying a-rhythmically to a soundtrack playing in his head. 'The Hacienda must be built, Michelle. If you build it they will come.'

'Aye, very good. But this place has already been built an nobody came. It needs major renovation for a start.'

The beat in Andy's head kicked in and he started to shuffle his feet from side to side. 'It needs a lick of paint here an there. Nothin major. It's no a nightclub for trendies. No dress codes, guestlist, or snobbery. It's all about the music.'

'It's a deathtrap. Can you no see the place? Can you no smell the place?'

'You've no heard DJ Quantum,' dismissed Andy as he continued to approximate the whitest man ever to take to a dancefloor.

'I'm no sure your entire business plan should depend on a DJ no one's ever heard of.'

'He's new. Cornelius found him. He's been locked away for years perfectin his style.'

'An if that doesn't work? What about Plan B?'

Andy waved his hands in the air. 'Well, he was dubstep wasn't he? I'll probly ban dubstep.'

He looked to the sky and raised his arms to the heavens, stopped dancing and looked briefly entranced before continuing.

'Stop bein pessimistic, Michelle. Feel the energy. Feel the soul.'

'I'm bein realistic. IF you can find some more money. IF you make sure it's done up well. IF you market it properly. It could, maybe, with a bit of luck, work. Promise me you'll have a look at these figures.'

'But it's art,' huffed Andy. 'You can't overthink these things.'

'Andy, look at these fuckin figures or I'll leave you.'

Tutting, Andy finally accepted the papers Michelle had been thrusting at him. Although not the most numerically literate of fellows, he couldn't help but notice the disparity between Michelle's calculations and his inheritance and meagre savings. In fact, the situation was even more grievous given he had exaggerated the resources at his disposal and the extent of his investment to date. But with DJ Quantum on board, it would all work out somehow, he told himself. The Hacienda must be built. Or at least reopened under a new name.

THREE

To his manager, Cornelius appeared to be the model employee as he sat in his glass-walled corner office staring intently at his computer screen while absently mindedly rubbing the space where his moustache used to be. He was actually embroiled in a frantic attempt to buy a mirrorball. One billed as the world's largest, in fact. His bid stood at £3000 with less than a minute of the auction remaining when his concentration was broken by a knock on the door.

'Hey Cornelius. How's things?' asked his manager, entering without waiting for a response.

'Err...in the middle of something important here,' he replied, flashing his superior a concerned look before turning back to the screen which revealed he had been outbid at the last second by £15.

'Bastard! Sorry, what's up boss?'

'I think I might have some good news for you.'

'Oh?'

He leant on the desk, checked no one was listening and leant in so close that Cornelius began mentally filing a sexual harassment complaint. Under instruction from Emma, who remained angry about her Dad succumbing to a lifelong Scottish diet, his legacy being frittered away, and her husband's abetting of said frittering, Cornelius had agreed to shave. As his manager whispered to him inches from his face, Cornelius wished he still had his moustache to act as a spittle sponge.

'Well, we really like having you here, and there may well be an opening as partner coming up.'

Cornelius looked wary and reclined away from his manager's bad breath. 'Right...and why's that good news for me?'

'You said promotion was the most important thing to you.'

'Well, yeah. But I meant Watford. I thought we'd a real chance of the play-offs but the way we've started the season we'll struggle to finish top half.'

'Football. Ha! You crack me up. But seriously, how would you feel about that?'

Cornelius squirmed as he attempted to hide his growing discomfort. Luckily for him, the cavalry had arrived in a sweat-soaked Soup Dragons t-shirt and was currently shuffling from one foot to the other in the adjoining open-plan office.

'Err...decent. S'pose. Sorry,' he nodded in the direction of the corridor. 'One of my most important clients just showed up.'

Cornelius didn't wait for permission before bounding towards his brother-in-law past rows of accountants pretending to pore over spreadsheets while wondering what had become of their life.

'Hey man! How's the nightclub world treating you?' Cornelius and Andy exchanged their traditional "cool" handshake, although one of the participants' hearts was clearly more in it than the other. Andy was struggling to find the energy for the move and could only answer with a gasped breath.

Cornelius' employers were headquartered in an under-occupied business park to the north of the city. To anyone who had decided the outlay required obtaining a driving licence would be better spent on records, gigs and club nights, this meant catching four buses to reach it. The journey wasn't so much the issue as the nearest stop being a good mile away from Cornelius' work on the opposite side of a busy dual carriageway that Andy had been forced to dash over. As the beads of perspiration streamed down the crimson sphere balanced precariously on his shoulders demonstrated, he was not a man who walked a mile, or dashed any kind of distance, lightly.

Andy wiped his brow and screwed his face up as he surveyed a scene unnervingly similar to the one he had thought he'd escaped forever. The sterile room was silent but for the odd click of a mouse button and the ever-present hum of an air conditioning system like the one in InsuranceInsurance.com.

Composing himself, he looked at Cornelius' beaming face. 'You heard from DJ Quantum at all? I need to know he's still on board.'

'Course he's on board. This's his big moment. But if you're worried I'll send him a postcard.'

'A postcard?'

Cornelius nodded. 'You don't speak directly to DJ Quantum. You drop him a postcard and arrange to meet. It was how Morrissey and Marr did it. Don't worry. The man digests music and craps it out even better. All he cares about is getting behind the decks and blowing minds.'

'But he's no actually done that yet has he?' Andy's voice betrayed new-found doubts over the wisdom of buying a nightclub with little financial acumen and even less idea how to run it.

'He blew our minds. And his mum's.'

Andy's face crumpled. 'If I'd one criticism of DJ Quantum it'd be the fact he still lives with his mum. Doesn't exactly scream sex an drugs an rock an roll.'

'Quantum inhabits his own space, that's what he always says.'

'Right. It's just I'm screwed without him an Michelle keeps pointin out things that supposedly need done to the place. Personally, I've shat in much worse toilets.'

'Ask me.'

'Have you ever shat in worse toilets?'

'No, ask me about the Jumpin Jack Flash.'

'But what about Emma bein pregnant an stuff?'

'It's not Emma's money.'

Andy gasped as the enormity of what Cornelius was saying sunk in. 'But...all they years of savin.'

'Andy, man, you're family. My best friend. And I want in on this.'

Cornelius broke into a smile that would melt the heart of anyone not unfortunate enough to have been married to him for the past 10 years.

'You think I'm going to let you have all the fun? Who found Quantum? Who nearly just purchased the world's largest mirrorball? And look!'

Cornelius handed Andy a CD, bowing slightly as he did so. The cover sleeve, bearing the title CORNELIUS' GREATEST PROTO-FUNK COMPILATION EVER VOLUME III in glitter had been lovingly crafted. At least four different colours of highlighter pen had also been employed.

'Dunno what to say.'

'You don't have to say anything. Best in the series for me.'

'I mean about the wedge.'

'Look, we're slaving away in jobs we hate, never getting the appreciation we deserve.'

It was true that having to divide numbers into odd and even factions had never sat well with Cornelius but he had never understood Andy's occupational frustration. David Porter was an insurance salesman, after all, and he and Isaac Hayes were the finest songwriting partnership in R&B history. Then again, he did become a penniless alcoholic. Mind you, Isaac ended up becoming a scientologist and dying on a treadmill so David actually got the better deal in the end. Like John Lennon getting shot before he had a chance to do his Mull of Kintyre.

Cornelius was confusing himself so he turned back to Andy. 'You know what my dream is.'

'The world's rarest record.

'But what good's that? It's only two minutes and 33 seconds long. A record that cost 20 grand but I could never play. And don't need to cos Emma already downloaded it for 79p. I don't want to be one of those guys who's owned by his possessions. Not when we could have the world's biggest mirrorball instead.'

No matter how many times Andy told him his former employers specialised in home and contents rather than original pressing vinyl, Cornelius had on a weekly basis requested a quote for insuring a record he'd lusted after his entire life. The significance of the gesture therefore, in addition to his guilt about doctoring the balance sheet Michelle had seen, meant he was quickly warming to the idea.

'Me and you Andy, we'll be like the...the Chemical Brothers-in-law! I've already been thinking about names.'

'I thought about namin it after the man who's goin to make me – I mean us – famous.'

'Club Quantum!' squealed Cornelius.

'I was thinkin The Quantum Club!'

'We can discuss specifics later. Let's hug this shit out.'

They embraced enthusiastically, but separated after finding themselves tenderly kissing each other's cheek. Four dozen number-crunchers were staring in amazement at the most exciting development to have taken place in an industrial estate practically on the outskirts of Aberdeen for many a year.

'But what'll Emma say?'

'Don't worry about my baby. I just need to pick the right time to tell her.'

FOUR

Emma knew the community centre well. As a teenager she and her then boyfriend, under the influence of White Apocalypse cider, had broken in and had unsatisfactory adolescent sex under the monkey bars.

And here she was again, 21 years later, legs apart, panting and wondering when the ordeal would be over. Only this time, there were more than two people in the room and (Sittin' On) The Dock of the Bay was being whistled in her ear.

'Breathe in, breathe in...' the antenatal teacher cooed to the dozen or so couples sat in a circle around her.

'You're a natural at this, baby.'

'It's breathin, Cornelius. I've been doin it for 36 year.'

'You know what I mean. I'm just trying to offer support.'

'And...exhaaaaaale.'

She squeezed Cornelius' hand and tried to talk whilst breathing out. 'Youareaspectacularlyuselessmaninsomanyways...phew...but I've never doubted you in that respect.'

'Breathe in, breathe in...'

Emma followed the instructions as Cornelius continued to chat. 'Cos I do think about the future, you know. We've got to plan for it.'

'And exhaaaaale.'

'Phoooooooooooooooooooooooooooooooooooo....'

'That's right, breathe baby. And you know how important family is to me. And we need to pull together in a time of loss.'

Each page of Emma's diary contained the triple-underlined sentence "BE NICE TO CORNELIUS TODAY" as she really did need reminded that, aside from the foibles she bore the brunt of, he was a good man. Emma had initially been puzzled by his "Hey baby, do you prefer Stax or Motown?" patter when they first met and told him to fuck right off. Cornelius was persistent, however, and didn't use the cover of strobe lighting and dry ice to sexually molest her, which set him apart from the rest of the male population of Dundee clubland.

Despite a cringeworthy rendition of 'My Girl' (the Otis rather than Temptations version, naturally) outside the Sheesh! kebab shop she agreed to meet him again. Emma's abrasive personality meant she had trouble forming relationships that lasted longer than the hours between dancefloor arse-grab and drunkenly faked orgasm. The fact Cornelius was oblivious to most of what goes on in life made them a good fit and, as he stroked her hair and talked about family, Emma felt her husband was finally maturing into a functioning and worthwhile member of society, something she had given up hoping for her little brother to achieve.

'Apart from that prick Andy. Me an him are finished.'

'Breathe in, breathe in...'

'Family's family. I mean, he's your brother. My best friend. We can't let him do this nightclub thing...'

'And exhaaaaale...'

'Youmeanyou'llhelptalkhimoutofthis?'

'...alone. We can't let him do this alone.'

Without instruction to do so, Emma blew out fiercely. 'What d'you mean?'

'Breathe in, breathe in...'

'Remember how much you loved Storm and how much you miss it?'

'And exhale...'

'IfuckinhatedthatplaceandonlyeverwentcostheyletyouDJ. EveryfifthMonday. Iwasgladwhenitclosed.'

'Well, it opened up again. And then closed down again. But Andy's definitely on to something. You know how you always said I should follow my dreams?'

'And exhale...'

A combination of Emma's unnatural breathing pattern and Cornelius' rambling caused her to begin hyperventilating, but she continued to loudly spit syllables out as her spasming diaphragm permitted. 'What. You. Mean? We. Are. Become. Parents. Can't. Go. Back. To. DJ. You. Cannot. Mix.'

'No, I've finally accepted that my destiny lies elsewhere. Like Everlast, when he left House of Pain to go solo. I've done something...brilliant...'

Emma began to hyperventilate quite badly, drawing looks from the other proud parents-to-be dotted around the room. The instructor crouched by Emma and smiled in her face.

'No, Emma. Now's the time to relax.'

*   *   *

It is perhaps unsurprising that so many residents of a city build on the slopes of a volcano are prone to eruption. While the Dundee Law had last spewed forth lava, ash and gas in the Ordovician era, Emma Morgan's latest sudden, violent outburst had just taken place.

Nursing a swollen fist, she paced towards their car whilst shouting threats and obscenities to no one in particular. Cornelius emerged from the community centre a few moments later and, unimpeded by bondage-tight trousers, took no time in catching up with her.

'I can't believe you got us banned from Lamaze class for fighting the instructor.'

'Just shut up, you. A nightclub? I can't believe you had thousands stashed away you never told me about an you've used it to buy a fuckin nightclub.'

'I didn't buy a nightclub. Me and your brother bought a nightclub. It's a family affair.'

'You selfish prick. I'm nearly seven-month pregnant. My Dad's just died. I've no slept in weeks. I've got piles the size of golf balls. An my fuckwit husband an arsehole brother have bought a nightclub.'

'Look, just calm down. Breathe in...'

Emma punched Cornelius' shoulder but succeeded only in further injuring her hand. 'There's a reason that club keeps shuttin down. What the fuck makes you think you can make it a success?'

'Hey, I had a residency in Ibiza, you know...'

'No. You didn't. You played a few CDs by the pool each afternoon when we were on holiday an nobody stopped you. That's no a residency.'

Cornelius ignored the slight. 'Look, this is for all of us.'

'So you bought a nightclub for our unborn baby? D'you have any idea how ridic...wait a minute. No...you're no stupid enough to quit a perfectly good job. Are you?'

Cornelius held his hands out to his wife in a display of impassioned, if ineffective, pleading. 'But they wanted to make me a partner, baby. You know how I feel about number apartheid.'

'Right, we're goin to stop this right now.'

Emma opened the car door, struggled into the passenger seat and slammed the door shut. Cornelius reopened the door and attempting to placate his wife on bended knees.

'I think the problem is that you've never heard DJ Quantum in the mix.' He shut the door again the instant he finished his sentence, his mind already drifting off into visions of Bianca Jagger riding through Club Quantum on a white horse as Fat Boy Slim slapped him on the back and congratulated him on the mirrorball.

FIVE

His wife would never credit him with it, but Cornelius was a man of foresight. Realising it wasn't impossible that the most exciting music news since Bowie stepped back into the studio wouldn't be received favourably, he had arranged for a tour of the club to sweep her up in the excitement of the venture. Michelle and Andy were to meet them there, partly to increase the good vibes, but mainly because the presence of witnesses would prevent Emma from following through on one of her frequent mariticidal threats.

The visit did not get off to a good start when Emma slipped on a used condom in the cloakroom, and her anger had not rescinded any by the time the quartet found Gibby propping up the bar, can of Export and pile of pornographic DVDs in front of him.

'I see our numbers have swelled somewhat,' he greeted the party. 'Nice to see you again chief. An the beautiful Michelle.' He winked at Michelle, who looked straight at the porn. 'Ah, don't mind these, sweetheart. If you should ever need a little help gettin things goin in the bedroom department, just give Gibby a shout.' He turned to the inanely grinning newcomer with his scowling wife. 'I'm presumin this is Cornelius an this must be Andy's sister. That's a family head, aye?'

'This place's horrible,' said Emma looking around in disgust. 'I mean, it was always a bit of a dive but...did someone die in here?'

'No for ages,' said Gibby as he winked to Andy. 'An an emergency exit wouldn't have helped.'

Cornelius placed a hand on Emma's shoulder that was swiftly shrugged off. 'Give it a chance baby. A mirrorball will brighten the place right up.'

'An where're the ladies'? I'm burstin. Must be the damp.'

'Out the hole in the wall where the door should be, right past the broken glass an down three flights of stairs. Watch out for the puddle where the basement floods.'

Emma tutted and lumbered off the dancefloor as Michelle looked around, desperate to make the best of a desperate situation. 'I mean it's pretty grubby but redecoration, some new furniture…'

'A giant mirrorball.'

'…sort out the floodin, broken windows etc an it wouldn't be unsanitary anymore.'

'But the main thing is the sound,' Andy nodded to Cornelius. 'The best PA since the Paradise Garage.'

'Great music every night,' enthused his brother-in-law. 'Imagine Aretha Franklin in a hot-tub with Underworld and Desmond Dekker…'

'But with phatter beats.'

'Yeah, wait til you hear DJ Quantum,' Cornelius continued. 'He's been in his room perfecting his sound for 10 years. It was him who actually invented dubstep just so he could have something to destroy.'

Gibby was appalled by this turn of events. 'DJ Quantum? Ooooft! I'll have to haul you up there chief. What about Tony?'

'Who's Tony?'

'Our resident. On a mission to weed out the pop sheep an identify the chosen few deservin of his genius, he says. Also a lawyer so he's handy to have around if the authorities start sniffin about. Brian won't be happy. Most nights he's the only punter in so him an Tony've got close.'

Emma burst back into the room shouting as she made her way back across the dancefloor. 'I can't go in there. It smells of death.'

'Got to put my hands up to that one I'm afraid,' said Gibby, literally holding his hands in the air. 'Had an omelette for tea. It was like the Barry White that killed Elvis.'

'Well, why didn't you go to the men's toilets?' asked an incredulous Emma as she clambered on to an unsteady bar stool.

Gibby shrugged. 'I just find it liberatin to use the women's toilets whenever I can. The government shouldn't be tellin us where an when to perform bodily functions. Every turd in the tarts' is one up the man.' Winking at Andy he continued, 'Sometimes I like to piss in sinks as well.'

'This place just gets better an better.'

'C'mon Emma,' said Andy, trying to raise his sister's spirits. 'There's nothin that a slap of paint an a strict gender-separation of facilities won't sort out.'

'Well said, chief. While I've got you here, we need to speak about sundries.'

'Sundries?'

'Think of them as miscellaneous expenses. Important for... Oooooft!' Gibby broke off and clutched his stomach. 'This'll need to wait for another time. That omelette's challengin my bowels to a re-match.' Gibby darted out the room in a half-crouch, leaving a trail of noxious gas in his wake.

Andy walked straight towards the nearest table, sat himself on the least filthy plastic chair he could find and pulled out the latest edition of Mojo, which he proceeded to bury his nose in, much to the disgust of his sister.

'You don't think we'd be better dealin with everythin that needs done about Dad's house an mibbe, I dunno, decide where to scatter his ashes?'

'I need to keep up with the latest sounds,' he replied before smugly holding up the magazine, the cover stars of which were The Beatles. 'I'm a nightclub owner now. Makin Dad proud.'

'You're in no way makin Dad proud.'

'Dad loved music. Which is why we should wait an scatter his ashes at Glastonbury.'

'Dad never went to Glastonbury.'

'But he wanted to after I told him about the caterin vans. We could make a weekend of it.'

Michelle stepped between the siblings before the situation deteriorated further and eased Emma into a chair at the opposite side of the table from Andy. 'What about we scatter the ashes next week once everythin's sunk in?' Andy and Emma both nodded. 'Okay, now as far as this place goes, what we need to do is get a proper plan, look over the accounts...'

'No need,' interupted Cornelius with relish. 'I've already done it.'

'An how they lookin?'

'Really, really bad. This place hasn't made a profit in years and all the bills are overdue.'

Emma swore under her breath before asking, 'So how come you're sittin there fantasisin about mirrorballs?'

'Oh, you know. I'm just really happy I own a nightclub. Even if we don't make the opening night, I'll be able to tell my daughter that her Daddy owned the coolest club that nearly was.'

He tried to pat Emma's belly but his advance was rebuffed. 'Well, you can tell her that every second week when me an her new Daddy let you see her.'

'Just get off his case,' said Andy. 'We've actually been puttin a lot of thought into our plan.'

'Oh really? What've you decided then?'

Andy nodded to his business partner and proudly announced, 'We've banned any singles that make the top 40.'

'And we're not going to tell anyone about it so it keeps its edgy, underground vibe,' added Cornelius. 'We don't want to reach people, we want them to reach us.'

'So, you plan to turn around a strugglin nightclub by no playin music people might actually like an keepin the whole thing a secret? What a pair of arseholes.'

Several minutes of silence followed Emma's not unreasonable critique of her brother's and husband's strategy. Try as he might, Andy was unable to absorb the words he cast his eyes over, so eventually he abandoned the task, berating the paucity of modern music journalism. It was an industry he had once harboured ambitions of working in and even managed to have a few pieces published in local fanzines before blotting his copybook by declaring Oasis to be a flash in the pan and hailing Kula Shaker as the future. Cornelius too was unable to concentrate on his reading, but only because he was biding his time before detonating the good news bomb he'd been keeping up his sleeve.

'The books aren't all bad, though,' he eventually said with a grin. 'Looks like all our staff are stealing from the club.'

'An that's a good thing?' asked Michelle, before Emma was able to offer a more profane alternative.

'Well, at least it means some money comes in.'

Emma had tired of what she was hearing and turned to her most likely source of support. 'Michelle, please help me talk some sense into these pricks. Surely you can't think this is a good idea?'

She didn't, but the sparkle in Andy's eyes she'd first seen when they were allocated adjoining workstations at the call centre had returned since he'd taken ownership of Stor. He'd never got over the grounding of the Seagulls and the past couple of years had seen the better aspects of his personality absorbed by resentment so, having got over the initial shock, Michelle was not as opposed to the plan as she might otherwise have been.

She smiled at Emma. 'Cornelius an Andy are a pair of spacers who refuse to grow up but the deal's done. Surely you want your daughter to have a Dad who loves what he does. I mean, Cornelius isn't suited to accountancy. He can't even count.'

'I can count. I just don't get odd and even numbers.'

Emma made a final plea for backing. 'You don't think this is the most fuckin insane thing you've ever heard?'

'Course it is. Look at the pair of them. But if this DJ Quantum is as good as all that then mibbe everythin'll be alright.'

SIX

'This is the worst thing that's ever happened. Literally. A tragedy, an absolute tragedy.'

Two days had passed since the grand tour and Michelle, Andy and Emma were once again congregated by the bar. The girls sat on unsteady stools while Andy nervously paced around them. Michelle eventually broke the tense silence.

'I'm sure he's okay. Cornelius'll phone as soon as he can.'

'The way he went down. He was screamin, properly screamin. We built this thing around him you know. It was gonna be us an DJ Q, changin the world.'

Emma shook her head and tutted. 'He's no dead you stupid prick. He was cryin when he went into the ambulance. Cryin an walkin.'

'Only 27. You know what happens to musical genii at 27, don't you? Hendrix, Joplin, Jones, Morrison, Cobain, Winehouse an now Quantum. So young.'

Knocking drew their attention to the double doors, which swung open as Cornelius entered, wearied consternation upon his usually cheerful face. The returning co-owner and his brother-in-law shared a tight hug as Emma muttered something about 'fuckin benders' under her breath before Cornelius addressed the room.

'He's not dead. It's worse than that.'

'What d'you mean? What's happened?'

'It was...horrible, Michelle. I mean, I didn't know what to do. I went into the hospital with him and, after a while, his mum shows up. She was nice, Mrs Quantum. Said she was sure we'd be a success. Then she went in to see him and when she came out she handed me a postcard and whispered to me, "It's my handwriting, not his."'

He passed Andy the postcard so he could read the grim diagnosis for himself.

'DJ Quantum has RSI. In his mixing hand.'

Fighting back tears, Cornelius nodded. 'They say it's the worst case since Andy Weatherall in '93.'

'In his mixing hand? Can't he work with one?' asked Michelle. 'Does that drummer no only have one arm?'

Andy sighed like a teenager embarrassed by his parents. Cornelius patted his arm and turned to Michelle to explain the seriousness of the situation.

'Def Leppard are shit. Quantum is a genius. He speaks with his hands, not his hand.'

'Well, just get another DJ then.'

Andy loved his fiancée dearly. He was well aware of his aesthetic shortcomings and sometimes still couldn't believe he was engaged to someone as funny, clever and beautiful as her. But no one who owned Bon Jovi's Greatest Hits should be allowed an opinion on music, these things were black and white.

'D'you no get it Michelle? He's the best mixer ever. He builds the crowd up an mashes things up that should never be mashed up. Our entire plan. Ruined at the stroke of the cross fader.'

Emma had heard enough. 'So we face bankruptcy cos some agoraphobic mummy's boy who's obsessed with obsolete forms of communication has hurt his hand? Fuckin great.'

'But you don't understand, baby. Quantum hears music differently to the rest of us. He's the only person who knows where Richey Edwards is. He worked out a secret code in a Manics b-side.'

'What a load of pish.'

'It's like a Magic Eye puzzle – most of us can't work it out but his brain isn't the same as normal people's.'

'Your brain isn't the same as normal people's.'

'Honestly baby. Him and Richey postcard each other now using a secret language they call Welsh.'

'I've had enough of this. If you two won't listen to reason then I'm gonna find someone who'll make you.' She stormed out, kicking her stool over in the process. Cornelius stood stock still, trying to process developments.

'Oh right,' he said after several seconds of Michelle staring to indicate he was expected to once again pursue his wife. He paused by Andy on his way out.

'He was good though, wasn't he? I mean, he only mixed Macarena into Leftfield but you could hear how good he was.'

*   *   *

The dynamic duo behind Club Quantum/the Quantum Club dealt with the devastating loss of DJ Q by sticking their fingers in ears already buried in sand. As Cornelius was banished from his marital bed he had plenty of time to work on his proto-funk compilations. In such circumstances he normally headed to the spare room, but it was currently out of commission due to him having begun converting it to a nursery some months ago. Lacking, as he did, any sort of practical skills, Cornelius found the project to be more arduous than originally anticpated and quickly abandoned it the second he realised being a club co-owner looked much more fun.

Andy, on the other hand, attended to the last of the affairs relating to his father's estate without the assistance of Emma, who filled her hours plotting intricate and violent revenge on her brother. Eventually, Michelle pointed out that each day's delay left them deeper in the hole and scheduled a high-level parley in the club's office, a cluttered and foosty room that had been used as a storeroom, venue for drug deals and knocking shop over the years. There, Cornelius and Andy decided the DJ Quantum situation should be put on the back burner until more practical matters had been dealt with, at which point the progress of his convalescence could be measured.

'Right,' said an unusually decisive Andy. 'Gibby says Licensin will be coming round next week. We should get the place lookin a bit sharper before then.'

'Yeah, but we can't get a giant mirrorball for a month at least. And I don't think we should let anyone see the place til we've got that on the go.'

'But – at the same time – I don't think Licensin are bothered about whether we've got a giant mirrorball or no. I'm thinkin we just move things in front of the dodgy sockets, cover up the damp in the cellar an put some posters up.'

'First impressions count though. A great painter wouldn't let anyone see a masterpiece before it's finished.'

'But the sooner we get the licence sorted, the sooner we can borrow more money to pay for DJ Quantum's rehab.'

A knock at the door prevented Cornelius from processing this suggestion and his brother-in-law from thinking too deeply about the ever-expanding web of lies he was spinning to cover his financial arse. The caller was beckoned in and a man several years younger than either of them entered. Though obviously dressed for business, his suit was tolerated rather than worn, and the battered briefcase he carried was as perforated as Cornelius' eardrum the time he fell asleep by King Tubby's speaker-stack. Acting on Andy's instruction to take a seat, the visitor weaved knowingly through the broken amplifiers, empty beer barrels, and other debris to join them at the ancient wooden desk.

'My name is A.P. Richardson,' the stranger informed them. "An I'm the legal representative of Emma Morgan.'

'Emma Morgan?' Cornelius, already surprised to be receiving visitors, furrowed his brow. 'My Emma Morgan?'

'Yup. She's served this injunction prohibitin you from buyin this club.'

Cornelius broke into a half-laugh. 'There must be some mistake. My baby wouldn't do that to me.'

The solicitor was unmoved by his protest and slid a transparent plastic folder across the desk to them. 'There's a coolin off period which allows stakeholders to object if their interests are likely to be adversely affected by the proposed transaction. It's all in these papers.'

'She's objecting?' asked Cornelius. 'On what grounds?'

'On the grounds that you are mentally incompetent an are placing the financial security of your unborn child at risk.'

A.P. Richardson produced a mobile phone, punched in some numbers and, passing the handset to Cornelius, explained that his wife would provide confirmation.

'Hey baby, it's me,' he said when Emma answered. 'What's going on? But baby…Just talk to me…It's our dream…No, ours as in me and Andy…Oh come on…Baby please.' He returned the phone to its owner. 'She says any communication has to go through her lawyer.'

'Anythin you'd like me to pass on to my client?'

'Yeah, tell her that she should trust me. And that if we build it they will come. And that…and that I love her.'

'Hello, Mrs Morgan? Your husband says you should trust him, that if they build it they will come, an that he loves you…. Ah-hah,…hmmm…absolutely…no problem.' He hung up and turned back to Cornelius. 'She says you're a prick.'

'This is ridiculous,' said Andy slamming his fist on the desk. 'Me an Cornelius are gonna make this the best club in the country. Well, the city at least. Once DJ Quantum's back nothin's goin to stop us.'

'DJ Quantum is also raising legal action against you.'

'What?'

'He's allegin that he injured himself in an industrial accident. The trauma he suffered, on top of his loss of earnins, amounts to a substantial sum. It's all in these papers.'

Andy could barely believe what he was hearing. 'Industrial accident? He spazzed his hand scratchin records. An he's on the fuckin dole! He'll get more if he moves on to disability. We've done him a favour. Give him a phone, Cornelius.'

'I can't. You know what he's like. D'you have a postcard?'

'Fuck the postcard. We're being sued.'

The solicitor silently handed Andy the phone and indicated it was ringing through to DJ Quantum.

'Hello? Err…Mrs Quantum? Is your son there? Thanks.' He covered the mouthpiece. 'She's goin to get him…Hello?

Quantum? It's Andy Brennan here. What the fu...Okay, here he is.' He passed the phone back. 'He wants to speak to you.'

Mr Richardson smiled and took the device. 'No problem. I'll let them know.' He hung up and turned to Andy and Cornelius. 'He says any communications should go through his legal representative.'

Andy and Cornelius shouted at DJ Quantum, A.P. Richardson and themselves without approaching lucidity.

'You know,' the solicitor said, placing the mobile back in his pocket and leaning back in the chair. '...there is another way.' He waited a second to ensure he had their full attention. 'I also happen to represent the club's former DJ.'

'Wait a minute!' Cornelius exclaimed. 'The old DJ is a lawyer. His name's Tony. A.P. Richardson. Anthony P Richardson. You're Tony! You're representin yourself!'

'Indeed,' he smirked.

Andy shook his head. 'You've engineered two lawsuits to pay us back for sackin you.'

'I couldn't possibly comment on my clients' motivation.'

'But presumably these lawsuits would go away if you were reinstated.'

'Fair to say no one wants to sacrifice their credibility on cases with no guarantee of success.'

Cornelius saw the picture unfolding before him. The white horse faded from view and his mirrorball glistened sadly over an empty dancefloor. 'But, Quantum's ace. And you're renowned for vibe-inappropriate music and contempt for the crowd.'

'Then again, even if my clients were to be unsuccessful it would be at the end of very costly an lengthy legal cases.'

'I think I need to consult my business partner,' Andy said, turning to Cornelius. 'We're snookered aren't we?'

A flash of inspiration hit Cornelius and his eyes widened in excitement. 'Unless...maybe I could take over on the decks?'

Andy turned back to Tony and held out his hand. 'Welcome aboard the good ship Quantum Club.'

'Club Quantum,' Cornelius corrected him.

SEVEN

The miseries Tony would visit upon the House of Quantum were only just beginning, as Andy and Cornelius were to discover as the appointed hour of ash-scattering approached. The morning began like no other in their working lives to date when they found the man they were relying on to keep the fledgling enterprise on the right track asleep in the office, naked as the day he was born.

'...an there it was – all over her back!'

Gibby threw himself back in a chair facing his employers on the other side of the desk. Andy prided himself on not being a willy-watcher, but he couldn't help noticing Gibby was almost completely shorn of pubic hair. He had regularly denounced the modern trend for pubic grooming as effeminate, but he had been feeling a tad curious since hearing of the alleged magnifying effects.

'Well, err, thanks for sharin that Gibby,' he said, attempting to focus on his eyes. 'Can I just clarify, you didn't actually have this burd here did you?'

'Had her here, on the bar, in the cellar, on that desk.'

In unison, Andy and Cornelius lifted their hands from the surface they had been resting on. Their response prompted Gibby to elucidate further.

'Well, I couldn't exactly take her home with my Angie there could I?' Gibby rubbed the enormous hipster beard he had grown since Andy and Cornelius took over. 'Relax. Stuff like this goes on all the time in clubs. I know it's a young man's game but...'

'What d'you mean?' interrupted Cornelius, sensitive to the fact Gibby was nearly twenty years his junior. 'We're still young. We're still cool. I was at Spike Island you know.'

Gibby picked up the packet of cigarettes lying on the desk of shame, and lit one, only for Andy to object by quoting passages of the Smoking, Health and Social Care Act 2005 at him.

'Chill out, chief. It's only a fag. I'll open the window. Although it's already a bit nippy in here so I'd just like to point out that as far as Gibby jr goes,' he pointed towards his groin. 'We're talkin an extra 15% at room temperature.'

Cornelius thought it prudent to change the subject at this point. 'So the staff are comin in today. And we want to reassure them that we're just all about the music, man. Cool vibes.'

'But cool vibes that turn a profit,' added Andy, aware that the hole he had dug for himself was getting deeper by the day.

Gibby shook his head and puffed away rapidly before stubbing the remainder out on the desk. 'You're no gettin it, are you? Leave all the profit,' he put quotation marks round the word with his fingers, 'to the superclubs, chief. Even in the glory days of the Boogie Room – an I'm talkin about times when we'd pull in 80-90 punters a weekend – it was never about the wedge. If you're about the music, the vibe, gettin your Nat King Cole, then you'll lose everythin but give people nights they'll never forget. Or remember. Fly too close to the sun, burn brightly, then burn out. Probly for insurance reasons.'

'Yes!' exclaimed Cornelius. 'That's exactly it! That's exactly what we're about.'

'Oooooft!' Gibby sprung up from the chair before Andy could correct his brother-in-law. 'First fag of the day. Always moves things along. I'll be lucky if I make the bogs. I'm crownin already.'

Andy and Cornelius watched him leave the office before their eyes fell upon the spot where he'd been sitting.

*   *   *

Having taken the offending piece of office furniture outside to await incineration, Andy and Cornelius turned their attention to the upcoming staff meeting. Keen to make the right impression on their inherited employees, they spent a significant period debating their plan of attack, an ergonomic layout that would exude both friendliness and authority, and the soundtrack for the occasion, which had taken up the bulk of the discussion.

While Andy suggested something cool and contemporary, such as Nightmare on Wax's 1995 album Smoker's Delight, Cornelius was insistent on something cheerier. Eventually they decided not to bother with music and realised they had argued about the matter for so long they were running late for the meeting and thus setting a poor example. They left the office and made their way to the main room, where they had previously laid out six chairs in a semi-circle. Only two were occupied. A now-clothed Gibby reclined in his as he texted, while an unimpressed-looking Tony sat cross-armed and upright.

'So anyway,' said Andy, taking his seat. 'Good to see you again, Tony.' He turned to greet the fifth member of the party. 'An nice to meet you, Lionel.'

Lionel, a stereotypically bearish bouncer who was approximately nine parts scar tissue and one part man, had stood by the door, silently staring straight ahead until now. He nodded solemnly in recognition of Andy's greeting without shifting his gaze.

'You no takin a seat?'

'A good doorman has no need of chairs. He must stand alone, ever watchful, ever ready.'

'Err...ok,' Andy continued. 'So we thought it'd be a good idea to get you here an talk through our plans for Quantum. First of all. We're all about the music. That's the guidin principle by which...'

He was interrupted by one-hot wonder Ini Kamoze, whose signature track, Here Comes the Hotstepper, happened to be Gibby's ringtone. Andy smiled at him, expecting him to lift his head in light-hearted apology before switching his phone off. Instead he answered.

'Alright chief...all over her back. What's that?' He whispered into the line, although still loud enough for anyone to hear. 'Bit of snow? Should be cool. Call you later.' After snapping his phone shut, he nodded consent for Andy to continue.

'As I was sayin. Music is the most important thing to us.

We've got big plans to build this place around the sounds. But we're gonna have to make a few changes.'

From over Tony's head, Andy saw a hand being raised. Pleased that Lionel, at least, appeared to be listening, he granted him permission to speak.

'Are you banning trainers?'

'Erm...no, everyone wears trainers these days so we're no goin to do that.'

'So my job won't be changing then?'

'Well, no, it's not changin. Anythin else you'd like to discuss?'

'No. A good bouncer has a zen-like calm that comes from effective compartmentalisation. It would be fruitless to dilute the efficacy of my performance by confusing the essential character of my role.'

He casually cracked his knuckles, a Kalashnikov-like sound that preceded the lyrical gangster's re-appearance. Gibby looked up at Andy. 'I'll need to get this. Snow on the horizon but none on the ground, know what I mean?'

'NO! Look. This is important. No dealin.'

'Here it comes. The reign of the Puritans. Sorry, chief but I'm no Roundhead.'

'Well, we saw that when you were running around starkers,' said Cornelius, before appealing to the staff's sense of solidarity. 'We're all in this together, right? Like The Beatles in Hamburg, away from home, in a strange place with nothing but good old fashioned rock 'n' roll to see us through.'

His enthusiasm failed to rub off on Tony. 'An this the big push? Bye-bye Stuart Sutcliffe, you were great but you're dead now, no use to us. Fuck off, Pete Best.'

Andy smiled in what he hoped was a reassuring manner. 'No, we're no sackin anyone. Although, Lionel, you do need to curb the violence. This place has a terrible record of hospitalisations.'

Another solemn shake of the head was forthcoming from the giant guarding the door while Gibby and Tony rolled their eyes. Andy steadied himself for the apex of his speech. 'An the skimmin has to stop. We need wedge to get things up an runnin. Which means a pay freeze. An no treating this place like a brothel.'

Andy directed the last remark to Gibby who was, perhaps for the first time in his life, rendered speechless as the new owner ran ahead to the section he was sure would win his underlings over. 'So back to the music. Music's why we bought this place. We want a club where people can hear the freshest an best sounds. You know, like New Order, the Stone Roses.'

'Hold on!' cried Tony. 'You won't get more punters in by playin their dad's CD collection. We don't want a load of fuckin MoJo readers turnin up.'

In Tony's opinion, there was no finer sight than an empty dancefloor. Each time he looked up from his decks to see hardcore industrial dance alienate the last of the revellers he felt vindicated in his belief that he was a genius and the rest of the world the idiots. He began working at the club as a barman to support his law studies during the Boogie Room era but was quickly demoted to glass-collecter. Proving equally inept in his new role, Tony soon found himself working the club's cloakroom before it became clear there was only one nightclub job unskilled enough for him to do.

'I get in all the white labels for real underground dance stuff,' he said. 'An all the avant garde funk you can shake a stick at. New Orleans voodoo rap, bhangra big beat, renaissance punk.'

'An people can't get into that unless they're out their heads,' added Gibby. 'Plus Lionel's big on the rights of the individual. If he wants to kick seven shades out of someone then he'll do it.'

Alarmed at the unforeseen turn of events, Cornelius decided now was the time for his piece-de-reistance. 'But wait 'til you see the mirrorball. The biggest going. Costs a fortune but it'll be worth it.'

'A mirrorball?' Tony rose to his feet in anger. 'What's this? 1975? You're tellin us we've to work for next to fuck all an can't even make a bit on the side while you're blowin a fortune on a mirrorball?'

'No a fortune,' pleaded Andy. 'But spendin a few quid to tart the place up might no be the worst idea. Paint, furniture…'

'I thought it was about the perfect beat, no the perfect seat. I'm withdrawin my labour.' He turned to his colleagues. 'Strike?'

The contract was sealed with a nod from Lionel and a 'What type of employer doesn't let you punt gear at work?' from Gibby. The erstwhile DJ and assistant manager walked out. Lionel nodded to the management once more and followed them out the door.

And that was how Quantum came to be the scene of the most ludicrious industrial dispute since Shaun Ryder refused to release the master tapes of Yes Please! until provided with cash, crack or both, one that meant its owners were almost certainly going to be late for scattering the ashes of the late Dave Brennan.

EIGHT

Having established a picket line outside the club's main entrance and got a brazier burning, Tony was somewhat stumped as to what his placard's message should be. He had been staring at the blank sign for several minutes, paintbrush in hand, without being touched by the hand of inspiration, so decided to check on his fellow travellers instead. Lionel was doing chin-ups on the gate and grunting while Gibby rolled a joint.

'You know, to the untrained eye it doesn't look like you two're committed to the workers' struggle.'

'Uuuuuuurgh!'

'You know how Lionel is,' said Gibby as he put the finishing touches to the bifter. 'Has to exercise every hour an a half otherwise his rage at life's injustices boils over.'

'An what about you?'

Gibby leaned over to the brazier and used the flames to light his joint. 'The workers need to relax.'

The club door opened and the owners stepped out to inspect the scene. It was Lionel who greeted them first.

'Uuuuuuuurgh!!!!'

'The brazier's a bit much isn't it?' Andy said, ignoring Lionel and noting that the chair they had disposed of provided ample kindling.

'Typical,' Tony said. 'You'd love to see us freeze our bollocks off, wouldn't you?'

'Actually,' Lionel said, dropping down from the gate and panting heavily. 'Your genitalia are one of the last areas to be affected by frostbite. As it's the evolutionary goal of every species to procreate, they have been handily tucked away, meaning they're usually quite warm.'

'I just meant cos it's July an there's a hosepipe ban on.'

Tony changed the subject rather than concede the point. 'Anyway, what brings you down from your ivory tower?'

'Look, things kinda got off on the wrong foot earlier. We understand youse are a bit put out but everythin we're doin is for the good of the club.'

'Yeah, man,' added Cornelius. 'And we're as into sounds as you are. Did I tell you about Spike Island? We like the odd bit of New Orleans Voodoo Rap as much as you do.'

'You two are so clueless you don't even know when a musical genre's made up an you expect us to listen to you? Pathetic.'

'You mean there's no such thing as New Orleans Voodoo Rap? That's deeply, deeply disappointing.'

Andy put a hand on his brother-in-law's shoulder. 'Never mind that. Anyone want to deal with this like adults?'

'We bargain collectively or no at all.'

Andy shrugged, keen to find a resolution that would allow him to scatter his Dad's ashes before he was forced to join him in the afterlife.

'Our demands are thus. The blanket ban on drugs is unworkable. We're all adults an it's good for staff to be able to earn a bit more on the side, especially given what we're paid. An if people know they'll be able to score, they're more likely to come.'

Andy snorted at Tony. 'That's ridiculous.'

'No at all, chief,' said Gibby, looking at him through blood-shot eyes. 'An we need somewhere to de-stress. Or where you can take someone to help you de-stress. Most important for morale, that.'

What passed for a turntable tyro round these parts nodded. 'An no micro-managin. If Lionel says someone needs to have an accident on their way out, they need to have an accident. Similarly, I must be given exclusive control over music policy. Plus the pay freeze is unfair.'

Lionel leapt up to the gate for another set of reps as Andy made the point, reasonably in his opinion, that drugs and violence were illegal. Tony countered that Simply Red weren't and thus the world they lived in was not based on fairness or sense. He looked to his sign, desperately wishing an iconic message which would come to define this conflict was emblazoned on it at that moment.

Cornelius held his palms out. 'Look man. I know you're upset about us trying to bring in DJ Quantum but...'

'DJ Quantum's backin the strike,' announced Tony.

'What?' Andy practically cried. 'Nobody's seen or heard from him for days an he's no even staff. How can he be supportin you?'

'I think he understands solidarity. Look, I've got a postcard from him here. It says "I am the Lech Walesa of the turntable".'

'Uuuuuurgh!!!!'

'This is ridiculous,' said Andy, growing desperate. 'Me an Cornelius. We're gonna...we're gonna...You haven't heard the last of this.'

He stormed back into the club. Cornelius smiled at his revolting workers and followed suit.

Andy retreated to the sanctuary of the office. He looked at his desk. Less than an hour ago, the fact it had recently been fornicated on was his biggest concern. Well, that and scattering his dead Dad's ashes. But now he had a full-scale industrial dispute on his hands and, even more greviously, Tony was threatening to tip the Dundee Courier off about developments. To most people, this wouldn't rank alongside Woodward and Bernstein being on your case, but Andy had held a fear of that particular publication ever since a withering review led to the demise of The Go-Ahead Seagulls. He also remembered what had happened to The Libertines after Pete Doherty started shagging Kate Moss and didn't want Quantum to suffer the same fate at the hands of the paparazzi, even if the two situations weren't quite identical.

Andy was shaken from his mawkish daydream by the office phone ringing and an accompanying racing heart. Had the Courier got hold of the story already? Or maybe it was a promoter offering him the latest band or guest DJ. He even, somewhat implausibly, imagined it might be Bobby Gillespie or Bernard Sumner calling to say that they'd heard the news, congratulations, and they were sure Quantum would be a great success.

'Hello? Quantum Club,' he said, savouring the moment.

'How come you're still there?'

'Sorry, meetin ran over,' was how he greeted his fiancée.

'How was it?'

'Oh, great. Really productive.' That made it around 10 lies today already, Andy calculated, residual Catholic guilt making him wonder what all the dishonesty was doing to his soul. 'Couple of minor issues to sort out but nothing major.' Eleven.

'Well you better sort it soon. Emma's goin mental an listin every single crime Cornelius ever committed. We're on the time he nipped out for a pint of milk an ended up goin to Amsterdam to see DJ Shadow. She's also threatenin to kill you if you don't get here soon. Oh, an you've to bring Cornelius's ghetto blaster an the CD she left in the car. It's Save All Your Kisses For Me by Brotherhood of Man. Apparently your Dad used to sing it to her, an she wants it playin when the ashes are scattered.'

'But it's a terrible record. It's cheesy an it's...'

'Andy! Mibbe just for once let it go, aye? It means a lot to your sister.'

Andy assured her he and Cornelius were practically on their way and hung up, huffily reflecting that his father had never sung anything from Brotherhood of Man's back catalogue to him. He sunk into one of the remaining non-tainted chairs and held his head in his hands. Even though the office door was open, Cornelius knocked, as he did every time he was about to enter a room Andy might be in.

This ritual dated back to the day, not long after he and Emma started going out, that he visited her family home. In those days, Emma was yet to be worn down by life with the world's most frustrating man and excitedly met him in the garden only for Cornelius to brush her off with a kiss on the cheek and race to her brother's bedroom, eager to show off the new Spiritualized album.

Unfortunately, Andy had spent that morning collecting scraps of pornographic magazines left in the nearby park. After hours of searching, he finally had all the required body parts for a full nude. Once home he assembled the scraps on his bedroom floor and reached into his bottom drawer for a headshot of Sleeper frontwoman Louise Wener he had previously cut from Smash Hits. The varying scales of the pictures meant Louise's right arm was like Popeye's and her left leg was, undeniably, black but the collage would do the intended job. Andy ripped off every item of clothing and kneeled before the object of every mid-90s indie boy's affection.

Cornelius was, of course, unaware of these events and threw the door over just as Andy reached the point of no return. He was still trying in vain to plug the leak as Emma, their father and visiting grandmother rushed to the room, alerted by Cornelius' screams. Most embarrassingly of all, The It Girl was playing on Andy's CD player when he was caught.

'You don't need to knock every time, Cornelius. That was a long time ago.'

He ignored Andy and paced around the room.

'I can't believe the New Orleans Voodoo Rap scene's over. 'Spose it's like capturing lightning in a bottle though. The Sex Pistols, acid house, REM before they signed to Warners, nothing good lasts.'

'I'm more concerned about the world's most militant nightclub staff to be honest. We need a change of tactics.'

'Absolutely. The problem is they don't think we're cool.'

'The problem is they think we're stupid. We need to show that we're smarter than them. Divide an rule. What's the most important thing to the future of the club?'

'The mirrorball!'

'No, Cornelius. The music.'

'Oh yeah. So we buy Tony off then?'

'Nah, he's a fanny. If we get the others to come round he'll be forced to fall into line an agree to play the music we want.'

Cornelius looked like he was considering this strategy for a few seconds before asking, 'D'you think there's still a market for bhangra big beat then?'

An object hurtled through the window Gibby had opened earlier and bounced across the office floor. This prevented Andy from having to debate the finer points of fake musical genres with his brother-in-law. He picked up what turned out to be a crumpled sheet of A4 paper, opened it out and found a scribbled message that turned out to be his first ray of hope that day.

'We can work this out, chief, but we need to be discreet. Meet me where no one in their right mind will follow.'

NINE

The men's toilets at the club had been called many things over the years – drug den, public health hazard, Dickensian relic – but never somewhere anyone in their right mind would want to visit. A puddle that could more accurately be categorised as a small lake covered most of the floor. Stale urine threatened to further submerge the facility as troughs edged dangerously close to capacity. A bare 40-watt lightblub provided scant illumination for the graffiti that covered every inch of wall, including the space where a mirror had once hung above a sink filled with broken glass. Distressed sounds could be heard emanating from one of the two adjoining cubicles. A pair of legs could be seen beneath each, trousers at ankles.

'AAAAAAAAAARGH!!!! OOOOOOHH!' cried Gibby. 'We're talking anal Armageddon here. How you gettin on, chief?'

Depending on your perspective on these matters, Andy was getting on either much better or much worse than his employee. 'Erm, well. Like I said, I don't need to go. I dunno why you insisted I try.'

'You can tell a lot about a man by the way he defecates, chief. That's when he's at his most primal. I need to know who I'm doin business with. I like a man who goes often an honestly. Gets rid of all the toxins. That's why I take liver salts twice a day.'

'Well, cheers for the tip. Now, back to this ridiculous strike. I've been thinkin…'

Gasping, Gibby interrupted. 'You know what I've been thinkin, chief? I've been thinkin about the Rolling Stones.'

Andy screwed his face up, both in confusion and in discomfort at the rustle of toilet paper being prepared for application next door. 'Eh?'

'Well, The Stones was Brian Jones' band, like this was Tony's place. But Mick an Keef sidelined Brian an everyone came round to their way of thinking. Hopefully Tony won't die in a mysterious aquatic incident, but we can't be held responsible if he does.' Though the partition meant Andy couldn't see him, he sensed Gibby winking at this point. 'Plus, unlike Keef I've no been bangin his missus. Although I might if he had one an she was tidy.'

As he listened to Gibby deploy the paper, Andy had a fair idea where the conversation was headed. 'An I suspect Keef operates best when his needs are satisfied?'

'Is that a penny or somethin else that I can hear drop, chief? Now, I've got somethin lined up with this little honey next week but my Angie's cancelled her Zumba so I could really do with gettin called in for overtime, if you see what I'm sayin…'

*　*　*

Cornelius was also saying a lot at that moment. As Lionel single-handedly manned the picket line, he discovered much of it was nonsensical, irrelevant and sheer fantasy.

'…so, you can imagine it, yeah? Here's me behind the decks and just to mix-it up right, cos I've mostly been playing acid house, I drop in White Lines and whoosh, place just goes crazy.'

Lionel had been staring straight ahead until this point, but now turned to face his employer. 'Cornelius, you've already told me about the night you met Emma's Dad. I am sure his suburban mind was blown by you commandeering his Aiwa stereo, but should you really be down here talking to me? I could be branded a scab just for talking to you.'

This broke the spell for Cornelius. 'You're not really serious about this are you, man? I mean, why not just give peace a chance? Or me and Andy at least?'

'Have you ever stood naked in a field, Cornelius?'

'Naked?'

'As God intended. We all stand alone in that field Cornelius. We all stand alone. Now, remember you are alone in that field. There is no one around. You are completely alone. What do you do?'

Cornelius shrugged.

'You are for all intents and purposes a God. Above all the other animals. You must create a moral code for yourself in your new world. You are the superman made flesh.'

'I am?'

'Now imagine David Bowie is standing next to you in the field, naked.' Cornelius imagined this. He feared becoming aroused, like the time he nearly poked his doctor's eye out after asking him to inspect a scrotal lump. I could just think about Emma in a Luton strip, he reflected. What a turn off that would be.

Lionel sensed Cornelius had conjured up a suitably vivid picture in his mind and continued, 'Do you touch tips?'

'Touch tips?'

'Yes,' replied Lionel, nodding downwards. 'Touch tips. It's David Bowie and he wants to touch tips. You are master of your own morality. Seconds ago you feared you were all alone in the world, now there stands The Thin White Duke. And he wants to touch tips.'

'Is anyone looking? I mean, I suppose…'

'And that's why I'm on strike. You and Andy have shown yourselves to be men with no respect for how things are done. Maybe David Bowie likes this club, but here you come in, demanding that every time he wants to experience the miracle of life that Celine described as drinking cold and pissing warm, he's got people like you wanting to touch tips.'

'Hey come on, you started this. Wait…David Bowie doesn't come here. Does he?'

'The point is, things have been done a certain way around here and suddenly here you two are and it's mirrorball this and don't break legs that. No wonder people are upset. As bouncer, my obligation is not to this club, sir. It is to the people inside.'

Cornelius scratched his head. 'Yeah, but your job isn't really changing.'

'What of the directive to curb the violence? My anger management classes have gone up 20% in cost. And you're suggesting a pay freeze?'

'Well. I mean, that was Andy's idea.'

'Unless you can show me you're prepared to stand on your own two feet then how can I trust you? It's your club too, and you're letting Andy make all the decisions, Cornelius.'

Lionel turned to stare straight ahead once more, hands cupped beneath his midriff, leaving a dumbstruck Cornelius to absorb what he'd just heard.

*   *   *

Gibby looked pleased with himself as he watched Andy try to locate a clean patch on a towel that looked old enough to have swaddled him in infancy.

'See? I knew you'd get there in the end, chief. I think you took a huge step lettin go in front of me.'

Andy shook his head. 'Did you have to peer over the partition like that? An are you no washin your hands?'

'Oh, aye. I always forget.' The tap reluctantly turned on at Gibby's equally reticent touch and a splutter of brownish water fell on his hands. Andy offered him the towel but Gibby shook his head and rubbed his hands across his beard instead. His employer thought it prudent to bring the conversation round to a subject more pressing than Gibby's child-like fascination with faecal politics.

'So, you think Lionel'll come round then?'

'Oh, absolutely. He'll prattle on for a bit, but he'll come round when I tell him he's free to start dispensin justice as he sees fit again.'

'But I never said…'

'I need to present it like we're all gettin somethin out of it,' Gibby placed a hand on his chest for emphasis. 'So it doesn't seem like you've singled me out for favouritism. Lionel's a sensitive soul so leave him to me. He needs to be handled delicately by someone with cunnin an guile.'

*   *   *

'If not Bowie, then Kenny Jackett,' someone almost entirely bereft of cunning and guile was saying to to Lionel at that precise moment. 'He's my favourite ever Watford player. I'd definitely touch tips with Kenny Jackett.'

*   *   *

Andy listened intently as Gibby outlined what he called 'Operation Hang the DJ', unable to escape the nagging feeling his vision for the club was being compromised and the essential austerity measures Michelle had demanded steadily eroded. But still, it gave them something to work on.

Indeed, so engrossed were the two in their strike-breaking plot they failed to notice Tony walk through the door behind them. Seeing his comrade and enemy conspiring, he sneaked behind the toilet door and waited for his suspicions to be confirmed.

'An if we play it right, Lionel might even stop skimmin off the top,' said Gibby.

'It's Lionel who's skimmin?'

'Course it's Lionel. Who d'you think it was?'

*   *   *

'Of course it's Gibby who's stealing. His only contribution to this place is the narcotics.' Lionel had eventually tired of listening to the surprisingly detailed reasons for which Watford legends Cornelius would and would not experiment with sexually and so had steered the conversation back to the club.

'Right, yeah. Good that,' said Cornelius, nodding.

'I thought you guys were totally anti-drugs?'

'Us? No, not us. Well, Andy is a bit. He's a bit more scared of authority than me, you know.'

'So you indulge yourself then?'

'Well, no. My wife won't let me. Plus, my asthma. At Spike Island, though. I was hanging out with all the drug casualties.'

* * *

'He was a volunteer with St John's Ambulance,' explained Andy. 'Spent the whole time givin cups of tea to guys that were freaking out. He never even seen the Roses.'

The portion of Tony's head that stuck out above the cubicle door shook. A benign smile spread across Gibby's face and he placed his hand on Andy's shoulder, an action that caused him to recoil, given recent events.

'Lovely guy your brother-in-law. Shame about his mirror-ball.'

'What d'you mean?'

'Well, I've looked at the RRP of they bad boys. If you want the thievin to stop, you'll need to hand out pay rises. An if you're givin me every second weekend off then you'll need to bring in someone else to run the bar.'

'But he's got his heart set on that mirrorball.'

Gibby sniffed, inadvisably given their location, and shuffled his feet from one puddle to another. 'It's a stickin point, chief. If I can't persuade everyone to come back to work then the strike'll escalate. An how would your sister react to you no bein able to scatter your old man's ashes today? I wouldn't want that nipper to grow up without its Daddy around, would you?'

'Well, no...'

'See, you're doin this for your family. You're a pragmatist. He's a mirrorball idealist. An if you do this then I'll get Lionel to stick to the puff when he's workin. Which is good cos you don't want a bouncer wired on powder.'

'But the actual dealin will stop?'

'Obviously. In future, I mean. But I need time to adjust my budget to legitimacy. Only fair after I helped sort all this strike out, aye?'

The feeling that all was not well nagged at Andy once more but he forced it to the back of his mind. 'S'pose so. What about Tony?'

'When he finds out we're back on board he'll fill his pants

quicker than I just did.' Gibby grimaced. 'There's definitely a down side to the salts. I'm off to speak to Lionel. Just hope he's no havin a down period.'

* * *

'It hurts, Cornelius. It really hurts,' Cornelius was now sitting on the club's doorstep with his arm round the hulking shoulders of the man who ferociously guarded his territory. 'I get depressed when people see my primate face and lack of neck and make judgements about me. A little smoke, the odd pill or line. It makes it easier for me to cope. I can look myself in the mirror and say, "You are Mark 'Lionel' Ritchie. You're not a joke." I own the complete series of "Idiots Guide to…" books but I am still stuck in a job where my brainpower is rated as secondary to my physical prowess. Yes, I may be capable of crushing a man physically, but I would prefer to crush his spirit with a well-timed bon mot. I am a lover, not a fighter, a poet not a pugilist, a man in love with language, not the language of violence. But are any nice girls interested in me?'

'I'm sorry man, I'd no idea. That's totally out of order treating someone like that just cos they…'

'I mean, there's the record for GBH and the restraining order as well. And the schizophrenia, but I keep that in check with self-medication. And, yes I did have some issues with uncontrollable weeping when I was younger but that was before I started balancing the uppers with the downers.'

With a weak smile, Cornelius assured Lionel that he too now viewed the drugs as non-negotiable and headed inside the club to appraise Andy of developments, knocking on every door he came across on his way to the office.

Thankfully Andy's hands remained clear of his reproductive organs throughout the resulting conversation, in which both partners reported substantial progress. Delighted that things appeared to be working out, Cornelius headed through the double doors and sashayed across the dancefloor towards the DJ booth with the intention of giving the decks a quick spin.

'Hello Cornelius.'

He jumped round to find Tony smoking by himself at a table.

'Holy shit! What a fright. Aren't you meant to be on strike? Why're you in the club?'

'Needed a shite. Gibby's been cuttin his gear with liver salts again. That okay?'

'S'pose. Strike's nearly over anyway, man. Lionel's crossed and Gibby…'

'I heard about Gibby,' smirked Tony. 'It was good of you givin up your mirrorball.'

'What? I've not…I'd never give up my mirrorball.'

'That's no what I just heard. Andy's struck a deal with Gibby. Turns out all that glitters costs too much gold.'

'Bullshit. He wouldn't.'

Tony tapped ash on the threadbare carpet that acted as an instant adhesive for anything that came into contact with it. 'Done deal I reckon. Bye bye mirrorball, we hardly knew you.'

Andy was family. He was his best friend. They shared everything together. But, at the same time, Cornelius feared that Andy lacked the mental sharpness to deal with Gibby. 'I won't stand for it.'

'Neither would I. In fact, I think the mirrorball's a great idea. But if you want them to take you seriously, there's only one thing for you to do…'

And so, the club's co-owner – despite ostensibly being the oppressor – joined the ranks of the oppressed. His mind full of mirrorball-related indignation, Cornelius stood shoulder-to-shoulder with Tony on the picket line. There was, however, still one force capable of dividing the workers united.

'Hi baby, look, I'm sorry I'm not going to…'

Cornelius was once again using Tony's mobile to try and make his wife see sense. The explosion at the other end of the line was clear enough for Tony to listen in with amusement.

'It's not really how I want to remember him anyway… Eating a steak and turning puce, that's how I want to remember your Dad. Crying on our wedding day. Not ash blowing across the hills.'

The shrieking became more measured at this point, and seemed to Tony to centre upon very vivid and inventive attacks on Cornelius' person.

'You won't be on your own…Andy, who's a backstabbing git by the way, and Michelle will be there…I know it's important to you, but this important to me. Andy? Oh, we're not getting a mirrorball, that's why I'm on strike.'

After inspecting the handset for clues why the conversation had ended abruptly, Cornelius handed it back to Tony. 'I think she got cut off.'

'Yup, that'll be it. Mobiles, eh?'

TEN

In a café barely two miles away, Emma's mobile was being slammed down on the table, causing Michelle to almost knock the lid off the urn she had been inspecting.

'That prick,' seethed Emma. 'That useless prick. That pair of useless pricks.'

'What now?'

Nostrils flared and eyes murderous, she turned to Michelle. 'Cornelius an Andy have fallen out. Somethin about that fuckin mirrorball.'

Emma had still not come to terms with the fact her husband had given up his solid, well-paid job to become the co-owner of a nightclub that opened and closed with the frequency of her teenage legs, less than three months before he became a father for the first time. Following his betrayal, the world's most litigious DJ had been added to Emma's list of people to extract revenge on but Andy retained top spot by some distance. He claimed to hate reality TV shows because they manipulated the intellectually challenged for their own ends but, in her opinion, that was exactly what he was doing by allowing Cornelius to tag along on this ruinous journey.

'I swear to God, I'm gonna smash that mirrorball an do medieval things to them with the shards.' Emma attempted to jump out of the seat but was thwarted by her condition. Michelle knew better than to offer her fiercely independent friend assistance until it was specifically requested, so she watched a heavily pregnant woman rock in her chair with gritted teeth before realising her limitations. 'Help me up, will you?'

Michelle sprung round to the other side of the table, lifted Emma to her feet and began steering her in the direction of the door, speaking in as soothing a tone as she was capable of whilst mentally carrying out a financial and emotional cost/benefit analysis of terminating her engagement.

'Oh, you better mind your Dad,' she said, nodding back in the direction of the table where the urn sat abandoned amongst used cups and saucers.

*　*　*

The staff and owners of Quantum had divided into two very clear camps. Tony and Cornelius stood round the brazier eyeballing the coalition of Andy, Gibby and Lionel. Tony's protest sign now read "(Mirror)balls to management" and was raised by the his comrade.

Andy shook his head. 'I can't believe this. My own brother-in-law.'

'Yeah,' Cornelius sneered. 'That's how I felt when I found out you went behind my back. You and Gibby. You double-crossing pair of...of...bastards.'

Shocked by a rare display of aggression from the world's most placid man, Andy attempted to limit the damage. 'Calm down Cornelius, it's no what you think.'

'The club needs a mirrorball! It's my dream.'

'We can't afford it. I had to make agreements.'

Cornelius waved his sign theatrically. 'The mirrorball will be the beating, glittery heart of this place and you know it.'

'You can't have it. Someone has to make difficult decisions an God knows I don't get any help from you.'

'So, the truth's coming out now. You don't trust me. You don't think I'm good enough for your sister.'

'Now you're bein stupid. I think Fred West's too good for my sister.'

'Speakin of which, I reckon that's her rockin up now chief.' Gibby pointed to a car that was drawing up by the front door. Shouted insults should be heard from within, and the air was turned even more blue when the passenger door was flung open and Emma attempted to extricate herself from the vehicle. Eventually she succeeded with the aid of Michelle and paced towards the picket line, urn in hand and future sister-in-law in wake.

'Cornelius! You utter, utter prick. You've ruined this day for me! We were meant to be scatterin my Dad's ashes.'

Without consciously planning her attack, Emma raised her right hand and, with as much power and aggression as she could muster, launched it towards her husband. Instinctively, Cornelius ducked out the way of the missile but Tony – not accustomed to dodging physical assaults by pregnant women – was unable to remove himself from its trajectory. The metallic cremation vase smacked him square in the forehead, knocking him to the ground where the urn and its lid parted company. The remains of Dave Brennan swirled around momentarily before the shocked onlookers watched them fall softly against the homeless shelter's pebble-dashed wall.

'Fuckin hell, that hurt,' Tony said as he picked himself off the ground. 'Youse all seen that. Assault. I'm suin.'

'ENOUGH!!!' screamed Emma with enough ferocity to send birds scattering from trees half a mile away. 'I'VE HAD ENOUGH OF YOU PRICKS ACTIN LIKE CHILDREN. TODAY WAS MEANT TO BE A SPECIAL DAY. WE WERE MEANT TO BE SCATTERIN MY DAD'S ASHES. WE WERE MEANT TO BE LISTENIN TO SAVE ALL YOUR KISSES FOR ME WHEN WE DID IT! I AM VERY PREGNANT, VERY UPSET AN VERY OFTEN VERY VIOLENT. SO LET'S GET INSIDE AN SORT THIS OUT ONCE AN FOR ALL. ALL OF YOUSE. NOW!!!'

Without hesitation, they filtered back into the club, led by Cornelius, who sensed that getting Emma back on side was essential to his mirrorball dream being realised. Andy held back at the door until it was just him and his sister left outside. She fixed him a stare that suggested violence remained on the agenda.

'In a way, it's what Dad would have wanted,' he said and tried to place an arm around Emma only to be shrugged off and forced into the club via its metal doorframe.

*   *   *

As the only sensible adult present, Michelle had taken charge of the crisis talks and stood before the rest of the group, whose factions were reflected in the seating pattern. Cornelius and Tony sat together to Michelle's right, while Andy and the other two staff members were dead ahead of her. A third group, comprising Emma, a dented urn and approximately 27% of her father's ashes, had been positioned on the extreme left to limit the chance of further incidents.

'I think this's a time for cool heads,' said Michelle, recalling the conflict management course she'd been sent on by work. 'Right, first of all. What you've to understand is that from now on, myself an Emma must be consulted on all major decisions affectin this hellhole.'

'What? C'mon...'

'No Andy, we've gone along with this shite long enough. If you an Cornelius can't be trusted then we insist on executive consultancy positions. Or I will leave you.'

'Michelle, please. Think of the mirrorball.'

Michelle carried out a hurried risk assessment and strode over to Emma and clamped a hand on her shoulder to prevent her from attacking her husband, before outlining the plan formulated during the car journey over. 'People can take drugs, but no earlier than 2am. That way you'll be compos mentis at work but comin up for the end of your shift. But absolutely no dealin.'

Gibby was disgusted. 'But that goes against the bargain I struck for us. Me, Lionel an Andy – we're on the same side here.'

'I have actually been considering where my loyalties lie, and I'm with a man who will touch tips with David Bowie for the good of the club. I can respect that.' Lionel shuffled his seat to the side, bolstering Cornelius' group. For his part, Cornelius beamed at Lionel before catching sight of Emma's spine-chilling stare at the far end of the line and turning away.

'Well, I'm stickin with Andy,' Gibby stated defiantly and crossed his arms. 'He let me watch him drop a Gladys Knight.'

'What? Err...well, that's all very sweet an disturbin,' said Michelle, addressing Andy. 'An we'll discuss it at home. But, movin on to music, Tony will have full freedom to choose tunes…'

'Thank you.'

'…til midnight when the place starts fillin up. Thereafter, music that people actually want to hear will be played.'

'But…'

'Quantum's on the mend. It says so on this postcard he sent from Lourdes.' The communication she described was passed around. Andy looked to Cornelius to verify its authenticity but was met with a shrug. 'Plus, your music is utter shite,' Michelle added to the scowling DJ.

'And, most important of all, absolutely no scammin, stealin or skimmin. It stops now.'

Lionel shook his head. 'How can you expect Gibby not to skim when you've cut off his main source of income?'

'Shut it, Gigantor. It's you who's been on the take.'

Gibby and Lionel continued to protest their innocence to each other before simultaneously realising the truth of the matter and turning to Tony, who stared at his shoes. Cornelius and Lionel shuffled their chairs away from him and towards Gibby and Andy.

Michelle shook her head. 'But I thought lawyers were loaded?'

'Yup, but I'm no allowed to practise am I?' said Tony. 'Some shite about no bein a fit an proper person. An what d'you expect? This place keeps openin an shuttin an then our earnins are interrupted again.'

'A fair point,' conceded Michelle. 'You have no real stake in this place. Owners come in with their big plans then go bust within a year.'

'Six month really, sweetheart.'

'So you just take what you can when you can an screw the long term.'

Gibby sniggered at Michelle's use of the word screw while Tony agreed with her conclusion.

'So, here's what's goin to happen. The ownership of this

club will be split five ways. Risk an profit likewise. That way, everyone has an interest in makin the place a success.'

'Woah!' cried a stunned Cornelius before turning to Andy for support, who undertook a form of protest, known in technical terms as whining like a bitch. They were, however, drowned out by Tony, who enthused about the potential of a worker's cooperative, Lionel, who gushed at the prospect of his potential finally being recognised, and Gibby, who considered how part-owning a club would exponentially increase his "hole opportunities".

'This is fuckin nonsense!' cried Andy, finally making his voice heard above the rabble. 'This is my place. Well, me an Cornelius' place. You've got no right to do this.'

Michelle smiled coldly at him, 'D'you want to be a single, outright owner of a bankrupt club, or a happily married part-owner of a barely sustainable one?'

'Doesn't look like I have much of a choice do I?' he muttered, unable to look his treacherous betrothed in the eye.

'Cornelius?'

'I still want my mirrorball.'

Loud sighs filled the air. 'Honest to fuck, Cornelius,' said his wife, leaning forward to face him. 'I've never heard of anyone goin to a nightclub cos of a mirrorball. That'd have to be one special fuckin mirrorball.'

Cornelius bounded to his feet to set the scene. 'You see! You're thinking about it already.' He began spinning one hand round and round to imitate the motion. 'Everyone is fascinated by the thought of an awesome mirrorball. They just don't know it. It draws you in and then the beats catch you,' he pounded out a beat with his other fist. 'And you belong to us.'

Michelle remained dubious. 'Even with Tony on the decks?'

Cornelius glanced at Tony as he bristled at this latest slight. 'Well...'

'An how big's the biggest mirrorball in the world anyway?'

'It's big, it's huge. It's 12 feet. In diameter.'

'So,' considered Michelle. 'It's 12 feet deep?'

'And wide and long. Oh yeah.'

'An how high is the ceilin? 16 feet? 18?'

Spatial considerations had previously failed to appear on Cornelius' radar and his face fell as Michelle continued.

'How long before some idiot, an I'm thinkin primarily of you, gets caught up in the beat, nuts the thing an brings it down on top of him?'

'Well, I mean. I s'pose when you put it like that,' said Cornelius, defeated but not quite sure how.

Michelle clasped her hands. 'Well lady an gentlemen. In place of strife I think we've brought about a new era of respect an collaboration. Anyone have anythin to add?'

Silence fell on the dark, demoralising dancefloor with its unmistakable odour once again. Finally, Emma turned to her husband and spoke in a tone more measured than any she'd managed in the past two hours. 'David Bowie. At least you've moved on from Kenny Jackett anyway.'

Cornelius giggled nervously before discreetly shaking his head at Lionel and pressing his index finger against his lip.

ELEVEN

It is 1997; the bathroom of a terraced ex-council house in Dundee. The exposed upper-arse belongs to Dave Brennan, who gracelessly lap dances the toilet seat as he digs into the cistern with an assortment of spanners and wrenches. Between puffs and pants, he explains the problem to his son, who sits on the bath, eyes closed and head bobbing to whatever plays on his Walkman. As the limitations of his current tool kit become apparent, Dave barks detailed instructions about which of the instruments strewn across the floor is required to complete the job. Tired of being ignored, he turns to face his son, whose hair – though already showing signs of retreating in the corners – is shoulder length. He is around a stone lighter than in the present day, and his clothes are less threadbare, largely because the exact same outfit is still worn on a regular basis. A bar of soap hits him in the face.

'Ow! Sake!'

'You listenin to me?' asked Dave as he shifted his considerable bulk to face his son. 'I said I needed a monkey wrench.'

He took his earphones out. 'Eh? What?'

'You're meant to be helpin, no standin around listenin to your personal bloody stereo.'

Andy raised a patronising eyebrow. 'Radiohead have just released The Bends, Dad. It's kinda important, you know?'

'An releasin the u-bend isn't?'

'Whatever.'

'I can't believe you still can't do this yoursel anyway. How many times have I shown you how to fix things around the house?'

Andy made no attempt to stifle a yawn, stretched his arms and mumbled 'Loads.'

'An you've never listened have you? What about that shelf

you put up for your Mum? I'm no sayin the head knock killed her but she was never the same again was she?'

His progeny made great play of checking his watch. 'Will this take long? Emma's new boyfriend is comin round an we're gonna work on some tracks. Now the band's split up me an Cornelius are thinkin of layin down some electro shit.'

Andy's Dad shook his head as he turned back to the task at hand. 'You sure it's no you he's goin out with?'

His son rolled his eyes. 'We're gonna be workin with old school samples.'

'You'd be better doin somethin about the old stool samples that have been floatin back up for days. I won't be around forever. Sooner or later you're gonna have to grow up an do things for yourself.'

'Look Dad,' Andy began, as if addressing the brain-dead offspring of a slug and a rock. 'It's no that I see manual labour as beneath me, but I just don't think my destiny lies in fixin bogs.' His earphones were back in and Sulk was flooding his head by the time his father responded.

*   *   *

It is a month since Dave Brennan's clotted arteries finally said enough was enough; a WC in a dilapidated nightclub in Dundee. The look of fear belongs to Andy, who stands in front of the toilet. He lifts the lid and immediately gags.

'For fuck's sake Gibby,' he gasped while attempting to hold his breath. 'That's abysmal...'

He looked at the wrench in his hand, tried hard to think what his father would have done in such circumstances, shut the lid and lifted the cistern. After inspecting its contents for a few seconds he shook his head and exited.

When Andy reached the bar, he found Michelle, Tony and Cornelius sitting round a small portable television. That his fiancée and brother-in-law appeared to be commenting on nuanced matters of interior design caused him to survey the room with confusion.

'When did we get a TV?' he asked after listening to Michelle and Cornelius debate the merits of flocked wallpaper for a few moments.

'Oh, hey man,' answered Cornelius without looking up from the screen. 'Gibby brought it in. Didn't want to ask where he got it.'

'Probly wise. D'we even have a licence?'

'Gibby says the TV Licencin aerial can't penetrate the walls here.'

'I wouldn't trust Gibby on matters of penetration,' said Michelle, eyes fixed on the screen and a Dulux paint colour chart on her lap.

Tony tutted loudly and exchanged disbelieving glances with Andy. 'This's meant to be a nightclub. We're meant to be all about the music.'

Michelle looked up to her fiancé. 'My main concern, as executive consultant, is to make sure this place is more women-friendly.'

'No! Fuckin no!' Tony cried. 'No fuckin cocktails. It takes ages to get served and…'

'I just mean so you don't want to cry when you walk in.'

'Turn it into somewhere soulless an bland you mean. Somewhere…somewhere normal people want to go. Twisted metal, leather furniture an neutral colours. Horrible. I blame this stuff.' Tony gesticulated to the screen.

Andy agreed with Tony for once, not least because he was presently of a mind to oppose anything Michelle said. He remained bitter about the fact his fiancée's intervention had resulted in him surrendering possession of his nightclub after little more than a fortnight. That said, his inheritance had been steadily eroded already so his share of Tony, Lionel and Gibby's buy-in was far from unwelcome.

'Look I'm puttin this off,' he said, marching to the wall and reaching for the plug. Medium-voltage current shot up his arm. 'FUUUCK!' he shook his hand for relief. 'Bastardin thing. Anyway, we've got business to attend to.'

Cornelius and Michelle protested that the episode had not finished and they had no way of knowing if this week's couple would lose a packet on their dream home, but Andy carried on.

'Right, we really need to get this place sorted out. I don't want it all fancy either but it needs a quick tart up.' Andy's original vision was of a kind of CBGBs-on-Tay, with the place deliberately grimy in order to set the correct tone. The reality of having to obtain the required permits to open the club and stave off bankruptcy had led him to re-evaluate. And besides, with the other partners required to chip in now, it wasn't all on him and Cornelius anymore.

'That boiler sounds worse by the day. Loads of other stuff needs fixed quick smart or we'll have to delay the openin. That costs wedge. We might need to sacrifice the new sound system for the minute.'

'No! Fuckin no!'

'No way, man. First the mirrorball and now the sound system. Everyone knows that's all you need to run a nightclub.'

'I'm pretty sure David Mancuso had less than that in The Loft. How else can we afford tradesmen to do the bare minimum – ie none of that fancy shite on TV – to get this place opened?'

Tony sat back in his chair with arms folded. 'Fuck gettin tradesmen. They're just robbin bastards who exploit the ignorance of the layman. Let's do it oursels.'

'Yeah, man,' enthused Cornelius. 'What about the punk DIY ethos?'

'I don't think Johnny Rotten was ever much of a plumber, Cornelius. You never seen Mick Jones fittin his own kitchen did you? Rat Scabies wouldn't have a fuckin clue about groutin.'

'I can fix the boiler,' insisted Tony. 'Piece of piss. That way we don't lose the sound system.'

Cornelius turned to Andy. 'Yeah, man. It's like your Dad was always saying...'

Michelle interrupted to add weight to Cornelius' point. 'It's a pity your Dad wasn't around. He was dead handy. Would've loved a job like this.'

'Never mind what my Dad would've thought,' Andy snapped. 'A mother of 10 has plumbin in better order than that bog. No way the council'll give us the all clear to open unless…'

'You're forgettin that Brian from Health & Safety is a huge fan of yours truly. Always badgerin me to teach him how to scratch. I'll get him round some night, show him the ropes – which is a huge sacrifice cos no one normally gets near my decks – an he'll sign off on anythin.'

Andy looked to Michelle for support but, for the first time since meeting Tony a month ago, she was in agreement with him. 'No point spendin money unnecessarily, Andy. All it needs is to be safe an look less like a sex dungeon.'

Bristling at this latest lack of support, Andy was about to point out that all he wanted was for people other than him to make it safe and non-bondage chamber-like when Cornelius sprung to his feet and outlined his vision for Club Quantum.

'Yeah, but cool, you know. A bit minimalist, but maybe a bit cluttered too. Some old furniture. And some new. Give the place a paint. Or strip the walls and put up new wallpaper. But new wallpaper that looks old. And DJ Quantum! He's a brilliant graffiti artist. He could do a mural. It'd be like The Roxy.'

'Absolutely,' agreed Tony. 'I'm thinkin a Mount Rushmore-style tribute to the great disc spinners. Mancuso, Grandwizard Theodore, mysel an Jimmy Savile.'

All heads turned to him. And then to each other as they attempted to digest what has just been said.

'Erm…what?' asked Michelle.

'Grandwizard Theodore. It was him who invented scratchin when his mum came into his room to tell him to turn the volume down an he got a fright.'

'No, the err…the one after him.'

'Jimmy Savile,' Tony said, sitting up straight, 'is one of the most important figures in the history of DJin.'

'But, he's one of the most notorious figures in the history of sex criminals,' pointed out Michelle.

'He was the first DJ to use two decks an switch between them rather than havin to take off one record an put another on.'

'Yeah, but man. Fuck...'

'Club culture as we know it wouldn't have existed without Sir Jimmy.'

'But...but...,' stuttered Cornelius, who looked to Andy for help only to find him staring in disbelief.

'Anyone who loves dance music or clubbin owes Sir Jimmy a huge deal of gratitude, despite some unproven allegations against him.'

'But...I mean...Man, come on...

'He's one of the biggest paedophiles in history. There's no way we're havin graffiti celebratin him in the club.'

Tony furrowed his brow at Michelle. 'Oh really, darlin? Mind you're only an executive consultant whereas I'm a full partner. An you know nothin about music.'

'But that doesn't mean I don't have a moral compass.' She turned to Andy expecting support but he was both reeling from what he had just heard and fearful of disrupting the labyrinthian management structure that was now in place.

The dotting of i's and crossing of t's on the partnership had proved predictably difficult to achieve and resulted in the adoption of a convoluted voting system. Every time an agreement seemed in sight, one or more of the parties objected for reasons far removed from Andy's original vision of a musically pure nightclub. While Gibby's insistence on primae noctis with any female staff and customers was quickly passed due to the unlikelihood of finding virgin maidens in Dundee nightclubs, others led to days of tense negotiations. Eventually an apportioning of responsibilities saw Gibby assume general maintenance and management duties, Andy finance and strategy and Lionel security. Tony was appointed musical strategist, although, in recognition of what Emma called his "cuntishness", any changes to the sounds policy had to be rubberstamped by at least one other partner. He was still proving impossible to placate, however, and regularly stormed off issuing his out-of-principle resignations. He had quit for three hours the day before when, in a conversation about studio bands, Cornelius said he preferred the Bar-Kays to the Fame Gang and Tony announced he couldn't work with people like him.

No one could define the strengths that Cornelius brought to the cooperative so the legally binding contract the partners signed listed his official role as "Vibes", as that was how Bez was billed in the inlay sleeve of Happy Mondays and Black Grape records.

Slowly recovering his senses after Tony's bombshell, Andy rued the fact that a clause detailing how to deal with apologists for paedophilia hadn't been inserted in the contract. 'Erm... well, why don't we kick the whole portrait-of-a-predator thing into the long grass for the minute? We'll get on with the rest of it an talk about this later.'

'All I'm sayin is mind what Oscar Wilde said about all the personally delightful artists bein bad artists. An give the man a chance. Somethin the savage media were unwillin to do even though he's never been found guilty of anythin.'

Tony nodded in celebration of a victory of sorts, while the others shivered, particularly Andy, whose letter to Jim'll Fix It asking to play Kenickie in the West End production of Grease remained mercifully unanswered.

TWELVE

Not having had sex since before his Dad died, Andy was suddenly ready to forgive Michelle's betrayal and had been studying his fiancée intently since awaking an hour earlier. Michelle wore a minimum of three layers of clothing to bed from late-September until mid-May, rising to five in December, January and February. She appeared to be having a particularly troubled sleep, and intermittently made grunting noises accompanied by spasmodic jerks, which Andy suspected was linked to the volume of wine she'd been consuming before bed of late. Her face was largely obscured beneath her brown curls, but patches of unremoved make-up now resembling primitive war paint were visible. This gave her the appearance of an epileptic Neanderthal who'd fallen asleep in 30,000BC and was about to wake up in Next's entire nightime range. Andy had never been so turned on.

He brushed the hair from her face using the back of his hand, but a particularly raggedy nail scratched her just beneath her eye.

'Uuuuuurgh. Naaaagh,'

'Shhhh….it's okay. It's all good.' He positioned himself on his elbow and kissed her on the scratched area as softly as he could manage before licking his lips and embarking on a trail of kisses that would lead to Michelle's mouth and then on to…

'Uuuuugh. Ih nh. Ih nh. Aff.' Spurning Andy's advances, she turned to face the wall.

He reached for a remote control that lay on his bedside table, pointed it at the stereo that lay in the far corner off the room and, as if by magic, Mr Big Stuff began playing. Andy caressed her shoulders, paused to remove hair from his mouth, and recommenced his campaign of woo by pressing his body against Michelle's back and arching his neck round to obtain access to her earlobe.

'Uuuugh. Tickly.'

There was nothing else for it. He was going to have to go nuclear.

Andy had never been particularly comfortable with dirty talk. He liked the idea but lacked the confidence to carry off the lines that popped into his head. Subsequently, his words were delivered in a whispered tone that would send shivers down the spine of a rhinoceros, before rising in a questioning intonation at the end. He sounded like a first-time sex offender who wanted to torment his victim but needed validation that he was doing it right. This new phase of the assault started with a series of promises which he knew he would do well to live up to given that Ramones songs generally lasted longer than him. Awoken by the filth being barked in her ear, Michelle shrugged 16 stone of horny fiancé off her back.

'Ewww. Mingin. Get off. I'll tell them it was rape.'

'C'mon Michelle, I know you want me as much as I want you.'

'I really don't.'

'Pleeeeeeease. Won't take a minute.'

With the one eye that wasn't glued shut by sleep, Michelle forced a look at Andy. 'You think this is your birthday or somethin? On a week day? What's got into you?'

'I'm celebratin the fact my nightclub's openin in a couple of weeks. But we'll have the painters in soon an so will you, so how about it?'

Michelle shrugged, 'Well, how could a girl say no to an offer like that. C'mon then Mr Big Head.'

'I don't have a big…'

'Just c'mere before I change my mind.'

Michelle attempted to undress Andy, but the Charlatans t-shirt he was wearing lodged around his neck. The pair of them attempted to work it free but it refused to go over his head.

'Told you.'

'Shut up. Must've shrunk in the wash. Hold on a minute.'

Andy sat up and Michelle watched him wrestle with the t-shirt. He was finally in the process of securing victory, red-faced and wheezing, when the phone rang.

'Leave it. I'll just be a minute.'

'It might be Emma. The baby might be comin.'

At least someone is, Andy thought as Michelle picked up the phone, cleared her throat and answered. 'Hello? Oh, hi Gibby…, I'm in bed…I'm wearin pyjamas, slipper socks an an engagement ring you fuckin pervert.'

She handed the phone to Andy. 'Alright Gibby, can we make it quick? Mibbe…hopefully…no she doesn't keep the slipper socks on. What? Oh fuck. Hold on, I'll be right there.'

* * *

Water dripped from the roof of the small room. All around, paint was blistered and peeling off the walls. The remains of a water heating vessel lay in the middle, a sad centrepiece to the scene that Andy, Cornelius and Gibby surveyed as Tony sat on a chair in the corner with an ice-pack on his face.

'Boiler's properly gubbed now, chief. Exploded.'

'So I see. Thought you knew what you were doin, Tony?'

'Yup…trickier than it looks. Fucker exploded in my face. We're lucky I survived.'

Andy felt Tony's conclusion was a matter of some conjecture but Cornelius waded into the debate with the intention of being the voice of reason. 'I think it was pretty brave of Tony to even try. I said last week that someone should see to that rancid old boiler but I couldn't face it. Gibby said he'd do it.'

'Aye, but truth be told I thought you were talkin about your missus, chief.'

Despite this latest set-back, Andy remained relatively posi-tive. 'We'll need to delay the openin, but it could be worse I suppose. We can use the insurance money to improve the whole place.'

'Ooooft'.

Andy turned to Gibby, instantly fearing what came next. 'Ooooft? What d'you mean ooooft?'

'Well, it's just this place's insured as my home, chief. Cos it's cheaper, aye?'

'What?'

'It's alright, everyone does it. Peter Stringfellow does anyway. Put a mattress down in the corner, say you're renovatin it an bob's your uncle.'

'Cunning.'

'It's no cunnin, Cornelius. I worked in insurance, mind? We generally didn't pay up when people said, "'Scuse me Mr Insurance Man, I'm renovatin my home so it looks less like a nightclub an I need some of your money. Ta."'

'What if we do the place up so it already looks like someone's flat, set the boiler off again, call insurance and then, with the money they give us, do up the club good and proper, mirrorball and everything?'

'Worth a shot, chief. You've got a fair set on you.'

Andy's even temper was fast disappearing. 'You don't think we'd be better off just doin the club up rather than spendin lots of money to convince someone to give us less money to paint the walls so it can look like a club again?'

'You don't understand, man. They won't know it's a club.'

'But. It. Is. A. Club. What's the point of takin a club, makin it no a club in the hope you can get money to turn it back into a club. Why're we even discussin this?'

'To avoid insurance fraud, chief. Which you could go to jail for.' Gibby and Cornelius shook their heads at each other. 'I know money's tight but you're jeopardisin the whole enterprise here.'

'Forget the insurance. We'll have to dig deep an get people in to do whatever else needs done.'

Tony's ability to form words was compromised by his recent facial injury and ice treatment but he made it clear that it would be over his dead body that the sound system would be surrendered. The prospect was a tantalising one in Andy's mind and he pledged to bring the subject up with Cornelius and Gibby at a later date, but for the moment he railed against his co-owners' enthusiasm for DIY.

'We don't have time to piss about,' he pointed out. 'We need the club ship-shape for the Health & Safety visit.'

'Told you, leave that to me. Brian's sound. He'll even turn a blind eye to this. All in hand.'

'Like the boiler was?'

Tony lowered his ice-pack to show a face redder than Stalin's piles. 'What say we put it to a vote? All in favour of wastin the entire sound system budget on gettin workshy builders, join-ers, sparkies an plumbers in to do work we could do oursels, potentially puttin the future of Club Quantum...'

'The Quantum Club.'

'...potentially puttin the future of Club Quantum at risk, raise your hand.'

Andy realised the futility in taking part in the referendum so instead curled his lip and stared at his opponents.

'Democracy has spoken, gentlemen,' announced Tony as he stood up and left the room. Andy went to follow, with Gibby immediately behind him. He loudly broke wind and put his arm around Andy's shoulders.

'Just you wait, chief. We'll have this place lookin like Kirstie an Phil's wet dream before you know it.'

* * *

Michelle was up, showered, and dressed for work by the time Andy returned. This was something of a blow as he'd spent the journey home hoping that carnality remained a pos-sibility. While Cornelius droned on about Sly and the Family Stone's place in musical history and his vision for a new chill-out zone, Andy could think of nothing other than the things he would do to Michelle when he returned. The filthiness of his thoughts progressively escalated until he was mentally degrading the woman he had pledged undying love to. He practically sprinted up the front path and through to the kitchen, where he found Michelle thumbing her way through wedding magazines at the breakfast bar.

Realising it wasn't to be his lucky morning, Andy headed straight to the fridge. He emerged 30 seconds later with a slice of cold meat between his fingers, and proceeded to swallow it whole, as a bird would a worm. He returned to the fridge, repeated the action with a cheese slice and then produced a bottle of Irn Bru, which was quickly gulped down.

Michelle looked over at her fiancé with concern and began to speak.

'Oh, that's interestin.'

'What's that?'

'It says here one of the biggest mistakes couples make is leavin it too long to start losin weight before the weddin.'

'Well they shouldn't have let themsels go in the first place.'

'Oh, absolutely. That's why I'm goin to the gym already.' She paused before striking. 'Ever fancy comin with me?'

Andy shook his head. 'No my thing. Body fascism, Michelle. That reminds me, I need to cancel my membership.' He paused to burp loudly and waft the odour he emitted around while screwing up his face. 'A healthy man shouldn't see £20 disappear from his bank account every month.'

'Okay, but maybe you shouldn't be too hasty.'

Andy turned and scowled at her. 'Are you sayin I'm fat?'

'No, no fat exactly. But I've noticed you snackin a lot more. An you've no been wearin that New Order t-shirt lately.'

'So?'

'So, you love that t-shirt. Even though it's full of holes an stained an all frayed around the edges. The only time you ever go a week without wearin it's when you're in one of your "up cycles" weight wise.'

'I can't believe this. I'm no fat. I've been fat in the past. But I'm no fat at the minute.'

'I never said...'

'You know how I know I'm puttin on weight? My head looks proportionate. It's like a tennis racket at the minute. The fact I'm no wearin my New Order t-shirt has no nothin to do with my BMI. I'm just tryin out a new look.'

Michelle's face displayed her cynicism.

'You know that t-shirt was bought at the Barrowlands in '93? My first ever gig. Unlike some people I don't just throw things out when they become frayed round the edges or if I've put on a bit of beef. I've got a nightclub openin in a month, mind? We don't have a drink licence or safety certificate, the boiler just exploded, my business partner runs around chasin shiny mirrorballs like a puppy, the bouncer is a pseudo-intellectual psychopath, the DJ worships at the altar of Jimmy Savile, an the general manager might be the biggest sexual predator since him.'

'True, but, you know, just with what happened with your Da...'

'An there's what happened with my Dad! I'm grievin, Michelle. Grievin an stressed. No wonder I'm grazin.'

'But you're havin four square meals a day as well. Emma was sayin that even Cornelius has started joggin.'

With a flourish, Andy swept past Michelle towards the kitchen door. He turned to face her once again. 'Look, I don't want to hear this. I don't need the extra stress.'

He opened the door with the intention of slamming it shut behind him, but instead paused at the sight of a biscuit tin on the worktop. Michelle's look seemed to challenge him to launch a raid but Andy shook his head at her and stormed out the kitchen, up the stairs and towards the spare room, where his emergency crisp supply was stashed.

THIRTEEN

Few people looked as at ease with the world as Gibby did reclining in the big office chair bought to replace the one he had previously soiled, feet on the desk and speaking on the phone. The contents of his conversation stopped Andy in his tracks as he walked in.

'Anythin you're into really. Hardcore, softcore, lesbians, bondage, two lassies an one laddie, two laddies an one lassie, gay, bi-sexual, bi-curious. All the best quality DVDs. Discretion assured. Absolutely no judgement...what? You dirty bugger, Dad...uuuurgh...no way.' He noticed Andy lingering in the doorway. 'Anyway, I gotta go. Business calls.'

He hung up and greeted his co-owner with a smile not befitting a man who had spent half the night clearing up the remains of an exploded boiler. 'Mornin, chief. How's tricks?'

'Better if I hadn't just heard you peddlin scud vids.'

'You wound me, chief. I'm operatin a non-physically located, high-end adult entertainment retail outlet.'

Gibby handed Andy a DVD, the back cover of which he proceeded to read.

'"See Emily Play With Herself?"'

'I thought my main stock portfolio should relate to music seein how I'm the co-owner of a nightclub now. Yours for a fiver.'

'Even though I do prefer the Syd Barrett era I'm gonna say no. I've got a full an active sex life at home.'

'I hear you, chief. But you never know when you need to set the mood for romance.'

Andy read on. '"Emily is a dirty little slut who loves it in all her holes." Flowers an chocolate just don't cut it anymore do they? Anyway, I thought everyone downloaded porn now?'

'It's a foolish man who puts all his faith in In Private

Browsin an his broadband connection. More an more men are realisin that it's wise to have the odd magazine an DVD stashed somewhere safe for emergencies.'

'What's In Private Browsin?'

'It's what the Government invented to lull perverts into a false sense of security. No that I'm operatin in that kind of market, of course.'

'What about Tony, though? He seems to hold Jimmy Savile in high regard.'

'Ah, don't worry about Tony. He just hates people an thinks art is more important. Plus he can't see what Savile did wrong on account of him being a-sexual.'

'Tony's a-sexual?'

Gibby nodded his head. 'So he says, but I just think it's cos he's the only DJ in history never to get his Nat King. I said to him, "Tony, speak to Gibby. He knows all manner of manky hoors. One of them must be willin to get their gums around it." No interested.'

'Amazin.'

'He did buy Viagra off me though,' said Gibby scratching his beard. 'Said you never know when it might come in handy, which was weird. Anyway, back to the matter at hand. No one realised the infallibility of the digital wank bank at first so I snapped up all the filth I could get my hands on an now I'm floggin it to the people who got rid of it in the first place.'

'See, I knew this Internet thing was a fad. I mean, down-loadin might give you access to every song, album, demo an rarity ever produced, an...'

Gibby stood up suddenly. 'I'm gonna stop you there, chief, both cos I've somewhere else to be an cos I've heard you go on about this a million times already. See me an my Angie? We've heard all each other's stories an spend most of our time together in silent resentment. I'd hate tthat to happen to us.'

He walked round the side of the desk, paused by Andy's side, ran his hand down his cheek, snorted with contentment and walked past him.

'Well, err...thanks for that Gibby,' he said, wiping his cheek in disbelief. 'Close the door behind you, will you?'

Andy heard it shut as he collapsed in the chair, closing his eyes and slowly lowering his head until it rested on the wood. His mind compiled a things-to-do list longer than an afternoon of Sting explaining the intricacies of Tantric sex. Get proper insurance sorted out. Start clearing up ahead of the refurb. Get things moving with the licences.

'I essentially see the licensin system like slippin it in the Gary Glitter, chief,' Gibby had said when Andy complained about how bureaucracy was stifling art. 'Better to ask for forgiveness than permission sometimes.'

Questionable as this stance was, Andy reflected that it may still be best to leave this side of the operation to Gibby. That would leave him free to work on the PR. Cornelius was meant to be sorting out posters and flyers but his mind was occupied by soft furnishings at the moment. And he really should do some sums and work out how much of his inheritance remained. If only Michelle had consented earlier that morning. He always thought more clearly after sex. Or masturbation. That's it. A wank. He would have a wank. The door was on the latch after all. Without opening his eyes, Andy leant back in the chair and reached down for the belt that was stretched to the limit by his burgeoning belly.

'Ahem.'

Andy leapt into an upright position slapping his hands down on the desk where they could be seen. Lionel stood by the door which would have concealed him while Gibby was conducting his disreputable business. He stared straight ahead with his arms folded.

'Jesus! I nearly had a heart attack.'

'That is perhaps something to do with the strain that having a head that size puts on your heart. Or because you appeared to be about to play with yourself. No wonder Cornelius always knocks when he thinks a room is unoccupied save for yourself.'

'I wasn't about to play with myself,' protested Andy, irate that Cornelius had shared their secret. 'I was...emm...I was...I just didn't expect an uncategorised species of super-gorilla to be hidin behind the door. What you doin anyway?'

Lionel broke his pose to stare hard at Andy. 'I am not hiding. I am, perhaps uniquely amongst my peers, taking my new role as the co-owner-slash-executive-security-consultant-slash-justice-dispenser seriously.'

'Oh? How so?'

'By clearing up this pigsty of an office.'

'But you're just standin with a weird look in your eyes.'

Lionel reached into his pocket, produced a bag of pills and presented them to Andy. 'That is because I found these. We took them off some miscreant who had the temerity to sell his wares without our express permission back in '05. His brain function is now permanently impaired to a level I am fast approaching. Want one?'

'God no. They can't be safe.'

'We'll soon find out. A life without risk is a life not lived. '

'Right, well if you don't mind I've got to make a call about insurance,' said Andy, intending to recommence his relief operation the second his colleague left. Lionel did not take the hint, however, and continued to stare into space. Reluctantly, Andy dialled the number of his insurer.

'Then we'll need to get on with the refurb,' he said to himself as much as Lionel.

'Everyone seems determined to make an arse of this themsels. Paintin. Plumbin. What's all that about?'

Lionel nodded solemnly as he processed the question whilst othewise remaining still. 'We are in many ways a generation emasculated by affluence. Of course, our fathers would have no problem carrying out these jobs. Simultaneously they attempted to instil a sense of practicality in us while bolstering our sense of entitlement to the point we rejected the principle.'

'This is nothin to do with my old man,' snapped Andy as a voice on the other end of the line informed him that the number he had dialled had not been recognised.

'Not your father in particular,' replied Lionel as he rolled his head around to a tune playing in it. 'I am merely saying that what our fathers showed us...'

'Look, Lionel. I understand you're off you're tits an want to chat, but really, I'm tryin to get on with things, no talk about what your Dad showed you, okay?'

A look of hurt came over Lionel's face as Andy re-dialled.

'My father showed me how to masturbate. Literally. It wasn't until many years later that I realised it wasn't quite cricket.'

The voice down the line asked Andy to respond to a series of automated prompts but he was too busy staring at Lionel with his mouth hanging open to notice.

*   *   *

An hour hence from his victim-of-incest bombshell, Lionel's impaired synapse function meant he had little memory of the incident but he was acutely aware that the laws of chemical gravity were kicking in with a vengeance. He considered delving back into his magic bag before deciding against it on the basis that his heart was already racing at a level The Idiots Guide to Cardiology warned was fatal in 98% of cases. As Lionel descended from a great height, his libido rose inversely and, in the absence of any realistic, or even unrealistic, sexual targets, he settled for the next best thing.

Entering Quantum's dilapidated hub, he found Gibby reading Lady Chatterley's Lover and supping a can of Tartan Special. Checking that no one else was around, Lionel tip-toed his way to the bar, as only a 20-stone bouncer can.

'Hello Gibby. How are things?'

Gibby looked up from the novel, which he was finding disappointingly tame given its infamy, to greet the gargantuan doorman. 'No bad, gigantor. You?'

'Fine, fine. Does the new business continue to prosper in spite of these harsh financial times?'

Gibby smiled at him. 'What can I say? Sex sells.'

'Absolutely. So, err...aah...have...do you happen to have any more of that CFNM material?'

'What's that then?'

'It's the stuff you sold me the other day.'

'Oh right. No idea to be honest, chief. You said you weren't fussy so I just grabbed the first DVD I could find.'

'Right,' said a disappointed Lionel. 'But perhaps it wouldn't be out of the question for you to perform a stock check?'

'Absolutely. Customer service is my forte. You'll have to remind me what it is again though.'

'CFNM.'

'CFNM. What's that stand for?'

'Clothed Female Naked Male.'

'What's that then?'

'Well, it's err...it's about ....men. Being naked. In front of women. That are not.'

Gibby closed the book, pulled himself out of his slouch and fixed Lionel with a disapproving stare. 'Oh right, so that's what you're into then is it? Flashin.'

'It is not flashing! It is…well, if you can imagine scenarios where a man surrenders his power to women by undressing while they remain clothed.'

Lionel's eyes went wild as he continued, through gritted teeth, to explain the fetish to Gibby. 'And the women love it. You should see them at the stripper shows. Drunk on smuggled-in vodka, wedding rings glistening in the artificial light of some seedy working man's club as they grab every part, and I mean every part, of the man. Brides-to-be wearing a white veil and L-plate getting their fill in front of family and friends.'

Gibby inhaled through his nostrils and slowly turned his head to the side. Lionel's demeanour changed.

'But I'm only interested out of intellectual curiosity,' he insisted while wiping drool from the corner of his mouth.

'You know what I hear when you say that, chief? "I am a horny, disgustin man that's clever enough to make it sound like I'm no just a perv".

Lionel punched the bar, a motion that shook the aged structure and caused Gibby to jump back in his seat. Lionel realised the reaction was disproportionate and apologised to his colleague before elaborating. 'I want to know, on an academic basis, what makes men, in a supposedly chauvinistic society, aroused by being exposed in front of women. Is this urge to be judged related to feelings of guilt about the ordering of gender roles? Maybe it goes back to our Eden complex and how man came to be ashamed of his own body, or maybe because of deep-seated insecurities which we bury beneath layers of clothes, the removing of which represents the exposing our true selves. Maybe it goes back to the fear of our pants being pulled down in public by our mothers as punishment, and if so is it an Oedipal thing?'

'Or mibbe you just get off on showin your toby to burds.'

Lionel shook his head. 'For a pornographer who prides himself for being non-judgmental, you're very judgmental.'

'Okay, okay, keep your clothes on. Just need to understand my customer if I'm to meet his needs. I'll see what I can do.'

Lionel beamed and clasped his hands together and motioned them towards Gibby as if thanking him in prayer. 'Obliged. Now if you don't mind I have work to do. Have you seen Tony by the way? There is a matter I wanted to trouble him with.'

'In the cloakroom last I seen him. His Ricky Gervais is still gubbed after that bother with the boiler.'

Tony did indeed appear incandescent, at least on one side, when Lionel found him sitting in the cloakroom, surrounded by abandoned items of clothing and bashing away at a laptop. He looked up when he heard Lionel approach.

'Remember that disco compilation you used to play to antagonise the students on indie night?'

Tony smiled, 'Affectionately. I finally found a use for disco.'

'Was that on CD or vinyl?'

'CD. How?'

'Oh, I just find myself, from time to time, in the mood for a boogie. May I borrow it to aid my quest?'

In all the years Tony had known Lionel, he'd never been in the mood for a boogie. Still, who knew what went on in that unbalanced mind of his.

'If you want. It'll be in my crate.'

'Obliged.'

Tony turned back to the screen in the expectation that Lionel would leave. He stood there staring at him instead.

'What are you doing?' Lionel asked, finally.

The DJ sighed. 'Seein how Andy an Cornelius are still stuck in the last century I'm takin ownership of our social media marketin strategy, an invitin people to the openin night.'

Without waiting for an invite to critique Tony's work, Lionel grabbed the laptop off him and squinted at the screen. He appeared to have started a Facebook page for the club in which he was attempting to be as offensive as possible to anyone who might stumble across it and consider visiting.

'Twenty-eight friends. Is that good?'

Tony nodded with pride. 'Absolutely. We've identified 28 people who realise this's a joint for serious music fans. We had loads more friends at one point but I've managed to weed out the dross. Same with Twitter.'

Lionel digested this information, nodded and stared at the cloakroom wall. There was a reason why he'd come to see Tony and something he was sure he meant to go and do now, but he couldn't for the life of him remember what it was.

FOURTEEN

Cornelius sat with his leg elevated upon a bar stool and a pack of ice on his ankle. He wore his jogging gear, an outfit of traffic-stopping wonder that consisted of a 1980s Watford tracksuit top, pornographically short shorts, a beat-up pair of Sambas and a headband. Andy and Gibby walked in, looked at each other in amazement, and approached their stricken colleague.

'Cornelius? What happened?' asked Andy, his eyes wide with shock.

'Hey, man. Nothing to worry about. Just went over my ankle a bit.'

'No, I mean what happened to your clothes?'

'You look like a cross between John Barnes an Leroy from Fame, chief.'

'Oh, this,' Cornelius said pointing to his outfit. 'Emma saw how much weight Andy had put on since we started here and didn't want the same to happen to me. I'm on a strict exercise regime.'

'I've no put on that much weight,' said Andy shaking his head and looking to Gibby for support, only for his intention not to be drawn into the debate to be signalled by the sucking of air through teeth.

Cornelius nodded his agreement. 'That's what I thought. I said you were looking good these days with your new hair-style.'

'What new hairstyle?' asked Andy as his hand instinctively reached for hair that had not been styled since the millennium.

Cornelius shrugged. 'I don't know. But your head was looking smaller so I presumed you'd done something to your hair.'

'So, you go over your ankle joggin here?' asked Gibby as he

wondered if the shorts indicated that Cornelius shared a fetish with Lionel.

'Nah, ran to the end of the road til I was out of Emma's range of vision then jumped on the bus. I've been going to the gym but Emma thinks I only go to perv on the girls so she says I can only go running. I did my ankle tripping on that pile of rubbish bags.'

'Why d'we have all these bin bags all over the place?' asked Andy, sweeping his hand round the room to point to several similar articles.

Gibby pointed upwards towards an open hatch that led to the attic and mouthed the words 'Lionel, chief' to Andy, who looked up into the darkness and a cranny of the club he'd never ventured into.

'What's up there?' he asked.

'What's up there, chief, is the flotsam an jetsam of good times an ruined lives.'

Andy and Cornelius stared at him blankly.

'Basically all the garbage that's been left here over the years that we didn't know what to do with,' he elaborated. 'Along with some stuff we needed to hide from the authorities an womenfolk. Hell, we even had womenfolk up there at one point,' he winked at Andy. 'But don't worry, they were illegal immigrants an needed somewhere to stay.'

'So what's Lionel doin up there?'

Gibby shrugged. 'Your guess is as good as mine. He just goes off on these little projects that cause everyone else hassle. Always been like that.'

'Lionel,' Andy called up to the hatch, only to be ignored. 'LIONEL! LIONEL!'

After a few seconds of banging coming from the roof, Lionel's face appeared at the hatch.

'When you gonna clean this shite up? Cornelius nearly killed himsel on a bin bag.'

'I will attend to it as soon as circumstances allow. My spring clean is picking up momentum, but that is no excuse for making Cornelius the collateral damage in my war on clutter. Sorry, Cornelius. '

'It's okay man. Good work up there.' Cornelius raised an upward-turned thumb to the hatch and Lionel disappeared into the attic again with a grin on his face.

'You shouldn't encourage him, chief. No good will come of this.'

'Whereas peddlin porn when you're meant to be gettin rid of all they dead birds from the roof will bring us nothing but joy.'

Gibby held his hands up in surrender to Andy's sarcasm. 'I'll get to that presently but, speakin of dead burds, if you happen to know any necrophiliacs in need of audio-visual stimulation, point them in my direction.' Noting the disgust on the faces of the other two men, he added. 'They're only pretendin to be dead so it's okay.'

'Porn is totally overrated,' said Cornelius with conviction. 'It just kills your imagination and, since I started going to the gym, I've all the material I need.'

'Right, we can't fanny about here all day,' said Andy, wondering whether Cornelius realised that Emma was his sister. 'We've got a million things to do before openin night an I'm the only one doin anythin.' Loud thumping could be heard from above. 'Well, me an Lionel.'

'So, what you up to the day, chief? Gettin the insurance sorted? Movin things forward with the refurb? Licensin? Health & Safety?'

'No. I mean, obviously I'll be doin all that as well but first things, first. I'm accompanyin Cornelius to the gym.'

*   *   *

It was as he and Cornelius climbed the steps of the neon-lit temple of narcissism that the full implications of what seemed a good idea 20 minutes ago became clear to Andy.

'Look at it this way,' Cornelius said, trying to put his mind at rest. 'We'll feel all the better for it when we get out.'

'S'pose it'll be good to feel healthy again,' said Andy with a complete lack of conviction.

'Quick fag before we head in?'

'Be as well.' He accepted Cornelius' offer of a Regal and the pair lit up. 'I've got Extra Strong Mints on me. Can't let Michelle an Emma know we've started smokin again.'

'Too right, man. What can we do though? Everyone at the club smokes, we've got to fit in.'

'I know, but try tellin that to Michelle.'

'Between the smoking and the gym, the weight'll fall off. Then you'll be looking so shit hot that she won't mind your lungs going the same way as your old man.'

Andy considered this as he finished his cigarette, but still couldn't make the prospect of suddenly becoming irresistible to Michelle seem worth the pain he was about to put himself through.

'Cornelius, I really, really, really, really, really hate the gym. I don't want to go.'

'We've got this far. Getting up the motivation to come is the hard part.'

'No it's no,' Andy insisted. 'The grindin boredom of the treadmill an the excruciatin pain of sit-ups are the hard part. An, well, the club's a state. We should really…'

'Just wait. Within seconds of walking in this place you'll forget all about boilers and licensing and Jimmy Savile and all the rest.'

Cornelius smiled sweetly at Andy and held the door open for him. Bad dance music was piped throughout the facility and the smell of cleaning products attacked their olfactory functions. A tiled walkway with chrome handrails led to a reception desk staffed by a girl who looked like she'd escaped from one of the movies Gibby was doing a roaring trade in. She was in her late teens and wore a crop top that showed off a perfectly toned stomach, and shorts that made those sported by Cornelius's look like cargo pants. She shook her long blonde hair as if in a shampoo commercial, looked at the door and greeted her two admirers with a smile that should be reserved for returning war heroes, or boy band members at the very least. Andy's jaw dropped while Cornelius simply nodded a "told you so" to him. They approached with eagerness as Cornelius fended off his brother-in-law's attempts to reach the counter first.

'Oh, hi there Chelsea,' he said. 'Didn't know you were working today.' This was a lie as Cornelius had stolen the staff rota from behind the counter so he could synchronise his visits with her shift pattern.

'Hiya Cornelius,' she said leaning on the counter to give them an eyeful of cleavage. 'You're becoming something of a regular, eh? Wouldn't think a big strong man like you would need to work out so much.' Andy was about to roll his eyes at this pathetically transparent attempt at flirting when she added, 'And who's this handsome stranger?'

'This is my mate Andy.'

'Brother-in-law, actually. Cornelius is married to my pregnant sister. Meanin any future partner would have a step-child to consider.'

'Cornelius! You never told me you were married. I didn't think you were old enough.'

'Yeah,' he replied with uncharacteristic harshness. 'And I'm best man at Andy's wedding next year.'

The pair looked at each other as Chelsea added, 'Well, I think they're lucky girls. What'll it be today?'

'Two for the gym please,' said Cornelius.

'You don't, like, fancy my Body Combat class instead?' Chelsea raised herself on her elbows and arched her back forward. 'It's, like, reeeeeally intense. Works, like, every single muscle.'

'I bet,' said Cornelius, who, positioned only around a foot away from Chelsea's cleavage, felt as if he was had pushed the God of Fidelity too far. 'But we need to get back to work, so just the gym please.'

Reciting his marriage vows to himself, Cornelius took a step back, only for his place by the temptress of the treadmill to be taken by Andy.

'We actually co-own a nightclub,' he said inching forward. 'The Quantum Club? It's just about to open.'

Chelsea scratched her head. 'Never heard of it. If you need, like, a dancer give me a shout though. I've been on the podium at, like, all the big clubs.'

'We'll keep you in mind.' Andy replied, flashing Chelsea a grin that gave lecherous a bad name.

'Thanks guys. Just go on through. And remember if you ever want to, like, reeeeeeally work your body you know where I am.'

FIFTEEN

Michelle had returned home from work to find Andy in a happier and more relaxed mood than at any time since his father died. Welcoming the change, she assumed it was due to positive developments at Club Quantum. The boiler must have been fixed or something, thought Michelle as she burrowed in beside Andy on the sofa.

The boiler had not been fixed, however, and had Andy's hour of gym-based procrastination leading to an afternoon of Chelsea-inspired masturbation, he would have been demoralised by how his dream project was turning out. Still, Michelle was in stitches as he shared with her the latest madness from his co-owners.

'...he actually offered me Anal Ray in the UK. You were right about him. Fuckin perv.'

'I dunno,' Michelle looked up into Andy's eyes. 'Nothin wrong with porn really is there?'

'What? Really?' asked Andy, irate that he'd dumped his not inconsiderable collection of magazines and videos – having upgraded from scavenged-for scraps not long after the most embarrassing incident of a life filled with such moments – before moving in with Michelle.

'I mean. It might even be...sexy. No that anal stuff but if we watched another film together...' Michelle kept her gaze locked on Andy, who shuffled on the sofa, to conceal the fact he had gone from flaccid to fully erect within seconds.

His throat dried like a Saharan puddle at midday, so his response that he could maybe see Gibby about acquiring some stuff tomorrow was somewhat croaked, but clearly understood.

'Why wait?' asked Michelle as she ran a finger up Andy's inner thigh. 'I mean, he'll be at the club now won't he?'

The drive downtown took 10 minutes, but for the duration Andy seemed to exist in a different time dimension. Each red light was cursed and every learner driver they came across threatened. As Michelle pulled up outside the club, he briefly worried about her seeing that the 'STOR' sign hadn't been replaced yet, but almost instantly went back to planning his surgical strike. In-out, grab Gibby, listen to his theories about what Michelle would be into, and home for another in-out.

'Right, you wait here,' he said unclipping his belt. 'I'll be literally a couple of minutes.'

'Oh, I'll need to come in. I really need to pee.'

'Here?'

'Yeah, well you said you'd cleaned the ladies toilet. That's what you were doin all day yesterday wasn't it?'

'Well,' began Andy, who had in fact spent the day ensconced in the still-disgusting toilet reading Peter Hook's How Not To Run a Club. 'I said Cornelius had done it. Said he said he'd done it anyway. No guarantee how good a job he's done. You know what he's like.' Just one more lie, he told himself. No big deal. It's not as if you're injecting yet.

'I really need to go,' said Michelle, who was clearly in some discomfort. 'As long as Gibby's no still usin it as his personal fiefdom it should be okay.'

'Well, be quick. I'll see you back here in two minutes.'

The noise could be heard as soon as they stepped out the car. Andy and Michelle looked at each other and back to the club. The door to STOR was ajar and a thumping techno beat loud enough to shake the Law back into life was coming from within. Concerned that he was missing the opening night of his own nightclub, Andy led the way. No one was by the entrance or in the corridor that led to the club proper. The noise boomed louder and louder as they moved forward, but there was still no sign of human presence.

Andy looked to the ground as he pushed the double door open and walked through. He raised his eyes, fearing they were about to gaze upon the disco equivalent of the Marie Rose. It was much worse than that.

Tony appeared to be losing his mind in the booth as he

punched the air in time with each frenetic, floor-shaking beat. Gibby writhed around by the bass bin with his shirt off, gurning wildly. Lionel swayed from side to side in the middle of the dancefloor whilst rubbing his stubbly head.

'WHAT THE FUCK'S GOIN ON HERE?' Andy shouted, to no avail as the trio remained lost in their respective worlds.

He walked over to the nearest inebriate and tried shouting at him but, even from a yard away, Lionel was incapable of hearing his colleague. Eventually Andy tapped him on the shoulder. Lionel turned marginally quicker than coastal erosion, processed the sight of Andy for a few seconds then broke into a gap-toothed smile and embraced him with such warmth that Andy feared his ribs would break.

As this scene was being played out, Michelle walked round the back of the booth undetected by Tony and pulled the plug, receiving a hefty electric shock as she did so.

'Awww! Here!' he shouted at her.

'What's goin on?' she asked, inspecting the damage to her hand. 'Youse're out your faces.'

Lionel bounded over to her, shaking the floor with as much force as a PA pushing the outer limits of sound pressure had managed seconds ago. 'Ah, Michelle, We are having a little party to say goodbye to the old sound system. All is transient, all is temporal, all is, all is...Holy fuck I'm smashed.'

Tony offered Lionel's bag of out-of-date pills, now severely depleted, to Michelle and Andy, who both shook their heads. 'Yup, should've been here earlier. Brian was down.'

Andy's heart nearly leapt out his chest. 'From Health & Safety? Fuck. What did he say?'

'He left a note.' Tony held out a piece of paper, which Michelle grabbed from him.

'He's failed the club on every count,' she reported before passed the note into Andy's trembling hand. 'Says the place could be condemned unless we carry out major repairs.'

'He and Tony had a disagreement,' said Lionel, nodding his head to a track that had stopped a minute ago.

Even through the haze of a drug famous for inducing empathy and love, Tony's misanthropy was evident. 'Yup, the arsehole says he doesn't like ambient cybergrind techno.'

'Tony kept playing it, even when Brian threatened to do an on-the-spot inspection and fail us if he didn't stop. Pollice verso they call it in the context of gladiatorial combat. Mmmmm, nice pills make Lionel feel nice.'

Gibby had by this time joined the quartet at the booth and was attempting to stroke Michelle's neck whilst smelling her hair. Reading the note Michelle had passed him, Andy barely even registered the fact she was fighting off a molestation.

'It says we've got a week to sort this out or our licence will be revoked,' he said, all colour drained from his face. 'Tony, just for once, couldn't you have just played the game?'

'Nope,' replied the DJ placing his headphones over his ears once more and reaching for the plug. 'He was ruinin my buzz.'

'Everyone says your father was something of a DIY guru, Andrew. Even allowing for a certain degree of generational variations you perhaps possess enough traces of his abilities to perform the tasks yourself. Unless the chromosomes he gifted you were mainly related to obesity.'

'Will everyone please stop goin on about my motherfuckin father?'

Lionel placed a gigantic arm round Andy's shoulder. 'Do you have unresolved issues with your father that you would like to discuss? I do group therapy every Thursday.'

'No! Just…just…aaaargh.' He stormed off, Michelle pausing only to berate each of the trio with an Emma-esque use of profanity before following. Lionel and Tony shrugged and the music started up again, as invasive and tuneless as ever.

SIXTEEN

The mood had been lost by the time Andy and Michelle returned home sans porn so he was reduced, once more, to masturbating furiously in the bathroom. A look of concern was etched on Michelle's face when he returned to the living room. Her fiancé walking out with a magazine under his arm usually signalled that his bowels needed moving, so Michelle had also given up on the idea of copulation. Frustrated, she decided now to return to issues she had previously decided to leave until a later date.

'I couldn't help but notice the club renovations haven't really moved on in the past few weeks.'

Throwing the latest edition of MoJo, which featured a Louise Wener pictorial retrospective, on the coffee table, Andy shrugged. 'I'm waitin for quotes to come back.'

'I told you before, get everyone to chip in an save money. Just get it done. How's the boiler by the way?'

'Waitin for quotes,' he lied again. Fuck it, he didn't need the reminder of how shambolic the Quantum Club remained. 'D'you no think I know what needs doin? I've got licensin comin next week. DJ Quantum's ghost is hauntin me at every turn an…'

'I know you've got a lot on but the point is you're no makin any inroads into it.'

'For fuck's sake Michelle. I can't believe…' Andy continued to rant but his voice faded out of earshot as he paced towards the kitchen and back in as he returned with more slices of meat and cheese in his hand '…an shouldn't need to justify mysel to you.'

Michelle opened the coffee table drawer and produced a neatly stacked pile of papers and folders and held them out to Andy. 'Okay, let's go over the latest figures will we? How much is left in the account? When will Quantum be openin? How much money's needed to get us there?'

This was the turn of events that Andy most feared so he steered the conversation to the one area where tangible progress could be claimed. 'Well, I've been largely concentratin on publicity of late.'

Michelle tired of Andy's refusal to take the papers off her so she placed them on top of MoJo, which itself had landed on top of Michelle's wedding folder. 'So, what you done then? Finally worked out the mysteries of Facebook?'

'No, although Tony's meant to have done somethin with that.' Which reminded Andy that Cornelius had signed up for the world's biggest social network for entirely libidinous purposes. Having made Chelsea the subject of his first friend request, he advised Andy to join so he could check out the 'otherworldly' pictures from her holiday to Magaluf last year, and he had to admit to being tempted.

'What about posters an flyers then?'

'Cornelius is on the case,' he replied, making a note to ask him for a status update as soon as he stopped cyber-stalking 18-year-old fitness instructors.

'So in the absence of any kind of digital or physical publicity, what've you been doin to take ownership of the Quantum Club's PR?'

'Club Quantum,' said Andy before realising it was he who had the name wrong. 'An, I'll have you know, that I have, as it happens, managed to secure a feature interview with no less a publication than the Evenin Telegraph.'

Michelle looked at him blankly. Andy blinked. She blinked. Then he blinked again. Then her. This went on for some time before Michelle spoke.

'The Tele?'

'Yes,' he replied with a smugness disproportionate to the news he'd just delivered.

Michelle gave her fiancé a slow handclap. 'There's me doubtin you but it turns out you managed to corner the market in dyin media. How no get DJ Quantum to send his mum a postcard sayin "wish you were here"? That'll have about the same impact.'

Red mist descended on Andy. He stared at Michelle for a few moments, nostrils flared and brain unable to process a suitably cutting riposte. Eventually he marched out of the living room, giving the door a theatrical slam as he went, and up the stairs to the spare room where he his stash of smokes and crisps were kept, as well as New Order's entire back catalogue and more than one book with pictures of Debbie Harry in her prime. And when it came down to brass tacks, what else did a man need?

*   *   *

Andy didn't bother leaving the room until he heard the front door close behind Michelle the next morning. There were three reasons for this – his resolute belief that he was in the right, to prevent smoke wafting throughout the house, and not wanting Michelle to see that he'd spent most of the night crying like a baby.

He showered and dressed with stealth, planning as he was to spend the whole day at Club Quantum ensuring there was concrete progress to report that evening. His mood darkened further when the batteries in his Walkman failed during the bus journey, meaning he was forced to endure the sounds as well as smells and sights of public transport. It also led him to reflect on the fact he could never get one of those MPfree players he'd spent the past decade railing against without looking like a hypocrite of the highest order.

Given the state of 3/5 of the club's co-owners less than 12 hours ago, and the fact that another 1/5 spent most of his time lusting after barely legal gym bunnies, he was surprised to find signs of life when he arrived. More accurately, he was surprised to walk past the bar and find his way blocked by cardboard boxes, bin bags and a ladder that lead up to the loft. Tables and chairs resembling a jumble sale stall were strewn with clothing and various other nick-nacks. Shaking his head, he delved into the pile and grabbed the first thing his hand fell upon, which turned out to be a deflated blow up doll.

Andy, who had squeezed himself into his New Order t-shirt in an attempt to prove a point, held the offending item up to his face, stared into its eyes and called up the ladder.

'Lionel? Can you come down here a minute?'

A bin liner containing indeterminate items was thrown through the hatch, narrowly missing Andy's head which, admittedly, was not the smallest of targets. Eventually Lionel's legs emerged and he descended the ladder.

'This place's supposed to be openin in a fortnight. Every time I come in here it gets worse. There's a right stink comin from up there.'

'Which is, Andrew, the precise reason for my determination to expunge,' said Lionel, whose wild-eyed expression and tense jaw suggested that sleep was likely to remain a stranger for quite some hours. 'It would be terrible for the patrons we welcome here on opening night to be thinking, "banging tunes but an inmistakable whiff of death from above."'

Andy rubbed his eyes and took in what looked like a scene from a Channel 4 documentary on hoarding. 'There's someone important comin to see me here tomorrow. I'm tryin to put across a certain image, an the fact the place's full of sex toys isn't helpin. Why's it covered in sex toys?'

'I believe those incredibly lifelike dolls were left after the visit of a stag party some time ago. '

'Why didn't they just get dumped?'

'I decided that it was prudent to keep them away from Gibby, lest he seek to fill the hours between shifts by filling something else entirely.'

Andy conceded that had probably been a wise move and looked around the fabric mountain range that had sprung up overnight.

'Coats I can understand, but miniskirts, bras, pants...'

Lionel shrugged his massive shoulders. 'The women of this town are not renowned for shyness. There's plenty of men's clothing there as well if you're after a new t-shirt. That one looks a little snug.'

'No, it's no. Nothin wrong with it. I got this on the Technique tour. It's just shrunk a bit over the years.'

'Ah well, looks like you'll soon stretch it back.'

Andy tried to give Lionel a dirty look, but it was at this time he took in his appearance for the first time.

'Happened to your pus?'

'This,' Lionel said, touching the sticking plaster that covered half his head, 'is a small partying injury. The scar will be in good company amongst its brethren.'

Andy had no interest in re-opening the issue of last night until in-roads into his things-to-do-list meant he could preach from a position of moral authority, so he began plotting his route through the debris.

'I've got things to be gettin on with so you assurin me this'll be cleaned up by tomorrow would help a lot.'

'My word is my bond.'

Andy started climbing over mountains of bags and boxes. Lionel showed surprising agility for a man of bear-like proportions who'd spent most of the past week out of his head and weaved between various obstacles to stop Andy's progress.

'Err...do you mind me asking where you're going, Andrew?'

'The office, no that it's any of your business.' Andy pulled himself up to his full height in the forlorn hope of intimidating his colleague.

'Oh yes, absolutely,' Lionel said before pausing to give his jaws a grind. 'It's just...it's just. It's perhaps best to leave the dancefloor to myself and Gibby as it is need of a little spruce up after our impromptu celebration last night.'

'Fine,' said Andy, deducing that if they did indeed take care of that room then it would be one more accomplishment he could claim to Michelle.

Lionel waited until Andy finally managed to negotiate the obstacle course he had created before grabbing several blow up dolls and throwing them up into the loft. He picked up a dress and, after checking that no colleagues were in the vicinity, held it against his monstrous figure. Impressed, he grabbed some more women's clothes, folded them under his arm and climbed the ladder.

SEVENTEEN

Cornelius appeared to be in some distress when his brother-in-law found him outside the office. Andy rushed over to assist him, only to be assured that he was just stretching off his latest visit to the gym. After apprising Andy of the latest developments with Chelsea (she'd bent over to pick up a pen whilst convincing him to sign up for the XL members package), Cornelius opened the office door for him. A barely conscious Gibby lay prostrate and groaning on the desk, while Tony filled the big chair, with a laptop on his crossed legs. He looked at Andy and Cornelius, removed the pen he'd been chewing from his mouth, and frowned.

'Jesus Christ! What you wearin?'

Andy smiled at this confirmation of Cornelius' stupidity. 'He's pretendin to go out joggin to his psychotic bitch of a wife so he can ogle women at the gym.'

'I meant you. That t-shirt looks like it was bought in Mothercare.'

'For fuck's sake. Okay, so I'm carryin a bit of timber. I'm goin to the gym with Cornelius to keep an eye on him on behalf of my sister anyway.'

'You know I'm a monogamist, man. Just a bit of harmless titillation.'

Tony shook his head, 'You're all slaves to lust. Just like Sir Jimmy an yet everyone forgets his seminal contribution to DJin cos of a few unsavoury allegations.'

'But, man...I mean...'

'Wagner inspired Hitler but no one says "oh, forget the Ring, he would have been knockin out somethin cheery on the old Joanna at the gates of Auschwitz to welcome inmates" do they?'

'Tony, we really need to talk about this Jimmy Savile shite.'

'I agree that it's shite that we try to forget a man's seminal contribution to DJin just cos of some unproven claims.'

Tony made Andy feel physically sick at times. This was one of them. 'It's no good for our reputation.'

'Speakin of our reputation, I've been workin on our e-marketin strategy.'

Andy shook his head. 'We're no marketin E's or any other drugs. Mind, Michelle put a stop to that.'

Tony sighed. 'I'm talkin about our digital footprint. I tried to tell you about it but you just started goin on about how downloadin is ruinin music an how if you had a time machine you'd go back in time an sabotage any technology beyond the twin tape deck an 808 samplers.'

'Yeah, well. All that's true,' he insisted, once again lamenting the impossibility of him owning an iPod without losing face.

'Shite. Thanks to the wonder of modern technology, the Quantum Club is about to go viral.'

'Club Quantum, man.'

'I'm creatin a real buzz online to get the club's name, whatever is might be, out there.'

Andy felt the shiver of the 21st century down his spine, just as he did whenever he heard dubstep on the radio.

'The club has over 26 Facebook friends,' Tony elaborated proudly. 'If even half of them sign up as a fan of the club then their friends will sign up and their friends's friends will sign up and so on an so on.'

'How many Facebook friends do you have?'

Tony dismissed Cornelius' question with a wave of the hand. 'That's no important. What's important is invitin people to the openin night. We've had 16 people accept and 309 mibbes.'

'Why so many maybes?'

'New series of Downton Abbey starts that night. People are hedgin their bets to see how the parties go before decidin whether to go out.'

Andy's spine was a-tingle once again. 'People actually have Downton Abbey parties? I hate the modern world.'

'In this instance I agree. Look, I've been invited to three.' He turned the laptop to them and held it with the disgust most people reserved for the former DJ, TV presenter and predatory sex offender that he worshipped.

Cornelius struggled to comprehend what he was seeing on Tony's Facebook page. 'Erm...why have you accepted them all, man?' You're working that night.'

'You don't understand how Facebook works, Cornelius. No one actually goes to anythin they accept. It's just to look grateful.'

Cornelius nodded, not really understanding, but grateful of the tip should Chelsea ever ask him to an event. Andy, however, remained unimpressed.

'So why's the fact we've had 16 yesses a good thing?'

'Cos 16 people sayin they'll come then no comin is better than no one sayin they'll come an then no comin.'

'Good thinking, man.'

'No, it's no. It's just technogarbage. Facebook, Twitter. It's just a load of pish for teenagers to chat each other up on.'

'Here, I worked hard on this. D'you know how many fake friends I had to set up for Club Quantum?

'The Quantum Club. An I'm guessin 27.' Andy felt as if he'd shaken the modern age monkey off his back. 'While you've been playin on your computer, me an Cornelius have been gettin down to some real, good, old school promoter's work. Tell him about the posters an flyers.'

'They're amazing, man. Probably the best piece of design since Harry Beck did the London Tube map.'

'Fantastic. An when'll they be here?'

'Opening night.'

'Openin night?'

'Yeah, we thought it would be good to hand them out as souvenirs on the opening night. Like the first Factory night at the Russell Club.'

Andy could feel his blood pressure rise. 'What fuckin use is that?'

'Well, it worked for them. It laid the foundations for the Hacienda.'

'Factory Records folklore doesn't always make for the best business model. Mind the time you got asked to DJ here in the old days? When you insisted on signin in blood cos Tony Wilson done it? Even though you were gettin paid cash in hand an the owner said he'd prefer no paperwork.'

'Yeah, so...'

'So you severed an artery an nearly bled to death.'

Cornelius contemplated this. 'S'pose.'

Andy knew the importance of good flyering more than anyone. Shoddy design had, he felt, contributed to the downfall of his beloved band by making them look like an Eagles tribute act, thus alienating punters and local music journalists from the off. Keen to build on this latest victory in the Common Sense v Cornelius Morgan War of 1972-2014, Andy asked, 'So, is there any chance of us gettin them before our grand openin that no one'll know about?'

'Well, we...'

'Wait a minute, who's we?'

'DJ Q. He's a fantastic designer. Very pop art. Shades of a young Richard Hamilton. Designs all his own postcards y'know.'

Andy sighed, 'Here we go again. Can you send him a postcard, whether it's his own or has a pair of tits with a saucy pun written on them, an ask him to get his arse in gear, please?'

'I'll try, man. He's pretty keen on the opening night idea though.'

Tony was delighted that the latest DJ Q-related difficulty would add weight to his alternative strategy. 'So, now that we don't have any posters, how else are your traditional methods goin to get the word out to the great unwashed?'

Andy puffed out his chest in preparation for his coup-de-grace. 'I'm glad you asked me that, Tony. As it happens I have been workin hard to secure high profile media coverage.' He paused, building his part. Tony and Cornelius stared at him in expectation. 'Gentlemen,' he finally continued. 'I have managed to obtain an interview with the Evenin Telegraph.'

Once again his big news was not received as he hoped and his co-owners stared at him motionless before glancing at each other.

'Well I'm stunned, Andy.' Tony said finally. 'You're right. Why would we want to use a communication medium that half the world has signed up to when we can place an advert in a local newspaper?'

'Because it's local. An it's no an advert. It's a quarter-page feature. '

'No one reads local papers anymore.'

'People still buy it for the gig guide,' said a defensive Andy. 'Where else would they find out what's happenin locally?'

'You could go online an find out. I can set up email alerts which...'

Andy had been boycotting all DC Thomson publications since the hatchet job the Tele's sister paper did on his band but became strongly defensive of the august publishing house at this point. 'People still buy local papers cos it features people they know, things that affect them an their communities. The Internet's just a fad, you'll see.'

'An why the Tele an not the Courier?'

Andy felt the tragic tale of The Go-Ahead Seagulls was something Tony would enjoy rather than sympathise with so he decided to mention only the second of the reaons behind his decision. 'Cos Gibby says the boy who does the music for the Courier doesn't give good press unless you're prepared to reserve half the club for his guestlist. That elitist shite's everythin that's wrong with clubbing. I don't see how some punters should shiver in a cold queue when others march to the front cos of who they're shaggin or cos they look a certain way. Plus, we need every penny from payin customers, no freeloadin parasites.'

Tony shrugged and turned his attention back to his laptop.

Taking his silence to be a minor victory, Andy announced with a flourish that he and Cornelius were off to the gym for a quick work-out.

He turned to leave but something, or rather the absence of something, caught his eye.

'Did there no used to be a couch behind the door? Where's it gone?'

Gibby came to life and groaned. He rubbed his head, whimpered, and managed to croak out a few word. 'Lionel... took...No. Idea. Why. Owww. Head hurts. Actin strangely... even by...his standards. Chief.'

EIGHTEEN

The 24 hours that followed saw something as simple as a wrinkled nose persuade Andy to join his brother-in-law in the XL members' club. The contents of his fridge were also emptied in an attempt to replace burned calories, silence prevailed in his house and a second tearful night was spent in the spare room.

It was far from the best night's sleep Andy had ever had, filled as it was with dreams of being trapped in Homebase while some sort of clubnight took place in the car park outside, with Michelle dancing provocatively as various predators in Gibby masks circled her. As such, he was treating himself to a quick power nap in the office when he heard a knock on the door and opened his eyes to see the man of his dream, once more effervescent, enter.

'Alright chief. Bloke here sayin he's from the Tele. What happened to Washie?'

'He'd cost too much in guestlist privileges.'

Gibby shook his head. 'Aye, but he's a top bloke. Good mate of mine. But this guy you've got here. Well, he seems a bit of a walloper quite frankly.'

Andy stretched his arms out in an attempt to waken up in preparation for the most important media interview of his career to date. 'Gibby, please tell me you've no tried to sell a reporter a copy of My Boy's Lollipop.'

'I've no, but why shouldn't I? It's no just listenin to voice-mails that gives journalists their kicks. Know your problem? You're repressed. Sex is perfectly natural.'

'I know that. But there's a time an a place.'

'Let me guess. Your bed. At 9pm every second Wednesday. Missionary. A hot piece like Michelle? She'll be expectin more. There's a whole wild world out there, chief, an no one should be ashamed of perfectly natural desires. Dressin up, role play, light bondage, golden showers, animals, it's all good.'

'Animals?'

'No my thing, but if no consentin adults get hurt, who's Gibby Wisdom to stand in judgement?'

'What about the animals? Are they consentin adults?'

'Well, I've only seen the one animal actor an he was no foal.' Gibby illustrated his point by holding his hands around a metre apart. 'An he seemed to enjoy himsel.'

Andy pointed at Gibby. 'That doesn't matter. Was he able to say "yes, I'm fully aware of why you're pointin that camera at me an what you plan to do with the resultin footage?"'

'Obviously no. He's a horse.'

'Well then it's abuse. An FBI job. I don't want that shite anywhere near the club.'

'But...'

Andy stood up and walked over to Gibby, pausing to place a palm on his shoulder. 'Bestiality, Gibby. It's wrong.'

He left Gibby to rethink his whole belief system and strolled through to the entrance area, where his guest investigated the room with a disapproving look on his face, jotting observations in his notebook and capturing pictures on his camera phone. Oblivious to the fact he was already a couple of goals down, Andy bounced over to him with confidence, only for his stride to be broken by one of several bin bags that Lionel had failed to clear away.

'Sorry about that,' said Andy as he slalomed round the rest of the hazards. 'Still in the refurb phase you see. Ben, I presume? Andy Brennan. We spoke on the phone.'

'Hi there,' the reporter said, shaking Andy's hand. 'How's everything going?'

'Oh, you know. Few teethin troubles but we're gettin there.' Andy held out his hands to draw attention to a project that was getting nowhere.

'So, what's your plans for the refit?'

'This an that. Nothin major. At the end of the day this place is gonna be about the music?' Andy heard his voice lift a little at the end of the sentence in the manner of the young people he despised, and a little bit of him died.

Ben looked around with distaste once again. 'Okay. I was actually surprised when you said you were opening so soon. Not just because of the erm...appearance, but because I hadn't seen anything online.'

'Well there'll be some of that stuff, but what we're about is the old school. Posters an flyers. Etc.'

'Haven't seen any of them either.'

'Well, that's one of the aforementioned teethin troubles.'

The sound of banging could be heard from above. Ben looked to the roof and when his eyes returned to Andy he found a false smile on his face.

'What's that?'

'What's what?'

'That banging from the roof.'

Andy continued to stare at Ben and hoped his grin would buy him enough time to invent an explanation more reassuring than 'a bouncer rumoured to have been raised in a library by bears has been higher than the International Space Station for the past week.' What he didn't need at that point was Gibby to join them with a look of determined concern on his face.

''Scuse me, chief. I know you're busy an that but there's somethin I need to say.'

Andy replied through his teeth. 'I'm sure it can wait, Gibby.'

'No, it can't. All I can think about is bestiality.'

Andy walked over to his colleague and spoke to him without dropping the smile. 'This really isn't the time.'

'But, what that horse was doin to that woman. I mean...' Looking back over his shoulder, Andy noted that Ben's eyebrow was raised and he was licking the end of a pencil as he flipped over a page in his notebook.

Shooing Gibby back towards the office, he whispered, 'Look, we'll talk about this later okay?' before turning the smile on full beam for Ben once again.

'Sorry about that. Care in the community job.' Andy pointed to his temple and rolled his index finger around. 'All goin well our sound system an dancefloor will be as good as anywhere. That's what's important. What punters want.'

'I would say developments in the leisure trade over the past 20 years suggests they want comfort, safety and cleanliness.'

'Right, that's what we're tryin to get away from. Take it back to the music.'

'So what music will you be playing?'

Andy held his palms outwards. 'We have a strict musical policy. It has to be good.'

'Good? By whose definition?'

'Tony, our DJ.'

Ben flicked back several pages in his notebook, looked over the passage he'd been searching for and raised an eyebrow at Andy. 'This is the Tony Richardson who was banned from practising law after threatening the judge who made a light-hearted remark about Pete Doherty during a case?'

'Well, we have to reign in his sophistication sometimes.'

Ben raised his pencil, ready to record the answer to his next question. 'So, how am I meant to describe the music? Dance? Indie? R'n'B? Alternative? Hard rock?'

'But we're no anythin in particular. We'll play any type of music if it's good. But no poppy, charty pish.'

'Right, so alternative then.'

'No, I don't see why anythin that isn't Pop Factor has to be dubbed alternative these days. We're on a mission to pull down the barriers between genres. If we were a record shop then the only way we'd separate our music would be alphabetically.'

Ben shook his head. 'But that would just confuse people. They like what they like and want to find that type of music. And who goes to record shops anyway? Almost every song ever recorded is available and neatly categorised on iTunes.'

'But that's what's wrong. People's minds are stupefied by Glee an Simon Cowell an mainstream cattle markets. We want to broaden their horizons, provide them with an option.'

'A-ha! So you are alternative.'

'Well, yeah. But in a different way. We hate big corporate nightclubs.'

'Well, you're in a minority. Those places are smart, accessible, play music that you don't have to like music to like and don't frighten punters. People know what they're getting and are happy with that. Take Fat Sam's here in town, for example. They also play a lot of indie stuff.'

'Like what?'

'Scouting for Girls. The Feeling. Maroon 5. Savage Garden. For starters.'

Until his point Andy felt he had demonstrated admirable restraint, but his buttons had now been well and truly pressed. 'That's no indie! Scoutin for Girls are the biggest pile of shite ever. They're worse than Steps. At least Steps knew they were fuckin ear-rot. Scoutin for Girls have the gall to call themsels a proper band. I hope they fuckin die.'

'I like Scouting for Girls. They make catchy, inoffensive pop songs.'

'No they don't! They're so bland they're massively offensive. I can't sleep some nights for thinkin how much I hate them. One time me an Cornelius spent an entire day thinkin about whether we could live with ourselves if we cut the brake cables on their tour bus. We could.'

'Well, I think we can conclude our business here.'

Despite his racing heart and pounding temples, Andy realised he had to pull things back for the good of the club, proving Michelle wrong when she claimed he was incapable of compromise. 'Sorry. I was in the wrong. It's just Scoutin for Girls are a band I feel particularly strongly about. Can we rewind a bit?' It was with some embarrassment that Andy realised he was doing the rewind-a-record gesture popular with hip-hop MCs imploring their DJ to keep hitting that break.

With impeccable timing, Gibby re-entered the room, a gas mask round his neck and a Hazmat suit on.

'Right, chief. I'm goin to the roof. As well as the birdlife I heard Lionel say somethin about a fox bein up there.' Suddenly his face screwed up and he rubbed his stomach. 'Quick comfort break first. You'd think I'd learn about the omelettes.'

Trying to force a smile again, Andy turned to Ben. 'It's no like that. We've got a load of dead animals up there.'

'Dead animals? This is something Environmental Health should know about. I feel a front page coming on.'

Andy tried to protest that they would deny everything and that Ben had no evidence but he calmly returned the pencil and notebook to an inside pocket of his jacket, from where he produced a smartphone and began fiddling with it. His technophobia meant Andy didn't fully appreciate the gravity of the situation until his own voice could be heard, loud and clear, discussing bestiality, threatening multi-million pound recording artists, and generally sounding like a prick.

*　　*　　*

At that moment, 12 feet above them, Lionel was congratulating himself on a good week's work. Since hitting upon the idea he'd kept himself permanently high in order to complete the project as soon as possible and now had the attic looking exactly as he wanted.

Whereas the roof space had once resembled an emergency waste disposal facility site, it was now cleared of all furnishings, save for the sofa he had re-appropriated from the club office and the ghetto blaster borrowed from Cornelius.

Lionel, who was wearing an oversize fireman's uniform, was busy inflating and dressing a series of blow-up dolls. After completing this task he picked them up one-by-one and seated them on the settee before standing back to admire his handiwork.

His harem consisted of three brunettes, one redhead and a blonde. Thanks to his efforts, all now wore short, revealing clothes of the type that young women might wear for a night on the town. Or that a girl group might dress in.

He paced back across the room, placed the requisite eight

A-size batteries in the ghetto blaster and pressed play. A synthesised hi-NRG dance track began playing, but no lyrics could yet be heard.

Lionel checked that the hatch in the floor was securely locked for a fifth time and, reassured that no one could ruin the moment he'd worked so hard to realise, closed his eyes and took a deep breath.

He turned to his dolls, opened his eyes and began talking to them in the style of a birthday DJ.

'Ladies, I know you are here to celebrate Cheryl's birthday but the co-owner of Club Quantum requires you to listen to a very important fire safety announcement first. So please. Members of Girls Aloud,' it was at this point Lionel took up the role of all five girls and began screaming to himself in anticipation of what was to come, '...give it up for Officer Mark 'Lionel' Ritchie who, assuming you are good girls tonight, may well allow you to slide down his magnificent pole.'

Lionel did some more screaming from the back of his throat as the lyrics to Sylvester's Do Ya Wanna Funk? kicked in. He began dancing around, his timing compromised by the fact he was excitedly singing along in a suitably high-pitched voice whilst removing items of clothing. Being something of a novice as a male stripper, his attempts at sexiness fell as flat as the deflating vinyl vixens on the sofa.

Firstly he threw his helmet at the group, succeeding in hitting Kimberley in the face. He then tried a few spins before mincing towards the girls. After a few moves that he erroneously believed to be provocative, Lionel began teasing the girls as he slipped his jacket off his shoulders, coyly slid it back on again, and repeated the motion until he was sure his audience was whipped into a frenzy of excitement. Eventually, he ripped it off and placed it round Nicola's neck.

Lionel's yellow trousers were now only held up by a pair of braces, which he decided to use as a prop for his performance. He slipped his thumbs under them and began moving the braces from side to side, revealing a tiny bit more nipple each time. After the strap finally fell to his side he imitated another scream and pushed his pecs together so that they resembled a cleavage. With confidence growing, he sashayed towards Cheryl and pushed his right nipple into her waiting mouth, grabbed Nadine's head and moved it toward the left one. After a few seconds of frenzied screaming by the other three, Lionel danced back until he stood before them with his thumbs under the waistband of his trousers. Again he teased the UK's most successful-ever female pop act a few times by threatening to remove the plastic yellow trousers he'd purchased from Utopia Costumes that afternoon for £19.99. Warming to the part, Lionel shook his head at his assembly and wiggled his finger to warn they would have to wait.

By now, the song was approaching its end and Lionel, clad only in the trousers and non-regulation fire brigade boots, turned things up a notch. He dived on the dolls in an attempt to lapdance for Cheryl but succeeded only in bursting her blonde bandmate.

'Ah, sincerest apologies Sarah.'

Ever the professional, Lionel recovered by grinding up and down Cheryl a few times, forcing more air out of her as he did so.

'I would wager that Ashley never did this for you, did he?'

Lionel stood up again and moved along the line, pausing to lick his fingers and rub them round his nipples for Nadine. He then turned and performed a strange wiggling dance before reaching down for his toes to ensure the girls were staring at his bum. In one motion he pulled his trousers off and spun round to his audience once more. Wearing just his boots and tiger-print thong, he jumped towards the girls and began thrusting his groin in their faces. Kimberley was singled out for treatment and he lifted his leg over her head so that the contents of his pouch bounced against her nose as he prodded forward. After a few seconds, he released her from his grip and stepped back to give them a full view of their entertainment, playing with the string of his thong a few times and losing himself in the act.

He let off a primal scream before shouting through gritted teeth. 'YOU WANT THE LOT? YOU WANT MORE?'

Lionel twisted round to face away from the concubines in various stages of deflation. He closed his eyes and slowly lowered his arms by his side, hooked his thumbs under the elastic and yanked the pouch off in a rapid, violent motion. Lionel led the appreciation of his efforts once again with high-pitched screaming he was attributing to his adoring, lustful crowd as the show's climax approached.

At this point, Lionel planned to turn 180 degrees once more so that the 2002 winners of Popstars: The Rivals would be treated to a full-frontal view of his exposed genitals before he stepped forward so they, driven wild by desire, would be grabbing for him like the girls in Gibby's DVDs.

What actually happened was that he opened his eyes to see a face looking in, amazed, through the skylight. The face of Ben, who had decided to investigate the goings on in the attic by climbing the ladder Gibby had left outside. The face of Ben with his mobile phone held next to it as he recorded the proceedings.

Clad only in his boots, Lionel looked him straight in the eye and danced over to the window, did a few moves for Ben, blew him a kiss, shut the curtains and collapsed on the floor in embarrassment as the CD started jumping.

NINETEEN

It was the first time Andy and Michelle had spoken in days. Given the gravity of the situation, Michelle felt the time for recriminations over Andy's continuing prevarication, lies and neglect could wait. The most pressing matter was spread across her fiance's lap as he read aloud.

'Best of luck to Dundee's newest nightspot, Club Quantum, which opens next week. I fear the management co-operative at its heart will need it. The place looks like it has gone 12 rounds with a bulldozer, the staff may have reason to fear Yewtree's wildlife-oriented sister operation, and the musical policy seems to be to alienate as many people as possible. A particular highlight of this reporter's visit was watching a steroid-fuelled primate attempt a bizarre mating ritual with a clutch of PVC vixens. The video of this incident (rated '18') can be found on our website. All in all, the place to be if you're a chin-stroking, shoe-gazing virgin in their 30s who enjoys standing around with like-minded people in conditions akin to a bombed-out building in the Blitz. But without the spirit. For anyone else, avoid.'

Michelle rested her chin on Andy's shoulder and rubbed his arms. 'Oh well. Nobody reads local papers anymore.'

Certainly no one was likely to read the large forest's worth of papers their breakfast bar was close to buckling under the weight of. Andy had spent the day running around every newsagent, supermarket, petrol station and corner shop in Dundee, rambling about the principles of truth, disclosure, and objectivity as he did so. This damage limitation operation was effectively an investment, he reasoned, as the Press Complaints Commision would surely uphold his objection and awarded damages at least equal to the cost of 18,000 copies.

He closed his eyes and sighed, grateful of the supportive

words and human touch. He tilted his head until it touched Michelle's only for this brief moment of succour to be broken by a text message arriving on his fiancee's phone.

'Oh fuck,' she said holding the screen out to Andy for him to read. 'That's Emma sayin the article's online as well. 876 people have liked it on Facebook, includin Cornelius.'

Andy shook the paper with anger. 'This is a hatchet job. What happened to journalistic integrity? Impartiality of the press? Right to reply? They even got the club's name wrong. An steroid-fuelled primate? That's slander. He'd been on pills for a week straight. If I don't get a retraction then, I swear to God, I'm goin Leveson on them.'

Michelle stood up and massaged Andy's shoulders. 'Okay, honey. It'll be okay.'

Andy stood up and kissed her. 'I'm goin down to the club to sort this out.' He grabbed a doughnut from a packet on the table in front of him. In spite of the thawing of household relations, Michelle grimaced, a gesture that was not lost on Andy, who was tired of his waistline serving as a punchline.

'Any comments?'

Deciding to return to the issue of Andy's ballooning weight, along with all the rest of their issues, once this latest disaster had been mitigated, she forced a smile. 'No, you're fine. I'm more worried about what the stress is doin to your blood pressure so, if it helps, munch on.'

Andy nodded, 'Good, cos I've been goin to the gym every day. Look – my head's gettin bigger again.'

The sound of the house phone spared Michelle having to pretend that Andy was looking in any way healthier so she grabbed it as quickly as she could.

'Hello...Yeah, he is here so no need to come over an keep me company...I'm gutted about that too,' Michelle raised her eyebrows and handed the phone to Andy.

'Alright Gibby, you seen the paper?'

Andy heard smoke being exhaled before his partner responded. 'Seen it, chief? I've been fieldin follow-up calls all day. It's all over the web. David Hepworth, Paul Morley, they're all bloggin about it. Radcliffe an Maconie were laughin about us on 6music. The boy from Keane with the kiddy-on drug problem says it sounds like his kind of place. Even as one of life's optimists, I'd have to say this is about as positive a development as Dylan findin Jesus. Still, could be worse.'

Andy looked at the receiver in disbelief. 'Could be worse? How exactly?'

'Well he never seen the main room, did he?'

* * *

Andy stood with Gibby, Lionel and Tony by the bar. He turned one way to see a couple of head-shaped holes in the wall, then the other, to where the DJ booth has been all but demolished. An axe was jammed in the bar top and the remains of a fire smouldered in the middle of the dancefloor.

'What in the name of fuck have you done to my club?'

'Our club, Andrew, please. It's recherché.' Noting Andy's vacant expression, Lionel added, 'It means sophisticated. You know, cultured.'

'Like gettin your cock out for a load of blow-up dolls, you big freak? The whole world now associates my dream of restorin credibility to an industry contaminated with bland-ness with you stickin your hairy nipple in a plastic orifice.'

Lionel, already reeling from his recent brush with fame and the fact no exotic male troupes had been in touch yet to offer him work, looked to his feet. 'I wouldn't say the whole world. The Evening Telegraph has a circulation of about 20,000 plus an online readership of...'

Tony, sidling up to Andy, led the next attack. 'What about the DJ booth? It's in fuckin pieces.'

Lionel and Gibby exchanged shameful looks. The other night's revelry had gone on until Tony got bored and wandered off in pursuit of new distractions. His colleagues were far from finished partying, however, and decided that hedonism and interior design needed to be wed, chemically inspired as they were to take the renovation bull by the horns. And direct it to the nearest china shop.

'It's like that wall, Lionel,' Gibby had pointed out as they listed Quantum's shortcomings. 'What's that wall doin there? It's all wrong. It's hurtin my perceptions.'

'I concur. Allow me.'

He gently pushed Gibby aside with one arm, let out a low-pitched growl and charged the wall in an attempt to demolish it. His head made contact with a sickening thud and he bounced back on to the floor without registering any success in his mission.

'Good effort, chief,' Gibby nodded, reached for a bong that was handily positioned on a nearby table and lit it up.

Lionel pulled himself upright, rubbed his head and shook his body off as he studied the offending two feet of stone and plaster. 'Perhaps if I was to vibrate my molecules fast enough, like The Flash, I could materialise halfway through and destroy it that way.'

Gibby half-protested and half-coughed as a plume of smoke rose from his lungs and out through his mouth. 'Mibbe that wall's only messin with our perceptions cos we, if I've diagnosed the symptoms correctly, are well an truly banjo'd. It's a bendy wall. The wall's bendy.'

'So you're saying it should be a feature wall then? It should be afforded a stay of execution?'

'Aye,' said Gibby as he lowered his lighter to the bong once again. 'But take another run at it anyway.'

Lionel charged again, this time with even more force. Again, he rebounded and landed in an ungainly heap. He rolled around nursing an open wound to his forehead while Gibby sucked hard on the bong.

Eventually Lionel managed to stagger to his feet as Gibby was setting the water pipe down on the table with a fair degree of uncertainty. He moaned loudly and fell to the ground where the doorman had been lying seconds before.

'Perhaps I would enjoy a greater degree of success by honing my destructive skills on something less substantial,' said Lionel before pausing to catch the blood that ran down his face with his tongue. 'Can you think of any unambigious reason the DJ booth should inhabit that precise space?'

* * *

Only half the structure remained as the group inspected it, much to Tony's chagrin. 'I got enough paint to fix the walls but what about the booth? We can't just paint it beige an hope no one will notice it's in pieces.'

'An another thing, this isn't beige.' Andy pointed to the two dozen pots of identically coloured paint sitting in the corner next to the pile of vomit that Gibby had not got round to clearing up yet. 'It's more like flesh. You got flesh-coloured paint for the club.'

Tony moved back into his own space and tutted. 'It was on special. An I got it mysel cos I felt guilty about the boiler an Brian. Wouldn't have bothered if I knew you'd be such a prick about it.'

The quartet were interrupted by the tuneless impersonation of song coming from the corridor. It got louder and louder until there was a knocking on the double doors that were then thrust open as Cornelius appeared.

'Woaaaaah! I feel good, do-do-do-do-do-da, I knew that I would now, do-do-do-do-do-da, So good, do-do, so good, do-do...holy shit. What happened here?' He walked over to Andy, turning this way and that to take it all in.

'These aresholes got out their faces an trashed the place. Then they didn't tell me about it for days.'

'So why's the dancefloor still on fire?'

Gibby looked at him with pride. 'Well, that only happened last night, chief. You see, Lionel's fear finally kicked in an he phoned me in a panic sayin we had to burn the place down. Now, I wasn't thinkin clearly on account of no havin evacuated the old beach towels for 12 hours. So we got the fire goin, then the salts finally kicked in an 10 minutes later I was like, "nah Lionel, this is wrong." Quite frankly I was expectin a bit more gratitude.'

Andy's fingers gripped his temples. 'What did we say in the legally bindin contract? Any insurance burn-out has to be unanimously agreed by all partners. This was bilateral action an the place's absolutely fucked now. There's no comin back from this.' He looked for the nearest non-broken or burnt seat and collapsed on it.

'Nah…nah…I like it,' enthused Cornelius. 'It's like, it's like a blank canvas. Yeah, we can totally make this place our own.' He faced Gibby, Tony and Lionel in turn and nodded his approval to each of them.

'Have you finally flipped?' Andy wished that his brother-in-law would, just for once, take a glass-half-empty view of life. 'Youse said you would sort it out an all you've done is make things a million times worse. We pay whatever it takes to get the place sorted,' he held up his hands to silence the protests from all present. 'We put the sound system in the long grass beside the mirrorball an we use our time productively to try an turn our miserable reputation around. No more fannyin about on daft projects. No exposin yoursel to lumps of plastic…'

'Hey, I saw that video, man. Nice moves.'

Andy shot Cornelius a look that even he recognised as malicious enough for him to retract the thumb he'd just raised to Lionel.

'No floggin porn, no alienatin council officials an no skippin off to the gym to perv on teenagers every five minutes.' Andy felt the same stab of hypocrisy at this point as whenever he was alone in the house and played the Grease: Original Soundtrack he mercilessly mocked Michelle for owning. 'We're runnin out of money. If we don't sort this shite out soon we won't even make it to openin night. Got that?'

Andy wiped the spit from his chin that had flown out of his mouth during his speech and looked at Gibby, who nodded in a rare display of meekness. Lionel continued to stare at his feet while Cornelius mouthed the word 'sorry' to Andy.

Even Tony had been rattled by the ferocity of Andy's rant

and he looked to the wall, unable to meet his gaze. Eventually he worked up the courage to speak. 'Thing is, that paint's non-refundable. It was so cheap cos it's no exactly British kite standards so no legit painter would touch it.'

'True, chief. Best handle that oursels. I'll go see a guy who owes me a favour an get some dust sheets an protective gear.'

'Yes. I should probably get some sleep, Lionel yawned. 'I have been up longer than Keith Richards' time.'

Andy's mouth hung open as the three of them walked. He turned to his brother-in-law for support, but Cornelius was already bounding after them. 'I've got some other colours at home that'll complement the flesh perfectly. Watched Grand Designs last night. Epic ideas. Epic.'

TWENTY

Cornelius had piled the tins of paint by the foot of the stairs and was darting around trying to locate brushes, trays and other decorating paraphernalia when the front door flew open with such ferocity that it was nearly divorced from its hinges. Emma was struggling with shopping bags and angry that Cornelius had not responded to the repeated blasts on the car horn indicating that assistance was required. Her face brightened when she spotted the tins.

'Finally. I thought you'd never do it.'

Cornelius side-stepped the pyramid of paint and bent down to kiss his wife's bump while leaving her to deposit the bags on the ground herself.

'I know, baby. But I'm totally into it now. Watched Grand Designs. Dead inspiring.'

'Bollocks. I know all about your short-term obsessions. Like the scuba divin. We've still got a fuckin wetsuit takin up space in the wardrobe. I want guarantees that if you open they tins then you'll see it through.'

'I won't rest until I'm finished, baby. I've never been as committed to anything in my life. Even our marriage. '

Emma had heard all this before. In addition to the scuba diving and the mirrorball, she had competed with zorbing, potholing and the Nation of Islam for Cornelius' affection at various points in their marriage.

'Repeat after me. I, Cornelius Morgan, bein of partially sound mind…'

Cornelius placed his right hand on his heart and held the other up as it taking a presidential oath. 'I, Cornelius Morgan, being of partially sound mind.'

'Do solemnly swear, under pain of castration…'

'Do solemnly swear, under pain of castration…'

'To undertake, persevere with, an see through to the end…'

'To undertake, persevere with, an see through to the end…'

'The job of paintin my unborn daughter's room.'

'The job of painting my un…what? The baby's room?' Cornelius tried to shrug off this bombshell by playing it cool, something that didn't come naturally to him. 'Course. No probs. Just need to nip down to the club first.'

Emma raised an accusing finger to within an inch of Cornelius' face and edged forward. 'Un-be-fuckin-lievable. You're tryin to back out of it already.'

'Err…yeah. I'll be home for tea time though.'

'No you won't.'

Cornelius realised he was now backed up against the wall but Emma's finger remained the same distance away. 'No, honest I will.'

'No, you won't. You're goin nowhere until you've painted the baby's room.'

'But I said I'd be back. They're relying on me.'

Emma's bloated features fell into a smirk. 'Cornelius, no one relies on you cos you're fuckin hopeless in almost every regard. You can go an play with your friends once you've done what you said you'd do months ago. Or I'll cut your balls off an hold them in front of you as you writhe in agony.'

Emma reversed whilst holding her gaze on Cornelius. She swerved round the tins and stood by the door, crossing her arms and nodding her assent for her husband to begin his new assignment. He trudged towards the tins, picked them up and climbed the stairs. Emma followed Cornelius until he had reached the room and put the tins down as the door was locked from the outside.

*   *   *

Andy and Michelle lived only minutes from Emma and Cornelius in Lochee, the traditional home of Dundee's Irish community. Cornelius, who regularly told stories of growing up in North London and seeing the infamous 'No Blacks, No dogs, No Irish' posters wherever he went, felt an immediate affinity with his similarly opressed new neighbours upon moving to the area. This was an affinity missed by both the deathly pale locals in Celtic tracksuits and the Staffordshire Bull Terriers that dragged them up and down Lochee High Street when Cornelius unfailingly greeted them with a Black Power salute.

Both couples' homes were situated on a modern development of privately owned detached and semi-detached houses on the outskirts of the area, something that made a mockery of Cornelius' claims to have "never been able to escape the ghetto, like Chuck D". Despite their proximity and the love he felt for the man, Andy rarely visited his friend's home. However, not having heard from Cornelius since he fled the club in a fit of Nick Knowles-inspired passion the previous day, Andy felt compelled to brave the company of his sister. He rehearsed pleasantries for them to exchange as he approached the house, but whatever banalities he thought of always seemed to lead the conversational journey towards violence.

The garden was covered in sand and unlaid paving slabs piled against the wall. Cornelius had abandoned his landscaping project a year ago after claiming to have heard Louis Farakhan declare gardening to be un-Islamic. The lack of progress in this area was unlikely to have lifted Emma's mood any.

He reached the door and kicked sand off his trainers against the pebble-dashed walls as the first drops of rain could be felt on his back. Without Andy ringing the bell, the door was opened as far as the security chain would allow Emma squeezed her face into the gap and addressed her younger sibling.

'If you've come for Cornelius, you can forget it. He's busy paintin the baby's room.'

Andy tried to look above and below Emma to see if Cornelius was around, but the Brennan head always proved a worthy opponent at such times and he eventually gave up.

'But we need him at the club. It's an emergency.'

Emma narrowed her eyes and flared her nostrils. 'What kind of emergency?'

'Well, I dunno how much he told you but it started when the boiler blew up. Nearly killed Tony.'

'Only nearly? Shame.'

'That's what I said,' Andy climbed the step so he stood taller than Emma and could shelter from the increasingly weighty fall of water from the heavens. 'Look, this is ridiculous. Open the door so we can speak properly.'

Without a further word, Emma closed the door and Andy was left wondering whether that was the end of the conversation before he heard the chain being undone. He tried to enter as the door opened, only for Emma to push him back as she emerged. The door was closed behind her and she took her brother to task from the top step.

'I don't want Cornelius to hear your voice. He'll start whinin an want out again. An he doesn't know anythin about boilers.'

'That's no what Gibby says. Anyway, he's goin to be paintin.'

'He's useless at paintin, which is why he's doin that room again. The wall looked like it had alopecia.'

'Plumbin.'

Emma shook her head. 'He can't deal with faeces. He's got a phobia.'

'Electrics then. I get a shock every time I turn the lights on.'

'Well, now you know how Michelle feels. Anyway…' she gulped before mentioning the name. 'Dad showed you how to do all that stuff.'

Andy sniffed. 'I see mysel more as a project manager.'

'Well, you'll have to project manage without Cornelius. He's grounded.'

'Grounded?' Andy asked, decibels rising, 'He's a grown man for fuck's sake, Emma.'

Emma had placed her hand on the door knob but turned round to point at Andy in an escalation of this latest phase in their lifelong conflict. 'Yes! A grown man who you manipulated into throwin his life savins into a black hole called Club fuckin Quantum!'

'Quantum fuckin Club.'

'Whatever,' she snarled while waddling back over the threshold. 'Fuckin do it yoursel for once. Leave us alone or I swear to God you'll pay a hefty price. A hefty fuckin price.'

The door slammed in Andy's face before he could respond. Shoulders slumped, he rued the lack of protection that his New Order t-shirt offered against the rain and trudged slowly over wet sand towards the street without looking back. Had he done, he would have noticed Cornelius looking miserable and waving his paintbrush at him from a top floor window as the distance between the two friends grew once again.

* * *

After a drenching that made him consider whether it might be time he learned to drive, Andy changed into a Smiths t-shirt and played their first album as he attacked a deep-fried pizza with animalistic frenzy. Like Morrissey, Andy hadn't had a dream in a long time. Throughout his sleepless nights in the spare room he reflected on how the luck he'd had could indeed turn a good man bad and partially absolved himself of blame for his treatment of Michelle as a result. Please, please, please let me get what I want, he offered to no one in particular. Please don't let me go back to that fuckin call centre. Please somethin turn up. At least he had his fiancée back onside, he reflected, unaware that at that precise moment she remained enraged with him and was fucked if she was going to watch grease run down his miserable face all night.

'Are you seriously just gonna sit there when there's so much needin done at the club? They three knobs trashed it an you're just sittin around eatin an drinkin.'

Andy looked up at her with his face smeared in sauce and cheese. 'Well, that was kinda my plan.'

Michelle knelt down beside him. 'Mibbe if you were a bit more hands-on the others would fall in line. They're like dogs, they need a leader.'

Andy knew his fiancée had been exceptionally supportive over the past few months and that she continued to speak sense. At the same time, if she would just let him forget his problems for a while he might get a proper sleep and something might occur to him. He looked in the other direction. 'You know how I feel about DIY. It gives me the fear.'

'But…'

Andy wiped his face and stared straight ahead as he recalled the time his father had tried to show him how to strip wallpaper in conditions, his memory assured him, that made a Native American sweat lodge seem airy.

'This is a scraper. You stick it into the wallpaper an work it loose like this, see?'

Andy wasn't listening to his Dad, however, as he attempted to ventilate his chest by pulling at the neck of his Black Grape t-shirt. He pointed a sweat-glistened, trembling finger at the device in the corner of the room that he blamed for his plight.

'Does that thing need to be on? It's worse than 'Nam in here.'

'Aye, that's right. The hearts of they poverty-stricken, war-torn Vietnamese must be breakin for you havin to help do up a room. The humidifier needs to be on cos it makes it easier to strip the wallpaper.'

'But Glastonbury's on telly.'

'Andy, one day you're goin to learn that if you want somethin done, you have to put in the effort. You wanted your room redecorated.'

'But I thought you'd, y'know, pay someone to do it.'

'Oh aye? Made of money, are we? I dunno what's rattlin around in that giant head of yours sometimes. You're a man now, even with your long hair. It's time to start actin like one.'

When he finished telling the story, Andy's giant head was being cradled by Michelle as he blubbed on her shoulder.

'Shhh…it's okay, honey, let it go. It's okay.'

'I just…I just miss him so much.'

'I know, honey, I know.'

Andy wiped a handful of tears, snot and pizza residue from his face. 'He'd want me to do it, wouldn't he? He'd want me to do the club up mysel, wouldn't he?'

'Well, he wouldn't have wanted you to buy it in the first place, but yes. Kinda.'

'He had faith in me, didn't he?'

Michelle coughed, followed by, 'Yes, of course he did.'

'I'm a leader of men,' Andy insisted to himself. 'It's time I started actin like it.'

Finally, thought Michelle. 'So you'll go an start work then?'

Andy blew his nose, inspected the contents, then looked to Michelle. 'Nah. I'll get the rest of them to do it. Well, I'll really get Cornelius to get the rest of them to do it.'

'Cornelius?' Michelle was aghast that the apparent progress of the past five minutes had counted for nothing.

'He's mibbe no the sharpest key on the Casio but he inspires people. What about that racist?'

'The guy who ended up bein usher at his weddin?'

'Yeah. He embraced multiculturalism thanks to Cornelius. He looks at people with they big eyes an they just do what he says.'

Michelle had spotted the obvious flaw in this logic. 'You mean apart from his wife? Who hasn't said a good word about him since their weddin day an psychologically bullies him?'

Andy sprang to his feet. 'What a brilliant idea, Michelle! Thanks, I love you.' He planted a kiss on her forehead on his way out as she sat there pondering the precise physiological reasons for selective deafness and wondering whether there was any wine left from last night.

TWENTY-ONE

The coded message arrived in the form of a postcard created by the world's greatest undiscovered disc spinner and composed by one of its worst. After numerous calls to Cornelius' house were intercepted by the enemy, Andy wondered if he had been hasty in speaking out so vehemently and consistently about mobile telecommunications over the years. He finally managed to speak to his brother-in-law by calling during EastEnders when Emma was least motivated to answer. Cornelius, conscious that Emma was monitoring his every movement, whispered only 'I'll be in touch' before pretending to passionately appeal to a Delhi-based double glazing salesman to stop harassing him and his eight-months pregnant wife.

Quite why Cornelius felt the need to encode the postcard which arrived the following day, Andy didn't know. In order to crack the cryptic clues he had to watch Otis Redding live at Monterey, read half of Kenny Jackett's autobiography and listen to Exodus. The upshot was that Andy finally managed to piece together his instruction. "Meet me. Back Garden. 8pm. Come alone. Be quiet."

The rendezvous point required Andy to trespass through some dozen gardens, risking the wrath of angry dogs and irate householders as he vaulted more fences than Red Rum in his entire National Hunt career. Looking suspiciously like an out-of-shape housebreaker dressed all in black, he finally flopped into Cornelius and Emma's garden with a minute to spare. He wiped dirt from his clothes and attempted to catch his breath before straightening his back with some difficulty. Guessing that a light on in an upstairs window indicated where he would most likely find his brother-in-law, Andy threw a stone in its direction. Cornelius' head emerged from beneath the frame, making Andy think he'd probably been lying in wait for some time, then ducked down again.

Thirty seconds passed before Andy could hear the sound of voices from within the house.

'Baby! I'm just taking out the rubbish, be back in a minute.'

'You better be. I'm timin you.'

Andy shook his head as Cornelius walked out into the night, bin bag in his hand.

'Right, so what's happened is…'

'Shhhh! Emma might hear. Although Corrie's on so we should be good until the ads. What's up?'

Andy briefed Cornelius on the latest developments and his plan to have their co-owners inspired into transforming the club into the venue that he and Cornelius had dreamed of all along.

'Holy shit! I've never heard you sound so decisive in your life. Maybe you are the man, man! Maybe your Dad was wrong about you.'

Andy's brow furrowed. 'What d'you mean? Wrong about me?'

Cornelius shrugged. 'Nothing really. It was just that impression of you he did.'

'He did an impression of me?'

'Yeah. You didn't know?'

'No.' Andy's face wrinkled like Yoda's ballbag. 'What'd he do?'

'Well, he kinda minced about wobbling his head like it was too big for his body and talking crap about music in a really whiney voice.' Cornelius chuckled to himself. 'It was pretty funny.'

Andy spat on the ground. 'The cheeky fat bastard. I got that from him. My mum's head was like a peanut.'

'Don't sweat it man, it's just families messing around. He loved you and just wanted you to fulfil your potential.'

'No, he did it 'cause he was a bully. It's where Emma gets it from.'

'What d'you mean? Emma's not a bully.'

A high-pitched scream could be heard from inside the house. 'COOOOOORNEEEEEEELIUUUUUS!'

'Oh shit. I better go.'

'But, we've no discussed my plan yet.'

'Yeah we did. You're going to inspire them to stop arsing around.'

Andy's head wobbled around. 'No exactly. I was hopin you'd do it for me. Mind that skinhead?'

'Kev? Yeah, I'm godfather to his son.'

'You inspired him, didn't you?'

Cornelius smiled. 'He was giving me all sorts of abuse and I just said, "Hey man, let's talk this shit out. I like reggae, d'you like reggae?" Turns out he did and we went to see Jimmy Cliff at the Barrowlands.'

'See, that's what we need at the club. We, I, need you Cornelius. People respect you.'

'CORNELIUS! WHAT THE FUCK'RE YOU UP TO?'

Cornelius looked at the house, down to where his family jewels were located and then to his brother-in-law again.

'Sorry man, this is a fight you need to fight on your own.'

'But…'

'I'll be in touch as soon as I can,' Cornelius said, dumping the bag in a nearby wheelie bin. 'Expect a postcard.'

With that, he spun round and dashed the short distance to his back door. Andy reconsidered the idea of burning the club to the ground as a dog barked angrily from the direction he was travelling to. It was while struggling over the third fence that he remembered that he had to sort out insurance before that could even be considered an option.

* * *

Andy's words echoed around Cornelius' head all night. His brother-in-law, his best friend, needed him, and he was not the type of man who would fail to respond to such a plea, so

Cornelius set about his decoration duties with renewed vigour. After spending two hours choosing music of a suitable BPM to help him finish the task more quickly, he then spent an hour painting the skirting board, which was the only job left to do.

'Why's all the furniture been moved?' To be fair, Emma had commended him on a job well done before raising the issue.

'Feng shui, baby. I want the baby to have all the luck in the world.'

'The cot's in the middle of the floor.'

'I want her to feel like she's got a sense of space all around her rather than thinking one route is always closed off to her.' Cornelius placed an arm round his wife and hoped he sounded convincing enough to postpone further investigation until the big paint spill in the middle of the carpet could be dealt with.

Poor Cornelius, thought Emma. He wasn't as stupid as he first appeared, and could boast a third class Accountancy degree in addition to his encyclopaedic knowledge of rare soul labels. She was gazing upon his kind face and thinking that she really should cut him a break when he started beatboxing and air scratching.

'Cornelius! You're gettin on my tits. Shut the fuck up.' Emma instantly felt guilty about her reaction to such a minor transgression so nuzzled into her husband's chest and squeezed him tight. 'Anyway, I'm glad you finished so we can spend some time together. I thought we could...'

'Sorry baby,' interrupted Cornelius as he shook his wife off and picked up a coat to slip on over his painting clothes. 'Andy needs me. Quick slash then I'm Club Quantum-bound.' He paused to check he had the name right, then disappeared.

Cornelius was whistling in celebration of a satisfactory urination and the triumphant appearance he was about to make at the club when he jogged down the stairs to find his wife blocking the front door.

'I'm no kiddin you Cornelius, leave this house an I'll do to your balls what Joe Pesci did to that man's head in Goodfellas.'

'That's Casino, not Goodfellas.'

'I don't care. You're no goin out. If we're no spendin quality time together then you're finishin that driveway. There's no way I'm pushin a pram across half the Gobi desert to get in my own home.'

'But baby,' he cried. 'You were the one who said go for the house with the big front garden. Phil and Kirstie said that you should look to make on the back what you lose on the front, remember?'

'Cornelius!'

'You're always on about priorities and right now, as a father and a provider, the priority should be getting the club ready.'

Emma adopted a cross-armed stance and tilted her head, angry that Cornelius still wasn't getting it. 'This isn't even about the driveway. It's about us. What's really important to you?

Attempting to defeat her with body language, Cornelius rolled his head and brought it to rest inches from what could pass for jazz hands. 'Emma – baby – you know you're the most important thing in my life. I love you more than Otis. But you're not being fair to me right now.

'I'm tired of your procrastinatin. I'm tired of your fuckin short-term infatuations. I'm tired of you smokin on the sly. I'm tired of you pretendin to go to runnin when you're really goin to the gym to perv on lassies who aren't the size of a hump-backed whale.' Emma let the fact she'd rumbled Cornelius sink in before taking a step forwards and pushing his hands down. 'Most of all, I'm tired of you indulgin that fuckin prick of a brother of mine an that fuckin hellhole of a club. Just accept it's never goin to happen, write off your daft record fund, which I'm still very pissed off about, an go back to accountin. You can stick the Quantum Club up your arse.'

Cornelius deflated like one of Lionel's hussies. He rubbed his head and slowly raised it again to look at her.

'Emma, do you have any idea of all the things you tell me to stick up my arse? I keep count you know. We're at 86 individual items this year alone, including, inexplicably, that Bootsy Collins Gold Disc I got when you sent me to buy a pram. Well, not today.'

Emma stepped back towards the door in shock. 'I beg your pardon.'

Cornelius nodded to himself. It was time to drop some wisdom. Grandmaster Flash-style. 'In here. It's like a jungle sometimes I wonder how I keep from going under.'

'What?'

'There's people pissing on the stairs they just don't care.'

Emma shrieked. 'An d'you think I'm proud of that? I'm pregnant an we were nowhere near a toilet.'

'Metaphorically Emma. People are metaphorically pissing on my metaphorical stairs. You are. Don't push me cos I'm close to the edge. I'm trying not to lose my head.'

'Honest to fuck. Start speakin fuckin sense.'

Cornelius stepped towards Emma and gave her his best puppy dog eyes in order to soften her up for his grand finale. 'You are a beautiful, formidable, and hard-working woman and I love you. But things have to change around here. I mean it. Now, I'm going to make my nightclub the best goddam undercover joint in a 30-mile radius and nothing you can say can stop me.'

He stood tall and proud as he gazed directly at his wife, whose stare had become even more intense than normal. Cornelius' face fell as he realised his performance hadn't opened up the small window of light in Emma's soul that he'd hoped for. Without warning he turned and ran down the hall in the direction of the back door, careering into every piece of furniture in his way.

TWENTY-TWO

Eighty per cent of the management co-operative stood round the hole that had been burned in the dancefloor. They had been commanded to wait by that exact spot in a series of impassioned phone calls from the other twenty, who, having cautiously knocked first, threw open the double doors and danced towards them.

'Fuck, you're no high now as well are you?'

Cornelius took his place in the circle that had formed around the hole. 'High on life good buddy brother-in-law. I stood up to Emma, and you know how it went?'

'Terribly?'

'Well, yeah, to be honest. But until Emma catches up with me, which won't be for a while as she's eight months pregnant and I've got the car, I'm a real man. And real men get down to action.'

'That's all well and good, but why were you so explicit about meeting round the hole?'

'Because, Lionel, this hole is a metaphor for what happens to us if we don't work together. Look deep into that hole. Look into the blackness.' The eighty looked at each other then back to the twenty, who was staring downwards. They reluctantly did likewise.

'Now,' began Cornelius. 'If one of us was here on our own then we could fall into that hole and into the abyss below. But with all of us here, the others will catch them and stop that from happening.'

There was silence followed by, 'But the hole's only a few inches deep. Sprained ankle's probly about the worst you could expect, chief.'

'An that's no so much a metaphor as a health an safety lecture.'

142

'See! You're getting it already!' Cornelius put his right arm around Tony and his left around Gibby.

Andy shook his head. 'What the fuck're you on about?'

'I think your brother-in-law is rather clumsily attempting to articulate the point that, together, we stand a chance of making opening night, but divided we fall a matter of inches,' Cornelius nodded at Lionel as if he was Obi Wan passing on the secrets of the Jedi to Luke. 'But I am still on the return leg of my journey into the pharmaceutical unknown and Gibby's digestive system has been damaged, perhaps irreparably, by the stress.'

'Totally. I spewed takin a Betty Wright yesterday. My insides moved in two opposite directions at once. I feel all distended an wrong, like my own guts are sobbin orphan tears.'

Equally uninspired by Cornelius was the man who had approached him for the purpose of inspiring everyone. 'There's no point. We're fucked. We'd be as well just cuttin our losses.'

He sank to his haunches, a move he was finding more difficult to pull off by the pound, put his head in his hands and began groaning as he rocked. The others looked to Cornelius, who knelt down beside Andy.

'Man. We can't give up. This is your dream. Did I give up when I had my mirrorball snatched away from me?'

'No, but face it. We can't pull this off.'

'Andy, you're your father's son. Somewhere inside you there is some trace of his practical abilities. You just buried it under the soul and ska and indie and hip hop and house. Go back to that time. Think deeply.'

Andy raised his head off his hands. 'Well, he tried to show me how to wire a light switch just after the Roses announced they were splittin up.'

'And?'

'An I was thinkin about how it wasn't a bad thing cos of the guitar solos on the Second Comin an Readin bein a shambles an...an...yes! Yes! Give me a screwdriver. I know what I'm doin.'

He sprung to his feet and moved over to the light switch to the sound of whooping from Cornelius.

'Erm...chief? Just a suggestion, like, but should you no switch it off at the mains first?

'No, I don't need to do it until...' The unmistakable sound of live voltage meeting flesh and bone could be heard and the club was plunged into darkness as Andy jumped back screaming.

'Holy shit, man. You okay?'

'I think so,' he said shaking his arm and looking towards the light switch.' But. Fuck, I've made it worse.'

From nowhere, the lights flashed back on and everyone turned to see Lionel standing by the fuse box.

'You just tripped the fuse, Andrew. Actually, all we need to do is to run a new wire from the mains to here and that should sort everything out.' Noticing all eyes on him, he added, 'I served a year of my time as an electrician before I went to university.'

'An at no point you though it might help to impart this information before now?' Tony exhaled with disgust.

'I did not, Tony. Must be the methylenedioxymetham-phetamine.'

Cornelius clapped his hands. 'Guys, come on. If they can build an extension in a day on DIY SOS then we can do this. This is our place, this is our time. Only we can stop us from achieving greatness. Or at least making it to opening night. Because, by God, I am going to be castrated like no man has ever been castrated for this so we have to make it count. Who's with me?'

*   *   *

The next 12 hours were a time of blood, sweat and tears as the management co-operative co-operated for the first time in the months since circumstances threw them together. Working harder than Buster Bloodvessel's braces, they attacked the task with ruthless determination and very little ability, much like Cornelius behind the turntable.

Wearing the protection suits that Gibby had procured, Andy and Cornelius took no time at all in painting the worst bits of the club fleshy-beige. Taking a step back they realised how poor a job Andy had done with his sections so Cornelius had to go over them again.

Gibby took the axe to the bar top dozens more times so that it looked deliberately careworn, an idea Cornelius had gleaned from Nick Knowles, who he currently held in almost as high regard as Otis. Gibby's dubious acquaintances also came in handy when he managed to secure part of the actual Wigan Casino dancefloor courtesy of a Dundee soulie who had moved to Bolton to be closer to the action back in the day and had ransacked the place prior to demolition. Andy had been uneasy about the £5000 asking price, but was out-voted on the basis that Quantum would be able to boast a piece of clubbing history even if it lacked the spring-loaded system that gave the Casino its legendary bounce.

Responsibility for laying the new dancefloor fell to Andy, who smashed his thumb on only the third swing of a hammer and had to be replaced by Lionel. It was at this point that the wannabe-exotic dancer revealed he had spent a particularly fruitful period of Community Service laying floors and would complete the task in no time.

While this was happening, Tony painstakingly superglued the DJ booth back together and Gibby finally got rid of the bricks, broken glass, dead birds and other potentially lethal hazards littering the estate. Windows were opened wherever possible to air the place out, music posters were stuck over the wall areas where damp was most visible and masking tape was applied to any slashed or burnt upholstery.

Having significantly mitigated the risk of electrocution and roughly fitted the dancefloor, Lionel set about fixing the toilets, only for Andy to insist that this was his job and receive a faceful of foul brown water for his troubles. On his way back to the office to locate a towel, he found Cornelius in the corridor immersed in sandpapering. On closer inspection Andy saw that he was working on a giant wooden orb with little rectangular indentations and several feet of tinfoil by his side ready to be applied.

Andy walked over to his brother-in-law and placed a gentle hand on his shoulder. Cornelius turned round to see Andy slowly shake his head. He looked at his mirrorball-replacement project with sadness before following Andy through to the dancefloor, where the others stood waiting.

The Quantum quintet's hands came together in a giant high-five that gave way to an emotional group hug. Eventually they broke off to take in the new Club Quantum/Quantum Club.

Andy looked to the sky and said, 'See Dad, I told you I could do it,' then turned to his colleagues. 'Know what? I think the job's a good 'un.'

'It's…' began Cornelius.

'It looks…' continued Lionel.

'Well…' added Gibby

'It still looks a bit shite doesn't it?' finished Tony.

Three-quarters of the walls were fleshy beige, while posters reflecting various musical influences were dotted around at apparently random intervals. The DJ booth was a riot of tape and glue and the possibly famous old dancefloor featured a new sooty black mark courtesy of Gibby falling asleep while smoking around 5am. Having run out of flesh paint, the wall to their left now featured a graffiti mural.

Andy was determined that his broken thumb, faceful of faecal matter and electric shock weren't for nothing. 'Look, when the lights are down it could be any crappy provincial nightclub. That's some achievement.'

'And DJ Quantum did a great job with the graffiti,' added Cornelius.

Andy nodded. 'I really like that portrait of Mick Jagger.'

'It's not Mick Jagger. It's Robin Asquith. See the ladder? It's a scene from Confessions of A Window Cleaner.'

'Ah, that's why he's on the job then? I thought the dame was Marianne Faithfull.'

'Nah, just some bored suburban housewife whose husband is about to return from work early. DJ Q wanted to subvert the preconceptions of the music buff by referencing substandard 70s sex comedies. He's pretty deep you know. One of the bravest and most dangerous street artists around.'

'Where's he now?'

'Home. His Mum said he had to be back for midnight.'

Everyone nodded their appreciation of DJ Q's work but Tony rubbed his nose to suggest unease in his nasal cavities.

'You can still smell the spray paint though, aye?'

'I'm high as a kite to be honest with you, man. Never used a face mask. You'd never see Nick Knowles embark on a project without the appropriate safety material.'

Gibby produced the bag of pills that he had somehow managed to wrest ownership of. 'Aye, but you never see Nick with the magic either, chief.'

They laughed and gave their jaws a collective grind.

'Nick Knowles could do with Lionel on his team, aye?' Andy asked with a smile. 'Jack of all trades here. Where'd that come from?'

Lionel blushed as Gibby added, 'Always the ones you least expect.'

'Much like Sir Jimmy in that regard.'

No one had the energy to pull Tony up on his latest declaration of misguided support so they fell into silence instead. Eventually a buzz at the door broke the spell.

'I'll get it on my way out. Better get home before Emma comes looking for me.'

Cornelius gave each of his associates a hug before exiting, leaving Andy to last. The pair shared a lengthy and poignant embrace and Andy whispered 'I love you, Cornelius. Thanks,' which caused his brother-in-law to make a sharp exit in an attempt to conceal the tears streaming down his face.

Andy took the scene in again with pride. 'I actually quite like the colour you know. What d'you think Lionel, recherché enough?'

'Absolutely. A triumph for collectivism and one achieved under budget as well.'

Andy screwed his face up. 'Well, aside from that £5K dance-floor, but I'm sure once word gets out we've got the Wigan Casino here in Dundee people will be flockin in from miles away. We might just be okay.'

As he finished speaking he noticed Gibby turn in the other direction whilst sucking through his teeth and muttering what sounded like 'ooooft!' There was something else he needed to speak to him about as well. That thing he said about miscellaneous costs or whatever he called it. He didn't have time to tackle him on either matter, however, before Cornelius charged back in.

'Holy shit, it's TV Licensing...'

'What? Fuck. Gibby. You said...'

Gibby vaulted over the bar and ducked behind it, re-emerging seconds later wielding the axe.

'Now's really no the time for recriminations, chief. Where's that TV?'

TWENTY-THREE

It could never be said that Andy was a man of great sensitivity but even he was aware that his behaviour over the past few months had left him somewhere between Bill Wyman and Rick Wakeman in the fantasy future husband stakes. But without any money to compensate for his flaws.

While Andy was to high finance what Skrewdriver were to race relations, his partners appeared to have inexhaustible resources to sustain them until the club finally opened. Gibby continued to play a pivotal role in the local black economy, Tony lived off various out-of-court settlements from parties unaware he was barred from practising law, and Lionel won hundreds of pounds each week at pub quizzes in addition to his cage-fighting earnings. Even Cornelius' record fund remained solvent, but Andy's financial situation was so bleak he had considered asking DJ Q's mum for pocket money.

But it was the lying rather than penury that was doing the most damage to his relationship. There might not be any portrait of him growing disfigured in his attic but he didn't dare look at his copy of London Calling for fear it was metamorphosising into Sandanista. With every mistruth his soul seemed to blacken further and made him more likely to turn on his fiancée as a defence mechanism. All that was about to stop though.

'So, everythin's ready for the council visits then?'

'Absolutely,' Andy was delighted to be able to tell her the truth again.

Michelle shuffled on her stool and looked down towards the figures that Andy had placed before her on the breakfast bar.

'An other than the openin night bein set back another couple of weeks an the two grand fine from TV Licensin, everythin's on track financially?'

'Completely,' Andy said, feeling the now-familiar sinking of his heart that accompanied dishonesty. The new-old dancefloor was completely off the books and his share had been funded by their wedding savings account. Best not to mention it until the club opened and you can start paying the money back, he thought. Ease your way back into honesty before then.

'Brilliant! There was me doubtin you too,' Michelle sprung up and kissed him on the cheek, which made Andy feel guilty and hopeful at the same time. 'So, what's next?'

'Well, we really need to mount an aggressive PR campaign to counter the damage from that hatchet job Ben did.'

Andy was about to follow up with a rant about Hugh Grant and Steve Coogan's failure to return his calls and blatant disinterest in non-celebrity victims of media vendettas when the phone rang. Michelle answered and listened for a few seconds before passing the handset to Andy. 'It's for you. Chelsea from the gym?'

Andy's guilt-hope balance dropped heavily toward the former as his voice rose an octave. 'Oh right. I'll take this next door. About my membership no doubt.'

*   *   *

Chelsea looked scared as she led Andy and Gibby, tongue hanging out, to the dance studio. She held the door open and explained. 'He's not been able to get up for, like, half an hour now. We tried to help but he insisted you came to get him.'

They followed her across the varnished floor to Cornelius who, wearing the same ridiculous exercise gear as before, was down on all fours.

'It's, like, his back,' she continued. 'I think the Body Combat was too much for him. Thing is, there's, like, a boxercise class about to start? We really need to, like, get him up now.'

'It's okay, sweetheart,' Gibby winked at her. 'We'll take it from here.'

Chelsea wished Cornelius all the best before leaving. As

soon as her back was turned, Gibby began simulating the types of things he would like to do to her.

'Ooooft! I'd rattle that until chaffage became life threatenin.'

'Tell me about it. She's costin me about thirty quid a month.'

'Ahem.'

They looked down to the folded lump of Cornelius, who tried to face them before indicating that was an impossibility. Gibby and Andy moved to his front so they could address their colleague.

'Andy, what's he doing here? You were supposed to come alone.'

'Aye, but I don't drive so I needed someone to get you to hospital.'

'Why would I need to go to hospital?'

'Cos your back's gone.'

Cornelius sighed. 'There's nothing wrong with my back.'

'Then why're we here? Not that I didn't enjoy meetin young Chelsea, like.'

'I...I can't get up.'

'Why not?'

'Cos...has Chelsea definitely gone?'

'Unfortunately, chief. Unfortunately.'

'And there's no one else in earshot?'

'No,' Andy said, puzzled by behaviour that was odd even for Cornelius. 'What's wrong?'

'I've...I've got a...y'know. A bricker.'

'A bricker?' Andy yelled involuntarily.

'Shhh! That's why I couldn't let anyone help me up. Especially not Chelsea and the other girls in the class.'

'So, for the last half hour you've been...?'

'Like a rock. It's going nowhere.'

'Is this a regular occurrence, chief?'

'No, it's not. I think there are three factors at work here.

The first is the girls in their tight lycra. Bending one way and jerking the other. Gyrating. It was like that video.'

Having failed to gain any traction on popular culture since the turn of the century, Andy was lost, but Gibby was confident he was following Cornelius' train of thought. 'Call on Me?'

'Nah, man. The Green Goddess fitness video. My Mum had it when I was a teenager. It was a confusing time and it had a big effect on me. Seeing all them girls brought it all back.'

Andy and Gibby smirked at each other. 'An what're the other factors?'

'Well, secondly there's the tightness of these shorts. They were rubbing at the most inappropriate time. And thirdly, and this might be the key, I suspect Emma spiked my Lucozade with Viagra.'

'Why would she do that?' asked Andy, shuddering at the thought of his sister and Viagra featuring in the same sentence.

'Well, I thought she was awfully calm after me standing up to her. She even smiled at me last night and said she had a surprise for me.'

Andy didn't want to ask the next question but curiosity got the better of him. 'Why'd she have Viagra?'

Cornelius angled his head as far as he could towards his brother-in-law. 'Gibby sold me it. Said it'd help when Emma got really huge but I had to do it anyway cos we had to bring the birth on.'

Gibby performed a little bow that exuded humility. 'At your service.'

'So what d'we do now?'

'Well, you two have to get me out of here in some way that doesn't reveal my boner while making it look like I genuinely have a bad back.'

'Fine. Right, Gibby. You take the rear and I'll take the front. An, Cornelius, whatever you do, please don't touch me with it.'

Gibby shrugged and placed an arm under Cornelius' ankles

and another under his chest. Andy hooked his arms under his brother-in-law's armpits and, on the count of three, they attempted to lift him. Unsuccessfully. A struggle between Andy and Gibby and coordination followed as a crowd of boxercisers expressed their impatience from the door. Several aborted attempts that resembled adventurous chapters from the Kama Sutra followed before they eventually succeeded in rolling Cornelius on to his back, knees tight against his chest. Wheezing as he wrapped his arms around Cornelius' ribs, Andy managed to elevate him enough for Gibby to slip between Cornelius' legs and obtain the leverage required to practically fold him in half. Taking short, quick steps they scuttled to the door muttering apologies to the inconvenienced class.

'That can't be good for his back,' said Chelsea as the unorthodox rescue party stumbled past her.

'Don't worry about us, sweetheart, we're professionals.' Gibby was about to wink at her when Andy momentarily lost his grip, causing Cornelius' head to smack off the ground and another part of his anatomy to stab Gibby in the midriff.

'Woah there, chief. Keep that for the missus, okay?'

TWENTY-FOUR

'How come Cornelius's got ice on his balls?'

Ignorant as he was to the events of the past few hours, Tony's question was not unreasonable as Cornelius did indeed have a large pack of ice on his groin as he sat by the nearest table to the bar. He turned to Tony with a pained expression on his face. 'It's a long story. We've got more important things to deal with at the minute.'

'Absolutely,' agreed Andy. 'Like where're these posters an flyers? At least if we can get out there an meet people face to face they'll realise we're no the weirdos we're bein made out to be. Apart from Lionel, mibbe.'

Cornelius raised himself out of his chair and limped forward, keeping the ice pack firmly in place as he did so. 'DJ Q's refusing to hand over the posters until the opening night. He says he won't allow us to interfere with his sense of history. Anyway, you don't want this place being like Studio 54 and having everyone queuing up outside.' With his spare hand, Cornelius produced a postcard from his pocket and handed it to Tony. 'This explains everything. See, the design's really good.'

'I'm pullin the plug on DJ Q,' snapped Andy. 'I've had enough of him.'

'But he's brilliant, man. He just needs help to come out of his shell.'

'He's a flake, a fruiter an a fraud. We're goin round to his house an demandin the posters an flyers that we've paid for. Or rather Lionel is. Where's the big bastard anyway?'

Tony sneered. 'Checkin his YouTube hits an gettin depressed about the comments, no doubt. He wrote a letter to the Guardian askin if they'd do a feature about CFNM in an attempt to legitimise his kink but they've no got back to him yet.'

'I've got a suggestion, chief.'

Everyone turned to Gibby, who had remained silent throughout the conference, not once interrupting proceedings to mention a man he knew who could help for a small price, provide an update on his bodily functions or regale the crowd with a lurid tale of fornication.

'I've been sittin here with the noodles workin overtime,' he continued. 'After millions of years of evolution we find oursels in a bit of a pickle, but humans have faced more pickles than your average chippy owner. The industry of leisure is driven by the pursuit of pleasure. So, in order to persuade the great Dundonian public we're worth takin a chance on, we have to make them believe that we can meet their pleasure needs.'

'Eh?'

'Turns out I was right all along, chief. Sex sells, an I recently met someone who can help me prove it.'

*   *   *

'So, you've never worked in PR before, can't name a single member of the Beatles, an list your likes as pink clothes, boys an Facebook. What exactly d'you think you'll bring to a musically uncompromisin indie club?'

Whilst Tony was unimpressed by Chelsea's credentials, his fellow interview panellists, Andy and Gibby, were captivated by the candidate, largely because she had chosen to wear the world's sluttiest business suit in an attempt to impress.

'Well, I'm not really sure. Mr Wisdom just said that I had, like, a lot going on that would, like, take the club forward.' Gibby winked at Andy, who nodded. 'And I do love music.'

'Oh, who's your favourite artist?'

Chelsea held her gaze on Tony as she considered her answer, professionalism and witlessness creating dissonance.

'Errr...I'm not really, like, into art? Although I like that painting with the woman with the funny smile. The one by Leonardo Di Caprio.'

'To be honest with you Chelsea, I'm no sure about your

interview clothes. I mean, I'm no actually sure whether you're under- or over-dressed but…'

'I, like, asked about that and Mr Wisdom, like, just said to wear somethin that reflected my personality.'

Gibby flashed a smile that could charitably be described as lascivious and more accurately as rapey.

Tony took a deep breath. 'I bet he did. Here, Mr Wisdom. What exactly d'you think Chelsea has to offer?'

His co-owner gave his pen lid a thoughtful chew before switching to full-on business mode. 'Well, primarily I see her role as bein promotional, handin out flyers an the like. I particularly see this as important in the hours prior to club nights. As you can see, Chelsea has a sparklin personality an I'm sure this will encourage young gentlemen to come along. Especially as she'll be accompanied by some of her pals from the gym as she does so. She also knows all about Facebook.'

'But I'm doin all that already.'

'I've got, like, more than 1000 friends.'

Tony sat bolt upright in his chair and stared at Chelsea.

'More than 1000? But that's impossible.'

He looked to Gibby for confirmation this was a wind-up only to be met with more free-flowing sales patter.

'An I believe there's a "check-in" facility on Facebook to let all your friends know where you are. Imagine, you're sittin in the pub, an up pops a message tellin you where Chelsea, with her sparklin personality an other assets, is at. You'd be sayin, "Cancel that round, chief, we're goin to the Quantum."'

Andy, feeling he should contribute more to the interview, managed to pop his tongue back in his mouth long enough to add, 'Yes, indeed.'

Tony shook his head in disgust. 'Well, thanks for your time, Chelsea. We'll let you know.'

Chelsea stood up and pulled her skirt down some distance so her modesty was protected and stepped forward to thank the panel for their time. As Chelsea bent forward, the white blouse with the top three buttons unsecured provided them with a clearer insight into their interviewee. She kissed Andy on the cheek, causing him to giggle like a schoolgirl before repeating the same move with Gibby.

Removing Gibby's hand from Chelsea's hip as she leant in towards him, Tony recoiled from her embrace. It was then that Cornelius, unable to knock due to the large carboard box he clutched to his chest, announced his arrival by whistling an unrecognisable tune. His view was obscured by the cargo he transported, rolls of paper protruding out of the top, and he walked with a slight, understandable, waddle but otherwise seemed buoyant as the group parted to allow him to pass.

'Result!' he cried out. 'There was a lot of swearing and tears but DJ Q finally gave me the posters. He swore he'd get his revenge on us, but his Mum said not to worry. Oh, and my pinger has finally gone down. So long as I don't get any more stimulation I should be okay.'

He threw the box down on the desk and turned to see Chelsea, who beamed at him.

'Hiya Cornelius! How's your back? What's a pinger?'

He crumpled into the chair that Chelsea had been sitting on only a moment ago and groaned. 'Oh God. Gibby, man, you're gonna need to take me to hospital.'

Grabbing his chance for the two of them to spend some alone time, Andy placed an arm round Chelsea and steered her towards the door.

'Tell you what, I'll show you out.'

He turned to wink at Gibby as they left the office, his attempts to impress clearly audible as they made their way down the corridor.

'I actually think we've got a problem with our computer here, Chelsea.'

'Really?'

'Yeah. It keeps playin Chasin Pavements on a loop. Thinks it's a Dell.'

Tony spat on the floor. 'There's no way she's comin to work here. You're all goin about with your tongues hangin out, or somethin else stickin out in Cornelius's case, cos she's dressed like a slut. I'm already doin everythin she can do…' Gibby raised an eyebrow at him. 'With Facebook an Twitter an that, I mean.'

'Oh really? Many friends d'we have so far, chief?'

'37.'

'Chelsea will quadruple that in a couple of hours. She's got thousands of followers on Twitter. If she tells them to follow the club, they'll do it.'

'But it's prostitution.'

'Aye, but only morally.'

'We were like a family before she came on the scene,' said Tony, displaying a North Korean zeal for revisionism. 'Now look at us. An what're you talkin about payin her? She's no gettin made a partner.'

Gibby lit a cigarette and offered one to Tony, who refused, and Cornelius, who accepted.

'Obviously no. All she's after is a free night out for her an her pals. Few bottles of Lambrini an some places on the guestlist an she's no lookin for a penny.'

'Guestlist? How many?'

'Well, 20 is a small price to pay for the impact havin them runnin around the place will have.'

'Twenty? That's 10% of capacity. Wait til Andy hears this. You know what he's like about guestlists.'

With perfect timing, Andy rejoined the party and took Cornelius' fag off him for a quick couple of puffs. 'What's this about a guestlist.'

'Oh, aye. There's somethin I didn't tell you about Chelsea's terms an conditions. An my plan to firefight in the press.'

TWENTY-FIVE

Tony's face might have been set to sour at the best of times but he exuded the charm of Mark E. Smith's spleen as one of the most influential men in the local music scene was chaperoned round the club. Washie's smiling tour guides didn't bother introducing Tony as they sidestepped him, choosing instead to point out exciting new features and gloss over particularly dangerous ones. Gibby outlined the future of Quantum, portraying Andy as some kind of latter-day saint-cum-musical visionary in the process, before his outsized colleague cut to the charm-offensive chase.

'As you can see, things aren't nearly as bad as your sister paper led people to believe. An we'd like you to tell people that.'

Washie grinned at Andy. 'Absolutely, mate. Place doesn't look that bad at all. I imagine it'll look right decent when you've done it up.

'Well actually, we have done it up already.'

'Oh. Never mind, I'm all about the music. An the guestlist.' His face grew serious as he leaned in to Andy. 'What d'we reckon? Twenty places a night? Mibbe the odd pint an lock-in thrown in? Oh, an a few extra places for the big dance nights?'

'Well...how vital is that to you writin a positive review?'

His expression remained stone-like.

'It's a deal,' Andy's hand was instantly accepted by Washie and the grin returned to his face.

'I'll give you the rest of the tour, chief. In particular, I'd like to show you a roof that is entirely free of animal carci. Unless there's been any developments overnight that is.'

'Perfect. Andy, a pleasure. I'll see you here for the openin night. Twenty-five tickets in the post, aye?'

'I thought the agreement was 20?'

'Big night, Andy. Big night.'

Feeling his profit margin bothered further, Andy grimaced. 'No problem.'

Gibby winked at him and led Washie outside. Andy spun round to find Tony lingering a foot behind him.

'Well that went well, didn't it?'

'I thought so.'

'Yup, a guestlist of 45 for a club that holds 200. Out-fuck-in-standin.'

'It's a temporary measure. We'll cut back once our reputation's restored an we get a vibe goin about the place. An besides, I think Chelsea's a valuable addition to the team.'

'Absolutely, so long as she keeps givin boners to you an your brother-in-law then we might be able to sideline you an run this place properly.'

'Nonsense. She's goin to show me how to use the computer an do Facebook an things.'

Tony screwed his eyes shut and rubbed his forehead. 'I offered to do that! You said Facebook was for the mentally ill.'

The door could be heard shutting behind them so Andy turned, expecting Gibby to re-enter, scratching his balls and offering to sell him porn.

'Hiya! Here for my induction.'

Chelsea stood before them in a a tight white t-shirt bearing the legend 'CLUB SLUT'.

'What can I say?' Andy asked Tony. 'I've finally been persuaded of its worth. Hi Chelsea. Please, come through to the office an make yoursel at home. Cos you're one of the family now.'

Tony looked Chelsea up and down before shaking his head and taking off in the direction of the bar. 'I'll leave you two to it. I'm goin to see if I can find a big-headed voodoo doll anywhere.'

Andy treated Chelsea to some more cringeworthy banter as he led her through to the office, where he sat down at the desk.

Chelsea shut the door behind her and moved over to Andy's side, chest at his eye-level, and tossed her hair back.

'So, what d'you want me to show you first?'

Andy gulped.

'On the computer?' she pointed to the screen in front of him.

'Oh right.' He coughed and composed himself. 'Well, mibbe you could show me how to get a Facebook page.'

'Yeah, that's dead easy.' Chelsea angled herself between Andy and the monitor so they were almost touching.

'Course, it'll be embarrassin not havin any Facebook friends. So you'll need to be my first if that's okay?'

*　　*　　*

The ladder was rickety, the weather windy and the tarpaulin-covered roof not a particularly welcoming location for Washie, who was wondering why Gibby had led him there.

'So, you see. No dead birdlife whatsoever.'

'To be honest mate, I'm more interested in the live orni-thology. Like that tidy piece who came in as we were leavin.'

'I know exactly where you're comin from, chief. That's Chelsea, our new PR.'

Washie leant against the window from where Lionel's moment of infamy had been captured the previous week. 'She'll pull the punters in no problem. Why d'you need to be throwin guestlist passes at me when the club can't afford it?'

'Cos once her an her pals have salivatin teenage spunkwads queuin round the block tickets are gonna be at a premium, chief. As you may have seen, Andy's no a businessman like you an me. He doesn't recognise that guestlist passes can be sold at a profit to said queuin spunkwads. That profit can be split 50-50. I launder the money back to the club in surpris-inly healthy bar takings, minus a small administration fee of course, an you put your share towards a bottle of champagne to share with Chelsea's pals. What d'you say?'

The grin was back on. 'I like your style.'

'It won't be proper champagne, chief. Most probly some cheap Chardonnay put through a SodaStream.'

'I know that.'

They shook hands, and Gibby eased himself over the ledge and on to the top rung of the ladder, which swayed in the wind before steadying under his weight. Washie watched him back down a few steps before hooking his leg over the side and doing likewise.

'I'll just warn you, chief. Scrambled eggs for lunch. You're followin through the eye of the storm.'

'Jesus Christ, Gibby. I should demand a couple of extra guesties just for that.'

Gibby reached the bottom, rubbed his stomach and pulled out a cigarette. 'That wouldn't be in the spirit of our agreement now, would it? Wouldn't want to have to tell Chelsea about your missus an kids.'

Washie reached street level and backed a couple of feet away while wafting the aroma away as Gibby lit up.

'She's a gym instructor as well you know. I've got a DVD of a green banana that looks just like her gettin rattled on an exercise ball. Called Twist an Spout. Yours for a ten spot.'

TWENTY-SIX

Andy's first Facebook experience confirmed his prejudices. His senses were offended by the banal pictures, comments and other information that everyone seemed to post, but, despite feeling the impending demise of civilisation more keenly than ever, he was eager for Chelsea to think he enjoyed it as much as she obviously did.

Eventually, though, the mask slipped.

'Fuckin bastardin thing.'

Chelsea, who was sitting on the sofa that had been restored to the office following Lionel's indiscretions, looked up from filing her nails and reading Heat. She put the magazine down and came to Andy's side once again.

'Here, let me have a look,' Andy pushed the chair back a few inches to improve his view as she bent towards the screen. 'D'you not have a computer at home?'

Andy scratched his head. 'I've got a Megadrive. Michelle's got a PC but I can't work it.'

'What's a Megadrive?'

'Never mind.'

'Well, I can give you a few tips but I don't know if she's got, like, the same hardware as me.'

Definitely not, he thought as he stared at a collection of physical elements that came with only a few years' warranty before the inexorable transformation to software began. Andy hadn't wanted to say anything, but Michelle seemed to be letting herself go a bit, what with the nightly drinking and lack of sleep.

'Right,' he began, returning to the digital dystopia in front of him. 'Every time I try to post a profile pic it asks me if I want to play somethin called Candy Crusher.'

She flicked her hair so that the ends brushed Andy's face, filling his nostrils with the distinct aroma of strawberries. 'Oh right, that's easy. What you have to do is this. See what I did there?' She wrinkled her nose at him and even though he was seated, Andy felt himself weaken at the knees.

'Yup,' he said leaning back in the chair with his arms behind his head then quickly closing his body again when he became conscious of the possibility of sweat patches as well as a familiar stirring in his loins.

Andy never heard Chelsea when she asked if he wanted to see her work on the club Facebook page to date, but as he generally nodded whenever she asked something he was soon unsurely reading what he saw before him.

'U.W.Less than.3.C.Q.C.U.M.2.O.P.N.N.T.N.B.I.N.G.U .R.P.L.S.L.O.L.colon.close bracket.X.X.X.X.X.X.' He turned to Chelsea and pointed to the offending passage. 'What's that supposed to mean?'

'You will love Club Quantum. Come to our opening night and bring your pals. Laugh out loud. Happy face. Kiss, kiss, kiss, kiss, kiss, kiss.'

Every atom in Andy's body wanted to scream that Quantum was a serious club for serious music fans, except those in the organ presently calling the shots. Maybe it could be passed off as postmodernist irony. Tony had been talking about playing some post-ironic modern garage so maybe a succession of random characters that the code breakers at Bletchley Park would struggle to understand could be reconciled to his grand vision after all.

He shrugged and changed subject. 'So, err…did you always want want to work at the gym?'

Chelsea inspected her nails and blew on them. 'Actually, I wanted to be, like, a beauty therapist to start with but the girls at college were dead bitchy.' She affected an American accent, 'Beauty-school sure wasn't like I thought it would be.'

Andy's heart would have pounded with excitement had all his blood not been surging to another part of his body. 'I love Grease! Do you love Grease?'

'I do! Isn't that the most? To say the least!'

'LOL!'

'Ahem!'

There weren't many people Andy would want hearing him verbalise his first internet acronym, or discover his dirty musical secret, but his fiancée definitely topped the list of those he would have preferred to have kept in the dark. He sprung out of his chair to greet Michelle and began walking round the table to her, only to become aware that he had lost control of his reproductive organs, half bending over and shuffling round the table with his posterior sticking out.

'Oh hi, honey!' He stretched his neck upwards to try and kiss Michelle, who moved out of the danger zone. 'Chelsea, this is my fiancée Michelle, Michelle this is Chelsea. She's just started workin here.'

'Hiya! I like your hair. I was just telling my Mum she should get it done like that. She's about your age.'

After noisily expelling air through her nostrils, Michelle replied, 'Well, thank you Chelsea. Would you mind givin me an Andy a minute please?'

'No problem. I'll see if Tony, like, needs a hand with his voodoo doll.'

Michelle watched her leave before walking to the door and slamming it. She turned to see Andy sinking back into the chair.

'Well?'

'I love you?'

'It's strange Andy. I seem to remember diggin you out of a rather large hole so that you wouldn't lose your nightclub. Now, the only thing I asked for in return was a say on any decision affectin the place. Such as mibbe, I dunno, decidin whether or no to hire lapdancers.'

'Sorry, we should've consulted you. But there wasn't time an it was a unanimous decision. We're all on the same page.'

'I dunno, I think she's on page three.'

'An she's no a lapdancer. She's teachin me how to use a computer.'

As soon as the words left his mouth, Andy knew it was a mistake.

Michelle ostensible calmness was both impressive and unnerving in her fiance's eyes. 'Which is exactly why I'm suspicious. Seein how I've offered to show you about a million times an been told how computers are for the mentally ill about a million times in response.'

'You think I want to learn this?' Andy pleaded, feigning martyrdom. 'It's for the club. She's doing PR. Gibby thought...'

'Oh God,' Michelle looked to the roof, noticing a bloodstain that she hadn't seen before. 'He didn't find her on one of his videos did he? PR doesn't stand for somethin horrible like that thing Lionel's into does it?'

'No, she err...works at the gym.'

Michelle crossed her arms tilted her head to the side. 'Your gym?'

'Yeah...'

'So, that's behind your recent fitness campaign is it?'

Deciding to stick with righteous indignation, Andy shook his head at her. 'If you remember correctly, I only started goin back to the gym cos you said I was disgustinly fat. So there's me sloggin my guts out every day to please you an you think I'm at it with the instructor.'

Michelle's stance softened and she dropped her arms to her side. 'I never said that. It's just funny you never mentioned Chelsea when you supposedly tell me everythin about your day.'

'I'd never lie to you,' lied Andy

'Okay. You have been workin hard to be fair. Were you at the gym today?'

Andy flexed non-existant biceps and nodded to Michelle. 'Oh aye, felt the burn. Big time.'

'Liar. You left your trainers at home. So I came down to drop them off.' She took them from her bag and threw them on the table before walking off.

'Michelle!' Andy tried to stand up but experienced the same

problem as before and covered his genitals. He was trying to work out why he remained is such a state of rigidity when Tony popped his head round the door.

'Hard work this computer stuff isn't it? Spiked drink. Up ya.'

Tony flipped Andy the finger and walked off, leaving Andy bent over the table, moaning and fighting the urge to thrust against it.

TWENTY-SEVEN

A DJ's booth is a place of sanctuary and creativity from where he wields power, manipulates emotions and provokes thought. Tony was doing all that and more as he jumped around twiddling various knobs and dials, taking his headphones off to sample the atmosphere he was building before putting them back on to cue up the next susprise. A haunting soundtrack evocative of a Highland Glen fell on Club Quantum/the Quantum Club as he manipulated the stereophonic possibilities of the new sound system, a much downgraded version of the one originally envisaged, to introduce birdsong from the bar-end of the club. Cheeps, chirps and cries built until the crescendo of high-pitched tweeting threatened to overwhelm the club's inhabitants. Then, out of nowhere, came gunfire, explosions, trumpets and, finally, cheering. A split-second's silence followed before Tony, writhing around in self-indulgent ecstasy, pushed the cross-fader all the way over to the left and a succession of bassy male voices reverberated around the room.

'AND THAT IS WHY MAN MUST CONQUER NATURE.'

'IT IS IN MAN'S NATURE TO CONQUER NATURE.'

'NATURE'S NATURE IS TO CONQUER NATURE.'

'GREENPEACE MUST DIE.'

Cornelius, Emma, Andy and Michelle were the only occupants of the dancefloor. To a man, woman and unborn child they were shocked and embarrassed by Tony's "revolutionary" new approach. The man in the booth looked ready to break a lifetime of celibacy with his mixer. He had now fallen to his knees, sweat-drenched as a trembling index finger exerted just enough pressure on a channel switch for a final sample, that of a synthesised child's voice.

168

'AND SO, THE CYCLE IS FINALLY COMPLETE.'

Tony took off his headphones and placed them on the booth with the reverence that a royalist would afford the crown jewels. He pulled himself to his feet and wiped away a tear before turning to face the others.

'What d'you think? Amazin eh?'

'An pile of utter shite.'

Tony sneered at Emma. 'I'll no take advice from a border-line personality disorder case with no taste in music if you don't mind. All psychos like classical music don't they? Like in A Clockwork Orange. An the Third Reich.'

'I don't know,' said Cornelius, trying to play the peacemaker. 'It's erm…interesting how…err…unlistenable it was.'

'Exactly!' cried Tony. 'Could you imagine how much everyone will lose their mind when they walk in here an that's playin?'

'I'd worry they'd all just walk out,' ventured Andy.

'Yup, but a few people will stay behind an mind the time they first heard the life-changin Sound Art of DJ Q.'

Andy muttered something under his breath but Cornelius enthusiastically played the role of Greek Chorus and explaining that DJ Q was concentrating on his art now that his disc-spinning career lay in tatters.

'But it's no art,' pointed out Michelle. 'It's no even music. It's just noise.'

'It's shite, I keep tellin you.'

Tony raised a DJ Q-composed disc and waved it at them like a bible in the hands of a hard-line Presbyterian minister. 'This, you heathen bastards, is the future. It was Q who tipped Susan Philipsz off about Sound Art when she was at Art College in Dundee an she won the Turner for it so he's tryin to take it to the next level. Wait til we get the installation installed. It's got video art as well, just 'cos he can do that better than anyone as well.'

Having watched several instructional videos provided by Michelle in an attempt to manage his colleagues more effectively, Andy decided to adopt an approach he called "sitting on the fence".

'I mean, there wouldn't be any harm havin the odd Sound Art night, on a Tuesday or somethin. But stick to the groove-laden floor-fillers at the weekends I think.'

The partisan jock did not respond to fence-sitting, however, and he slammed his hand down on the control console, causing a particularly loud bird squawk at the back of the room.

'This is a disgrace! You're all idiots. If I played that populist shite it'd be like Dylan goin electric. There'd be riots. I'm off to find a club that appreciates my vision!'

He stormed off, throwing several chairs out of his way and upturning two tables as he did so. The Brennan-Morgan-McKimmie clan watched the doors close behind him and shrugged.

'Wouldn't be the worst thing if he ever followed through on his threats to quit would it?' asked Michelle as she put her arm round Andy's midriff, or at least a portion of it.

Emma said, 'He's a fuckin tit. Anyway, we're out of here. Me an Cornelius are off to the cinema.'

'Oh, lucky you. I love the pictures but we've no been for ages, have we Andy?'

Andy ignored his fiancée and turned to his brother-in-law instead. 'What you goin to see?'

Cornelius slipped his hand inside his wife's and smiled at her. 'The Harder They Come. Special showing. I thought it was next week but Emma spotted that it was today.'

Andy sneered and turned to Emma. 'Your idea?'

'Somethin wrong with that?'

Andy shook his head. 'No at all. Just didn't think Jimmy Cliff singin his way through a Jamaican crime thriller was your thing.'

'Well,' she smiled sweetly at Cornelius. 'We're makin more of an effort to appreciate each other, aren't we?'

Cornelius bent down and kissed his wife, too passionately for a family audience. When his hand started running down

Emma's body towards her swollen breasts, Andy brought proceedings to a close with a cough.

'Sorry, man. Yeah, after all that stuff with the refurb we had a big talk, a big cry…'

'Well, you cried.'

'And then we made love all night long, didn't we?'

'Well, 10 minutes. An afterwards you did all the jobs you'd been promisin to do didn't you?'

Cornelius stared into his wife's soul through her eyes. Emma looked up at her husband and patted him on the head. 'Miaow,' squeaked Cornelius and began rubbing his head on her shoulder. Michelle struggled to contain the contents of her stomach.

'Right,' said Andy suddenly. 'Enjoy the film.'

'Cheers man. See you later.'

They walked off hand-in-hand. Andy turned to Michelle.

'Well that was fuckin disgustin.'

'It was,' said Michelle strengthening her grip round Andy. 'But it's nice to see them gettin on. Can we go to the pictures as well? We've no been for ages.'

'Hmmm…mibbe next week. I've got stuff to do.'

Michelle broke free and inhaled deeply. 'For God's sake, Andy. We're meant to be spendin more time together, remember?'

Andy did remember. Cornelius and Emma were not the only couple to have recently held a clear-the-air summit. Following what was now generally referred to as Brickergate, Michelle had made it clear just how hard the past few months had been for her and how she was no longer willing to accept the death of her one-time future father-in-law as an excuse for Andy's erratic behaviour and general disrespect. Since the talks were taking place while Andy remained fully engorged, he did not feel he bargained from a position of strength so he accepted all Michelle's demands and promised to himself that he would stop lying to her. As soon as the latest crisis was dealt with, the club opened and his – and therefore her – finances were more liquid, of course. He then offered Michelle the chance to take advantage of his inflamed member, an opportunity she passed up without a second thought.

'The guy from the council is comin round to see about our licence. Gibby's mate. I'll be home as soon as we get this sorted out, I promise.' Andy crossed his heart, a somewhat empty gesture given his recent proclivity for deception.

'Unbelievable. D'you ever stop lettin me down? Did you even get the things I asked you to get from the shop?'

'What things?'

'The natural yogurt. I asked you to get me natural yogurt.'

'Since when d'you need natural yogurt?'

'Since the thrush came back I would imagine, chief.'

At times it seemed like Gibby didn't so much enter rooms as materialise whenever conversation turned in a suitably lurid direction. He winked at Andy and Michelle, who looked at him, surprised and shocked respectively.

'Am I right, sweetheart? Wee bit fizzy down there? Here, no need to be embarrassed. That's the only reason anyone gets natural yogurt. We all get a bit fungal from time to time. Me, I just get my keks off an smear it all over my junk whenever me or my Angie get a bit itchy.'

He rubbed his groin as he might if applying natural yoghurt in the manner he had just described.

'Err...it's actually just used for oral thrush,' said Michelle, recovering from Gibby's diagnosis and recommended course of treatment. 'Which is what I have.'

Gibby leant in to Michelle and turned her away from Andy before whispering in her ear. 'Honestly, it's nothin to be ashamed of. If you ever need anyone to help you appl...'

'Tell you what Gibby,' Andy interjected. 'Why don't you just leave me and Michelle for a minute.'

'As you wish, chief. Mind you can talk to me if you ever need to speak about an embarrassin problem. I'm very discreet. I've never told anyone about Lionel's third ball.'

He bowed and exited.

Andy put his hands on Michelle's shoulders. 'Look, I'm sorry. But we can do somethin tonight.'

Michelle agreed that it was better than nothing and bent down to pick up her handbag.

'It is just oral isn't it?'

Although the look he received suggested that was not a subject up for investigation, Andy could definitely feel an urgent itch in his penis although, he conceded, this could certainly be as a result of his recent priapic incident.

TWENTY-EIGHT

As he leant against the wall enjoying the unseasonably good weather, Gibby's only concern was how his digestive system would deal with a 20th nicotine injection in a day that remained young. His good mood was broken when he noticed a familiar figure approaching.

'Here we go,' he said as a squat, balding man in an ill-fitting suit drew closer until only a few feet separated them. Gibby flicked the butt away and drew himself up to his full height.

'Well, well, fuckin well. If it isnae fuckin Gibby the fuckin glib. I swear tae God the only thing that wid survive a fuckin nuclear holocaust would be a bunch o' wee fuckin cockroaches an you, Mr Wisdom. King o' the fuckin cockroaches, that's you.'

'Alright Clive. Was wonderin when you'd show up.'

The smaller man broke into a smile that unnerved Gibby, no matter how many times he saw it. 'Nae need tae make a friendly fuckin visit sound like a bad thing. We've seen this fuckin club change hands so many times yet we always end up meetin here. The last great survivors o' the fuckin trade.'

'I heard you were into rough trade, Clive. An I don't mean the label.'

'Now, now Gibby. Homophobia disnae become a cosmopolitan fuckin man like yersel. That was a one-time thing.'

'That lasted three year?'

'Time disnae fly when yer residin at Her Majesty's Pleasure away fae the woman ye fuckin love.'

Gibby reached into his pocket again for his fags. Finding the packet empty, he crushed it in his hand, knuckles whitening as Clive grinned at the spectacle.

'Whatever. You're barkin up the wrong tree here. This place never makes any money.'

Clive stepped towards Gibby and half-whispered to him. 'Well, yer gettin a lot o' fuckin press these days. That's how I fuckin kent ye were open again and thought I should pay a wee fuckin visit, offer ye some alternative fuckin business models. Ways I can help ye out.'

Although uncomfortable by Clive's proximity, Gibby refused to back down and even edged towards his nemesis. 'No thanks.'

Clive leaned in further. 'A friendly fuckin chat's all I'm after.'

So this is how you want to play it then, thought Gibby and shuffled forward another couple of inches. 'You're out of luck, nobody's here but me an I'm no authorised to make any decisions on my own.'

Clive saw Gibby's progress and raised him an inch. 'How don't I just come in an fuckin wait for yer fuckin partners then?'

'I don't think so.' A centimetre. Gibby was rapidly running out of chips to gamble with here.

Clive butted the toes of his battered brogues against Gibby's trainers and shuffled forward, forehead to chin and what Gibby was sure was the beginnings of an erection to inner thigh.

'I dinnae ken how yer bein so fuckin obstructive, Gibby. Especially when I ken whaur ye fuckin live.'

Clive stared at Gibby's bottom lip and awaited his move, but clubland's premier wheeler-dealer stood stock still, heart thumping against Clive's shoulder. After what seemed like an age, he was relieved to hear the door open behind him.

'You here Gibby? What's this about Lionel havin a third spud then?'

He side-stepped his colleague and noticed a bald man marginally more substantial than a midget seemingly bumping atoms with him.

'No interruptin anythin am I?'

Gibby breathed a sigh of relief as Clive stepped back, smirked and approached Andy.

'No introducin me tae yer friend, Gibby?'

'Clive, this is Andy. He's the new guy they hired to collect the glasses.' Composing himself, Gibby winked at Andy to indicate that he should go along with whatever he was about to say. Unfortunately, Andy was so used to the gesture appealing to non-existent camaraderie, indicate sexual arousal, or seek approval for a particularly satisfying bodily function that he missed its significance.

Andy turned to Clive. 'I'm the co-owner of the Quantum Club.'

'Pleasure tae meet ye, sir. I'm a good friend o' Gibby's.'

'Course. Come in. I'm sure you'll find everythin's in good, workin order an that we're ready to open. I'm sure we'll be able to meet any demands you might have.'

'No, but...'

The invitation was accepted before the boy who winked wolf had the chance to protest further. He followed them to the office, where Andy sat down in the big chair and indicated that Clive should occupy the one at the opposite side of the desk. Gibby stood leaning in the doorway, arms folded across his chest. Andy nodded in the direction of the free chair but was met with a shake of the head.

'I'll hover thanks, chief. Bad smell over there.'

'For fuck's sake. Can you no just hold it until you get outside, just for once? We've got company.'

Clive leant back in his chair, belly flopping out between the lapels of his jacket, so he could see both his guests. 'I suspect Gibby's words were intended tae fuckin wound me. But this is business so I'll no let my emotions interfere with it.'

Andy pushed a pile of papers across the desk to him. 'Right, as you can see, everythin's filled in an correct. An I'm sure your committee will agree that myself an Cornelius are fit an proper people to hold an alcohol licence. We've never been in any kind of trouble an can have the application fee in the Council bank account first thing tomorrow.'

Clive's forehead wrinkled. 'I think yer mistaken, Andy. I'm no fae the fuckin council.'

'But, I thought you were Gibby's mate. The one on the Licensin committee.'

'I'm another friend.'

'I wouldn't even call you a Facebook friend. You keep sendin friend requests an I keep declinin. Thought you would've taken the hint by now.'

Conceding the point, Clive held his palm outstretched to Andy. 'We're business fuckin acquaintances then. I'm sure me an you can also reach a mutually advantageous agreement with regards tae insurin this fine fuckin establishment.'

'You're an insurance salesman? Used to be in the same game mysel so I'm insured to the hilt.' Andy had finally got round to completing this task the day before. 'I'm worth more dead than alive you know.'

'Probly the worst thing you could have said in present company, chief.'

'I dinnae think yer policy will provide the peace o' fuckin mind I can. What aboot…miscellaneous? Ye ken. For acts o' fuckin God. They happen a lot tae businesses that dinnae huv the right insurance.'

Andy shivered as he realised what was going on.

'Gibby kens how this works. So does Tony an my auld pal Lionel. An now you can relate the pertinent sections tae yer bra'ar-in-law. All nightclubs in this fuckin city pay a little insurance tae the fuckin Family, an' everythin fuckin works oot ok.'

'The Family? This is Dundee, no…are you for real? What if I go to the police?'

Clive raised his eyebrows, unfolding the bottom half of his face but causing the top portion to collapse in on itself. 'Wouldnae advise that. Seems a bitty fuckin hysterical.'

'Course I'm gettin hysterical!' Andy cried. 'You're blackmailin me.'

'Nah, I'm no. Yer buyin insurance against anythin untaeward happenin tae lovely fuckin Club Quantum here. Oor rates are very reasonable. Thank God this isnae a pub.'

'An what difference would that make?'

'We've nothin tae dae wi' pubs. They pay the MacTavishes.'

'The who?'

Clive leaned in and whispered. 'Big crime family. Scottish. Us Italians, we've been fuckin doin this a while so we've got a wee bit mair fuckin class.'

'You're Italian?'

'Sixth generation,' Clive nodded. 'Great, great, great Granddad was fae the fuckin Italian bit o' fuckin Switzerland.'

Andy rubbed his temples furiously. 'This is unbelievable. This really happens?'

He was addressing the question at Gibby but it was Clive who answered.

'It does. But it's no like the auld fuckin days. There's so many gangs aroond that the market's been divvied up. Too much fuckin immigration. Really, ye should be thankin God that it's us offerin ye this fantastic business opportunity an no the fuckin Jamaicans.

'The Jamaicans?'

Clive spoke as if he could taste the words on his tongue. 'Sandwich shops. Fuckin all o' them. Even fuckin Gregg's. An the Jamaicans are fuckin mean. Fuckin stylish, certainly, but mean. People're sayin they've moved intae fuckin museums an galleries now as well.'

This was starting to sound too ludicrous to be true to the beleaguered strategist. 'An the drug trade's entirely run by the Muslims, is it?'

Clive shook his head in disappointment. 'Ye sound like the Daily fuckin Mail. The Mormons control the drug trade, the Muslims are intae fuckin Bingo. Shias at least. Ye ken, it's a little insensitive tae lump the fuckin Muslims intae one homogeneous fuckin group. Racist.'

Having heard enough and keen to end the conversation before he found out that the car wash industry was really a money-laundering front for local Hare Krishna drug lords, Andy pushed against the desk and stood up as the chair rolled back towards the wall.

'Look Clive, I dunno what to think. We'll have to speak to Cornelius.'

'Aye, an don't think he'll take this lyin down,' nodded Gibby. 'He's a man of action.'

TWENTY-NINE

Cornelius' arms hung limply by his side, his shoulders slumped, lip petted and eyes crossed. All in all, he looked like the only dog in the pound unable to lick his own balls.

'I knew it wasn't on til next week! We've got to see that chick flick I said I didn't want to see now.'

Emma rubbed her shoe off the foyer carpet and looked to the concession stand in an attempt to conceal her grin. 'Look, I'm sorry okay? It's got that Isla Fisher in it though. You like her don't you?'

'S'pose. I like her accent.'

'Oh, an don't do that thing you do with accents.'

'I don't do anything with accents.'

Emma crossed her arms. 'Remember The Commitments?'

'So say it once, say it loud: Oim black and oim proud,' Cornelius giggled at the cod-Irish accent that he erroneously believed to have won him friends in Lochee. 'I'm gonna get some popcorn. D'you want anything before we go in?'

'Actually, yeah. Could you get me some sparklin water?'

Cornelius looked at her, unable to comprehend why anyone would voluntarily consume such a thing. 'Trapped wind again,' added Emma by way of explanation.

Cornelius walked into the shop and briefly considered the low-fat popcorn before picking up the buttered version, which he clutched to his chest as he selected a bottle of sparkling water from the fridge. He walked up to the till and placed the items on the counter. The acne-ridden teenage assistant with 'Adrian' on his badge looked at them and then at Cornelius.

'You sure you want this?' he asked, barely managing to control adolescent vocal oscillations.

'Course I do.'

Adrian sighed. 'You do know this is sparklin water?'

'Erm, yes.'

'Fair enough, he shrugged. 'Six seventy-five.'

Cornelius picked his items up slowly and deliberately and backed away towards the foyer. He paused at the shop front to stare at Adrian, whose attention had been stolen by his mobile phone.

Shaking his head, Cornelius walked into the foyer and handed Emma the water.

'You'll never believe what just happened to me. This cheeky little git at the counter is all like 'you do know this is sparkling water?' I mean, does he think I can't read or something? He earns minimum wage and I...'

'Will probly never earn that much again.'

'He was a patronising little shit, baby. Even blind people can tell the difference between sparkling water and still water. That's why the bottles are always different shapes, so thirsty blind people don't get a nasty surprise. Although sparkling water makes a sound when you open it, I suppose, so they could tell that way.'

In the spirit of their recent promise to show interest in each other's worlds, Emma indulged her husband while stifling a yawn. 'So what did you say?'

Cornelius raised his eyebrows and inhaled nasally. 'I was so taken aback. Couldn't think of anything.'

'Look, this is one of they things we discussed you no obsessin about. Either forget about it or deck the wee bastard.'

Cornelius shook his head. 'No. I saw too much violence growing up in the hood. I prefer to outdo a rival with my wits.'

'I really think a rap in the pus would be more effective,' Emma said as she dragged Cornelius by his arm in the direction of the screen. He was unable to forget the perceived slight, however, and swore revenge as Adrian, feet up on the counter, laughing at something on his phone, passed out of his line of sight.

*   *   *

As it turned out, Clive already knew what Cornelius' ill-fated visit to the concession stand had proved – that he wasn't a man of action. He knew a frightening amount about all Quantum's co-owners in fact – place of birth, date of birth, address, names of spouses and dependents (an accusation Gibby vigorously contested). Andy had to hand it to him – extortionist, would-be arsonist and all-round bad guy Clive may be, but his research was meticulous.

'I think you should go,' he said finally. 'This doesn't feel right.'

'Feels fuckin righter than haein yer fuckin club burnt doon I'd imagine. Or dealin wi the loss of a fuckin kneecap.'

Andy gulped, but Gibby swooped in to provide some temporary relief.

'Mibbe it's better if you come back later. Let things sink it a bit, aye?'

'Sure, anythin for friends.' He made the point to Gibby before turning to Andy. 'Ye hae four fuckin days. Ken how yev got four fuckin days?' Andy admitted that he did not. 'Cos I've been watchin the fuckin energy markets closely an I'm expectin petrol prices tae fall in that time. I didnae get where I am the day by bein fuckin profligate.'

Rising from his chair, Clive tried to button his jacket only to be foiled by his girth. He smiled at Andy in either an attempt to reassure him that there were ways of avoiding the worst-case scenario or in empathy with a fellow salad-dodger.

The office door opened and Lionel ducked under the frame before coming to a stop when he saw Clive. There was a moment of awkwardness as the two of them looked each other up and down. Clive eventually nodded to the head of security and broke the silence.

'Lionel.'

'Clive.'

'Still on the door here then?'

'Yes.'

'Seen your video on YouTube. Pretty fucked up, like.'

'Says the prowler of Perth Prison.'

Clive looked past Lionel to Gibby, who was sniggering at his own rapier wit, and back to the new arrival.

'Well, like I've always said. If ye ever want tae make some real fuckin money come an see me. Lot o' fuckin work oot there for a man o' your fuckin talents.'

Lionel's eyes lit up. 'As an exotic male dancer?'

'Err…no. The Jews huv that industry fuckin sewn up now. Ken what they're like for fuckin nepotism as well. There husnae been a fuckin foreskin seen at a hen do in this toon fur fuckin years.'

Clive looked around the room, clearly expecting some sympathy for his plight, or at least that of the non-circumcised stripper. Andy glanced at Gibby, who shrugged.

'In that case, no thanks, Clive,' Lionel returned to his default sombre look. 'It has taken years of soul searching and cognitive behavioural therapy to enable me to live with what happened the last time I was in your employment and yet it still ails me from time to time.'

'Well, I ken whaur ye fuckin are if ye change yer fuckin mind. I'll see mysel oot. I ken the fuckin way.'

He exited to sighs of relief from Andy and Gibby, while Lionel continued to stare straight ahead. Andy leapt out of his seat, pulled the door shut and turned to his compatriots.

'Gibby, I'd really like you to tell me I'm dreamin.'

'You're no dreamin, chief. Things must be tight though, Clive usually turns up once the place has been up an runnin for a month or two. No point puttin your head above water if there's no profit to tax.'

'An when were you goin to tell me we would have to deal with the fuckin Mafia?'

'Kept forgettin, to be honest. Had a lot on with this place an the DVDs an my Angie findin out about that webcam thing I had with that dame from Trinidad.' He winked to Andy before adding, 'Just as well monitors wipe clean, aye?'

Andy flopped back into the chair and drummed his fingers on the desk. 'We can't afford to pay protection. Wait a minute…you mentioned miscellaneous insurance before. What did you mean?'

'Well, knowin we needed to deal with Clive at some point, I've spent the past four month negotiatin with various shadowy underworld figures.' He looked at Andy, who looked confused, and Lionel, who remained impassive. 'You're welcome.'

'What? Why?'

'Cos this is a dirty business, chief. You need to do deals with bad guys if you're gonna survive so I figured that we'd best do business with the good-bad guys.'

'For fuck's sake, Gibby. Why didn't you tell me about this?'

'Well, I didn't want to worry you unnecessarily – again, you're welcome – til I'd somethin to report. It's no like you can just go to a price comparison website an get quotes for the best gangsters who'll fight their arsonist instincts for a reasonable price while lettin you keep the profits from sellin their drugs.'

'But we're no sellin drugs, mind? Michelle said the dealin had to stop.'

Lionel shook his head at Andy's naivety and Gibby smiled at him as he would an inmate who, after being served a luxury three-course meal of his own choosing, asked for tomorrow's menu. He walked to Andy's side and placed a hand on his shoulder.

'I sympathise, chief, I really do. You're there thinkin, "I've got this tidy piece who's far too good for me an I need to do everythin in my power to keep her sweet". But the bottom line is that guestlists, council officials, sound systems, beige paint – to say nothin of the fact Cornelius is likely to go rogue and buy a gargantuan mirrorball as soon as our backs are turned – it all adds up. We need to diversify our product range in order to improve our market share. Isn't that right, Lionel?'

Lionel nodded.

'But…I mean, she'll kill me.'

'Reckon she'd kill you if she knew you'd been tappin into the weddin fund, chief. Ah, no need for that look. Gibby knows. She might already know for all you know. Might even be the stress that's caused the flare-up in her phoo-phoo.'

Andy blinked at Gibby, knowing he'd do whatever he said and wondering whether there was a proven medical link between anxiety and fungal infections.

'So, what did these err…alternative insurance providers say?'

Gibby's face fell. 'Have to confess, chief, the feedback hasn't been good. Like Clive said, the lines have been drawn in thick black marker pen, underlined an underlined again. Everyone's scarred by the burger van wars. Everyone's stickin to their own turf.'

Andy nodded, thinking he understood then realising he didn't. 'So…err…what does that mean for us? Clive said somethin about alternatives.'

'There are always alternatives with Clive,' said Lionel with bitterness. 'He will have his pound of flesh whatever way he can.'

'What exactly did you do for him?' Andy asked the tri-testicled bouncer.

'It is a period of my life I am unwilling to discuss other than to say it taught me the wisdom of Nietzche's words that to forget one's purpose is the commonest form of stupidity.'

Without a further word, Lionel ducked under the doorway and stormed off wherever the unwanted memories were least likely to follow him.

THIRTY

A blanket of dread lay heavy on Andy as he stared at the phone, just as it had during his call centre days. He tried to make the call several times, but put the receiver down each time. What he had to say was not to the liking of the other party. Words would be exchanged, abuse was a certainty and tears a possibility. Eventually he plucked up the courage and dialled the number. Even as the phone rang, Andy was fighting the urge to slam it down again. Face it like a man, that's what Dad would have said. And with that new 1471 technology they would know it was him, anyway.

'Hello?' said the voice on the other end of the line.

'Oh, hi. How's things?'

'Well, I thought we could go for a walk then a few drinks,' said Michelle. 'Want me to come down an pick you up?'

'Well. The thing is...'

'Awww, Andy. No. I took today off cos I never see you. You're there all the time. I wouldn't mind but you never actually do any work. You just piss about with your new pals.'

'No. But...Right, the thing is. Erm...the visit didn't go as well as we hoped. In fact...'

'You know what? I don't even want to hear it.' Andy pressed his ear harder into the receiver in case he could hear the engagement ring being slipped off but the evidence was inconclusive.

'I'll be home later. We've just got a bit of a situation. I'll make it up to you. I'll take you out for a meal. Well, I'm a bit skint so maybe a takeaway. But no from the posh place.' Andy congratulated himself for subtly introducing his impending financial doom into the conversation. Gently get her used to the idea. Then break it to her about the wedding fund and becoming a drug pusher.

'You'd better,' she said, her tone curt and threatening.

The phone went dead. Andy considered returning the receiver to the cradle but decided to leave it in case a blood-thirty gangster or, worse still, one of those companies offering to sort out his PPI claim was calling.

He chewed his nails as he considered the options Gibby laid out for him – pay Clive, find another, bigger gangster to scare Clive off and pay him, or have the club razed to the ground. His Dad had always berated Andy for running from trouble rather than standing up for himself. Playground bullies who didn't go through a Cure phase and objected to your Robert Smith make-up were one thing though; ruthless mobsters that even Lionel seemed wary of were another. What his Dad had also failed to appreciate was that Andy was a man who believed in picking your battles rather than steaming in any time confrontation reared its head. If, for example, the Gatlin boys came calling and brutally gang-raped Michelle then he hoped that, like the Coward of the County, he would head down to their local and leave not one of them standing. On the other hand, he was unlikely to kill someone just because they called her a slag, which set him apart from the protagonist in Indiana Wants Me whose homicidal arse was eventually gunned down by state police.

Andy was congratulating himself on his wisdom when a brusque knock alerted him to the presence of his brother-in-law, who slammed the door behind him, started to speak, realised he was still too angry, then opened and slammed the door again.

'I'm bloody raging, cobber! Bloody raging!'

'Me too,' said Andy. 'But why're you speakin with an Aussie accent?'

Cornelius regarded his brother-in-law with confusion before realising what he was talking about and coughing. 'Sorry about that. Don't realise I'm doing it. Anyway, I'm still raging.'

'What the fuck're we gonna do Cornelius?'

'I'm touched that you've got my back like this, man. But this is something I've got to take care of myself.'

Surprised but delighted by this turn of events, Andy was perfectly happy to delegate responsibility for this particular task, even though it might result in his niece being partially orphaned.

'Good. So what're you gonna do?'

'Well, the way I see it, I go back to the cinema and...'

'Cornelius! D'you even know what's goin on? Gangsters are threatenin us.'

Cornelius stopped pacing around. 'Don't be silly. I'm dealing with something real here and you're talking about gangsters?'

'Real life gangsters who break legs an demand money.'

Cornelius dismissed him with a wave of the hand and went back to his pacing. Andy's eyes followed him across the room like he was watching tennis.

'I'm no jokin.'

'Neither am I. That kid needs a lesson. I'm at the cinema right and I go to by some popcorn and I get Emma some water, sparkling, right.'

'C'mon, I don't have time for this.'

'Listen, you'll be as angry as me. So I put the water on the counter and he's all like, "You do know this is sparkling water?" I mean everyone knows it's sparkling water. Even the blind know that. The bottles are shaped differently so they know.'

'Are you sure? I thought it was for the bubbles.'

Cornelius stopped pacing and stared at Andy, who was trying to make sense of half-forgotten chemistry lessons by jabbering about the danger of bubbles congregating at the gas ridges and dissipating. Even though he felt this hypothesis was a strong one, Andy felt the H2O tangent was distracting from the real issue at hand.

'Anyway, the problem is dealin with Clive the violent an dangerous gangster.'

'Clive the gangster? Stop babbling, man. I know what real gangsters are. You're forgetting I was dragged up on the mean streets of North London. Look, we have to prioritise and the number one priority is getting my own back on that hairless ballbag at the cinema. I was at it with your sister when we got home. From behind cos that's easier what with your niece being in there as well, and all I could picture was that counter assistant. I lost my wood, Andy. That little prick took my wood.'

Andy screwed his eyes shut to try to escape from the picture Cornelius was painting and opened them to find his brother-in-law shadow boxing, presumably in an attempt to demonstrate what he'd do to the teenage popcorn vendor if he ever got his hands on him. The Queensbury rules were quickly forgotten and Cornelius was stamping on his non-existent opponent with both feet and great force before Andy managed to derail the assault.

Under normal circumstances, there were only five things that enraged Cornelius to this extent – cruelty to animals, odd and even numbers, Watford losing, Luton winning and Prog Rock. At such times his decision-making prowess was even more impaired than usual, so, frightened as he was by the prospect of falling foul of the underworld, Andy spotted the opportunity to double his worldly goods.

'Bet you £20 this kid makes a fool of you.'

Although Cornelius departed immediately after the wager was sealed, Andy did nothing for the next two hours other than stare at the phone. It was time for honesty. Not complete honesty, of course, but partial honesty. He dialled the number and went over the version of events he felt would elicit the most sympathy. We've been threatened by gangsters, Michelle. I know, I might have to do things I don't like. They've made me withdraw money from the wedding account. And bribe a bank teller to backdate the transaction. I know! In the meantime, I need to stay here until we figure something out. No, not me and Cornelius. He's off fighting a war against an unsuspecting foe again. No, not …

'Hello.'

'Hi Mich, how're you?'

'Fine. Except you're still no here. Where's my curry?' She slurred her words, suggesting that the hour of the grape had been moved forward once again. His best-case contingency hadn't accounted for inebriation.

'Well, we've got a bit of a situation here...'

'What a shock. Whatsit this time? Lionel finally gone mad with a Kalashnikov? Gibby forgeto sign the register this mornin?'

'No, err...we've been threatened by gangsters.'

'Oh really? Like last week when you said the place was over-run by rats when you an Cornelius was really just gettin drunk an playn on the decks?'

'No, really.'

'Or the week before when you said there was a ghost but you were tryin to start a rap group.'

'A hip-hop collective. But this is serious.'

'Whatever. Know what? Maybe you ssshouldn't come homes for a bit.'

The phone went dead. Andy had never been kicked out before. In the months that followed DJ Shadow's Amsterdam gig, Cornelius had been a semi-regular resident of his spare room, but Michelle had never so much as threatened him with eviction. They had never even had a proper fight until he bought Quantum. As such, he was unsure how seriously to take her suggestion. Maybe it would be for the best to stay out of the way for a few days, though. Show her what she's missing. She might even be a bit more grateful when he did show up again. And all that stuff with Chelsea? It wasn't as if he would stray even if she threw herself at him. If she was insistent, then he supposed they could watch each other wank off or something. But he would never actually cheat on Michelle. But did she appreciate that? Andy was near enough indignant about his treatment when Gibby walked into the office.

'You okay, chief?'

Andy waved a hand in an attempt to keep his relationship issues private. 'Totally. Just thinkin what to do about Clive.'

'An about the earache from the missus?'

'How d'you know?'

'Every man has that look about him sometimes,' nodded Gibby. 'Plus I was listenin in on the other line.'

'For fuck's sake. That was private.'

Gibby pulled the face that Andy had initially thought radiated wisdom but quickly found out corresponded to noxious gas emissions. 'I was monitorin your call in case it was Clive. An anyway, I've got more bad news from my man at the council. Turns out he gave out the last nightclub licence this afternoon when he was supposed to be here. Apparently there's a limit.'

Andy brought his fist down on the desk. 'But he was supposed to be here!'

'Apparently he got a call from Tony an met him first. He's openin a private member's club in DJ Q's Mum's basement.'

It was now an hourly experience for Andy to wish he'd never heard of DJ Quantum. 'Fucked again. What're we gonna to do now?'

'Well, as it turns out, chief. I've got a brilliant idea.'

THIRTY-ONE

The empty bottles had steadily built up across the bar in the hours since Andy and Michelle's phone call. Both he and Gibby were considerably the worse for wear, and the ashtray which sat before them overflowed on to the axe-marked wood. Gibby took long draws on a joint the size of a dunce's cap as his business partner cried on his shoulder.

'So, I've been threatened by gangsters, I've been thrown out an I can't get my nightclub licensed. It's no been the best day of my life.'

'An your burd is riddled.'

'She's no riddled. It's oral thrush.'

'I'm jokin, chief. At least you'll win money when that guy takes the proverbial out of Cornelius.'

Gibby offered the joint to Andy, who surprised both of them by accepting it. He took a few puffs before handing it back and taking a sizeable gulp of his pint. When Andy launched himself brain-last into the nightclub game he expected to spend his nights swanning around making sure everyone was having a good time while being told how right he was about everything, including The Go-Ahead Seagulls who were enjoying something of a renaissance at the insistence of the genius-like DJ. Defective sewage systems, lovedoll orgies and Italian gangsters without a drop of Italian blood – they just hadn't featured in any of the books he'd read.

'What the fuck're we gonna do, Gibby? D'you think we could blackmail Clive? Lionel must know somethin incriminatin if he worked for him.'

Gibby shook his head. 'Thought of that. Just says he doesn't want to speak about a period of his life that ripped his soul apart.'

'Fuck. Must be bad. D'you think he...ended someone?'

Gibby shrugged and the pair fell silent again. Andy felt tears well up behind his eyes so turned to the side to make sure Gibby couldn't see. Luckily, his partner was deep in thought. Eventually, he spoke again.

'I keep askin mysel, what would Tony Soprano do?"

'No idea,' said Andy. 'I've never seen it.'

Gibby looked incredulous as he stubbed the joint out in the ashtray, pushing it so far through the piled up butts that his fingers re-emerged covered in ash. He patted Andy on the shoulder with that hand and picked up his fags and keys with the other.

'You've never seen The Sopranos?' Well, I think we need to redress that situation by retirin to mine an watchin from the start of series one. For research. We could take some beers down.'

Andy shrugged. 'Might as well, we can't sell them.'

*   *   *

The reefer that Andy accepted from Gibby might have been his first for over a decade but it wasn't to be his last. Over the next few days the pair of them made steady progress through an inordinate amount of weed, beer and episodes of the pioneering TV gangster series.

They reclined on a sofa in Gibby's darkened living room. Andy, practically horizontal amongst the empty bottles and take-away boxes, had learnt the hard way that repeated exposure to his host's airspace did nothing to build immunity against his flatulent excesses.

They faced a giant, wall-mounted TV screen, which flickered in the darkness before dimming as Don't Stop Believing by Journey filled the room, courtesy of a sound system that looked suspiciously like the one allegedly ruined by Gibby and Lionel during their drug-fuelled rampage.

'Outstandin,' said Andy as he wiped away a tear. 'I can't believe I'd never seen The Sopranos before.'

'I can't believe we watched 86 episodes back to back, chief.

What day is it?' With great effort, Gibby pulled himself to his feet and staggered over to the windows. He pulled the cord and the blinds shot up as brightness exploded into the room.

'Friday,' said Andy, shielding his eyes from the light. 'We've no slept for days.'

Gibby yawned. 'No that it hasn't been an honour an a pleasure to have shared this mobster marathon with you, chief, but it's mibbe time you were headin home. Or at least let the missus know where you are.'

Having spent the past four days trying to forget his relationship crisis, something suddenly occurred to Andy. 'Fogedaboutit. Where's your Angie by the way?'

'At her sister's,' sighed Gibby. 'For her own good.'

Reminders of his predicament began jabbing Andy from all angles and his Sopranos bubble was well and truly burst.

'In case Clive comes here lookin for you?'

'Well, partly. But more cos I had this thing lined up with this Swedish backpacker who asked if she could couch surf here.'

'Couch surf?'

'Couch surfin. Travellers stay with each other when they're in each other's towns.'

'But you don't travel.' The concepts of travelling and gap years were reminders to Andy that the world had peaked in 1997 and been in terminal decline ever since.

'No, but I enjoy the company of Swedish backpackers,' said Gibby with a wink. 'Anyway, she called off at the last moment. Somethin about a Google search an they accusations that should've been thrown out.' He shook his head bitterly. 'Never get Tony to represent you in court.'

Andy felt his bubble pop. 'For fuck's sake. That's another thing we need to sort out. DJ Q's basement isn't even a club.'

As soon as he said it, Andy's brain started to waken up. Very slowly. Like a factory loom that had lain mothballed for years, the spark didn't cause it to instantly return to full capacity but he definitely felt gears turn, rotors rotate and shafts shaft in his head.

'Anyway, I'd already packed my Angie off by then,' recommenced Gibby, who was unaware that Andy's frontal cortex was currently enjoying an industrial revolution. '...so this stuff with Clive came at the best possible time for me.'

Andy tried to focus on the very real threat posed by a very real gangster, but he was unable to shut out the noise of the wheels that kept on turning. He pulled himself to his feet, a smile slowly spreading across his unshaven face. 'It's like we seen on the Sopranos. Nightclubs pay gangsters. If only we weren't a nightclub...'

Gibby looked puzzled. 'Mind I said that about the insurance? You said it wouldn't work.'

'No for regular insurance, but for miscellaneous purposes... might be hard to categorise if we're somethin no one has their hooks into.' A flash of inspiration slapped him so hard across his face that he could practically feel like jowls wobble. 'Like a...like a pettin zoo!'

'Fryin pan an fire, chief. The zoos are the Dominicans.' Gibby was starting to get the idea now as well though and began pacing round the coffee table. 'No, you want to be somethin that hasn't attracted attention. Or money.'

'We need to save Quantum by pretendin Scotland's number one nightclub is a business that doesn't make any money.'

Gibby was just about to deliver a truncated breakdown of Club Quantum/the Quantum Club's financial prospects when Andy slapped him on the back and winked at him.

The blow dislodged a pocket of wind that had been trapped in Gibby's oesophagus for some minutes and, with the relief that came from belching days' worth of pizza, beer and cigarettes in Andy's face, a new clarity arrived.

He grinned back at his co-owner and nodded his head.

'Truth be told, chief. I'm startin to think you've got more balls than Lionel.'

THIRTY-TWO

For the fourth day in a row, Cornelius attempted to restore his dignity by pretending to be disabled. On each of his visits post-Watergate to the cinema he'd been disappointed to find his adversary hadn't been working – something to do with a Scout camp, according to the duty manager. As an unsuspecting Adrian stood behind the counter texting and yawning, Cornelius reflected that revenge was indeed a dish best served cold as the extended interval since their last encounter had allowed him to perfect his retaliation strategy.

The co-owner of Quantum was dressed in a purple overcoat, carried a cane and wore dark glasses. He took a deep breath before bumping into the doorframe, both for effect and to draw Adrian's attention.

'Good afternoon young man. Can I have a small popcorn please? Don't spit on it because I'm blind. I'll know you know.'

Adrian put down his phone and smiled at what he believed was a kindly old gentleman whose macular degenerations caused him difficulties choosing outfits of a morning. 'I wouldn't do that. Want anythin else?'

'Water. Do you have water?'

The pockmarked Explorer Scout ran over to the fridge and retrieved a bottle of water. He thumped it down in front of Cornelius with enough force for him to nearly jump out of his skin and gaudy wardrobe.

'Actually,' said the supposedly blind customer caressing the bottle as if it was a lamp he hoped a genie would emerge from. 'I'd prefer sparkling. Do you mind changing it?'

When the replacement was placed on the counter, Cornelius slipped his fingers round it. He moved his fist up and down a few times and produced not a genie but a satisfied gasp and beamed into space.

'Do you know how I could tell it was the wrong water? Cos of the shape of the bottle. It's designed for blind people.'

'I didn't know that.'

'No, I didn't think you did,' began Cornelius before realising he was now staring straight at Adrian and went back to gazing at the roof again. 'Everyone can tell the difference between still and sparkling water so asking someone if they knew what water they were getting would be quite patronising. Even to a blind man.'

Adrian's brow furrowed, almost causing several of the largest spots on his forehead to send pus spewing across the counter towards his unsettling customer. 'Err...£6.75 please.'

Cornelius turned to him and grinned. 'No, thank you. I am no longer hungry or thirsty. Point me in the direction of the door and I will leave.'

'It's over there, to your left.'

'Thank you, young man,' he said as he swept his cane off every obstacle he could see on the way to the door. 'The memory of this meeting will live with me forever, and you too should remember it. Especially the bit about the water.'

Adrian shivered as he watched Cornelius leave the shop before picking up his phone and sharing his experience with the world, or his 468 Twitter followers at least.

It was questionable whether anyone else would view the incident as the greatest act of revenge since the clouds in Carly Simon's coffee cleared and she wrote You're So Vain. Then again, few would see a misunderstanding over sparkling water as an insult equivalent to Miley Cyrus arriving at Riyadh International Airport in her stage costume. Once he'd rounded the corner and was sure he had gotten away with his ingenuous plan, Cornelius celebrated by swinging his cane around and striding up the hallway. He paused by a doorway and looked up to the LCD info bar above, which read The Harder They Come, and entered while whistling the eponymous title track.

THIRTY-THREE

The main room was in complete darkness, apart from several images projected onto the walls, a rabbit here, a flower there, a Ronald Reagan everywhere. The temple of dance was not silent, however, as Tony, lured back by rumours that a series of Sound Art enthusiasts were to be visiting the club, was once again interpreting DJ Q's adventures in sonic creativity. Wild industrial dance music followed its culmination before samples of evidently distressed animals competed for airtime with the sound of heavy machinery. The effect was not unlike an abattoir set to a beat.

'AND SO, THE CYCLE IS FINALLY COMPLETE.'

The room's lights were thrown on at full power, meaning the illumination barely allowed Gibby, Andy, Lionel and Gordon, the Council's head Licensin honcho, to see Tony, arms aloft and roaring like a lion that had just completed its hat-trick. The look of confusion on the faces of Lionel and Gordon were comparable to those of the other two following their first exposure to the world of Sound Art.

'So much more powerful with the light show!' cried Tony. 'Mind-blowin!'

Andy turned to the local authority official who he hoped was as scrutable as most of Gibby's associates. 'So, what d'you think?'

'Shite,' he shrugged. 'But it doesn't matter. All nightclub licences are gone.'

Gibby slipped an arm across his shoulders, causing Gordon to flinch. 'Ah, but we're no lookin for a nightclub licence, chief.'

'You see, we're no a nightclub,' added Andy who put his arm across Gibby's arm, locking them in an embrace that made Gordon feel like the unfortunate filling in a hobo sandwich.

'But you've got a dancefloor, DJ – an eccentric one granted – and you want to sell drinks.'

Andy and Gibby smiled at each other. 'For our Art Happenin.'

'Your what?'

'This whole place, Quantum, is a giant art project,' explained Andy, regurgitating the promotional postcard DJ Q had sent him that morning. 'An experiment in human nature. People pay to be part of a unique artistic expression using the medium of kick-ass beats an lights an everyone's happy.'

'So, how about rippin up the original application an we go for a licence as an Art Happenin? I'll throw in a couple of audio-visual marital aids as a sign of good faith. Can't say fairer than that, chief.'

Gordon shook off the space-invading applicants and rubbed his chin. 'Art Happening? Well…that's one of those tricky grey areas. It's neither one thing nor the other. Takes loads of investigation, and time and effort. What with the public sector cutbacks we normally just stamp it through and hope for the best.'

'So if we ask for a drinks licence an for our Art Happenin to stay open til 4am we'll get it?' asked Andy, with one eye on his partner.

'Probably. Then, if there's any issues we'll just switch the licence to a nightclub one on the quiet as soon as another shuts to cover our own backs.'

'Outstandin, chief. Outstandin.'

'Just one thing though.' Gordon nodded toward Lionel. 'I'm not comfortable with his underworld connections.'

'I find that to be most unfair,' protested Lionel. 'I only did the Kleeneze for Clive for a couple of months.'

'Kleeneze?'

Lionel nodded before shaking his head. 'Horrible work. Clive has the franchise for the whole Dundee area. They say you can make three pound signs in your spare time but the commission is negligible and the abuse from people still waiting for a detachable mop they ordered last year is horrendous.'

'That's the big secret?' asked Andy. 'That's what you couldn't live with?'

'Have you ever had an 87-year-old widow shut the door in your face because she cut herself on a cling film dispenser you sold her?' Lionel's voice cracked and he crashed down into the nearest booth.

Gibby slipped an arm round Gordon while he wasn't looking. 'No exactly a reason to withhold our Art Happenin licence is it?'

Gordon shook himself free once again. 'Three Betterware agents disappeared on that round in as many months.'

'I suspect suicide,' said Lionel as he tried to control a wobbling chin. 'If they were anything like me they would have struggled to cope with what they'd become.'

Gordon took pride in being an exemplary public servant and, as such, was keen to cut and run now that a plan had been formed that appeared to offer minimal personal aggravation. 'Well, if no one else on the committee has a problem then I won't object.'

'Fantastic,' said Andy. 'Lionel, will you show our guest out? Here's the relevant papers.'

Gordon accepted the bundle, but left Andy's free hand hanging in the air.

'I heard about that wee honey from the gym you've got doing PR. Any chance of a few guestlist places any night she's on?'

Andy looked to a shrugging Gibby then turned back to Gordon, who almost crushed his hand in gratitude. Never mind. Getting the place open even if no one ever payed in would be a kind of victory in itself.

'One down, one to go, chief,' said Gibby as he watched them leave. 'Suspect this might be a bit trickier though.'

*   *   *

Darkness had descended on the dancefloor once more. A child sung a haunting ditty over a jangly accompanying track of dolphin music and high notes played on a xylophone.

'Imagine yourself drawn,' the lyrics went. 'To the water at dawn, Come with me through the water, I am God, had a son but no daughter, With me you can breathe in the deep blue sea, But you don't believe in me, you believe in TV.'

The light, minus three bulbs which had stopped functioning in the past hour, came on once again to show that Gibby and Andy were now joined by Clive on the dancefloor.

'An it just goes on an on in a loop like that!' shouted Tony across to them. 'Til your very mind is blown.'

Clive was even less impressed than Gordon had been. 'What the fuck's this fuckin shite. Whaur's my fuckin money?'

'Well, as it goes Clive. We think there might be a bit of a problem.'

Clive spun round, causing dandruff to fly off his shoulders. Gibby and Andy took their cue to walk across to the nearest table and sit behind it, facing Clive.

'You see,' Andy's voice contained a confidence at odds with the nausea he was feeling. 'We appreciate that you Italians control the nightclub scene in this town. As such, we'd be happy to pay your very reasonable miscellaneous insurance rates...'

'...only we're no a nightclub.'

'No a fuckin nightclub?'

'We're more of an...' Andy looked to the roof for inspiration and found instead what looked like an old noose. 'Let me put it this way. Are you familiar with the life an work of Andy Warhol?'

Clive looked hurt. 'I'm a fuckin patron o' the fuckin arts, ye cheeky wee fucker. Course I ken wha Andy fuckin Warhol was. I even ken wha the fuckin people named in fuckin Walk on the Fuckin Wild Side are. Ye display a rather insensitive amount o' fuckin prejudice Andy. Just cos some cunt's involved in a life o' fuckin criminality doesnae fuckin mean he cannae appreciate man's better fuckin nature. Ye cunt.'

Andy raised his eyebrow at Gibby and turned back to Clive. 'Deeply sorry. But the thing is, we take our inspiration from his Factory. This place isn't a nightclub because, really, it's an Art Happenin. It's a project.'

Clive shook his head. 'This place has fuckin music an fuckin dancin. It's a fuckin nightclub.'

'Ask the Council, Clive. Your rules, remember. We can't pay you. It's like how they demark territory in The Sopranos.'

Clive, a huge fan of the series, nodded and for a moment was lost in long-form drama reverie before he remembered himself. 'Anyway, what if we fuckin decide tae expand intae the fuckin art world? Mak ye pay fuckin double for fuckin insurance. What wi' a' the valuable fuckin artworks in here.'

Clive looked around to back up his claim, but found scant evidence to justify higher premiums. Tired of the charade, he picked up the nearest chair and sent it crashing into Robin Asquith's distended lips. He sneered at his hosts, whose expressions now bore a distinct shite-scaredness. They backed against the far wall as he walked towards them with slow, sinister steps. In spite of his diminuitive stature, Clive seemed to stand significantly taller than either Andy or Gibby by the time he came to a stop before then. A pin could have been heard dropping on the dancefloor, so the double-doors being thrust nearly off their hinges caused everyone to jump.

Cornelius, still dressed in his blind man get-up, realised his error, retrospectively knocked on the door and bounded across the floor towards them, speaking very loudly and very excitedly in a Jamaican accent.

'Time to pay up Andy mon! I has come to collect!'

'What the fuck's fuckin goin on?' snarled Clive. 'Wha the fuck's this?'

'Who is I?' cried Cornelius. 'I is the fire and the vengeance is what I is. Who is I my little friend?'

Uncertainty swept across Clive's face. He looked from Andy to Gibby then to the DJ booth and back to Cornelius. 'I'm Clive. How's Andy payin you when he should be payin me?'

'Me nah know who you is, mon, but this is nothing to do with I. This a Jamaica 'ting. I is on fire today. BOOM!'

'Jamaica? But youse hae the...'

Gibby slipped out the booth and got between the two men.

'Mibbe you'd better go, chief. Before it kicks off. I'll walk you out.'

Clive didn't object as Gibby led him gently by the arm in the direction of the exit. He and Cornelius remained locked in a staring contest as his guide attempted a plausible explanation for what had just occurred.

'Seriously, chief. People thought they had it bad with you. Apparently the black mafia are all over the art world. I don't think you want to start a turf war over this place.'

Clive stopped Gibby and pulled him as close as they had been just days ago.

'I'm no happy aboot this. Nobody'll be happy aboot this.'

'Mibbe, but you don't want to mess with this guy.' He hooked a thumb back over his shoulder in the direction of Cornelius. 'Even Lionel's scared of him.'

'But…'

'See ya Clive. I'll message you on Facebook.'

Gibby pushed Clive out the door, breathed a deep sigh of relief and walked back towards the dancefloor that Cornelius and Andy were now rolling around on. After Gibby pulled them apart, Cornelius and Andy stood puffing and coughing for their brief exertions.

'Give me my money. You said you'd pay!'

Andy shook his head. 'I only said that to get rid of the gangster.'

'What gangster?' Cornelius looked around. 'That little man? You were scared of the tiny little man?'

Gibby chuckled and patted Andy on the back. 'Just give him the money, chief. It's worth it.'

Tony, who believed the previous several minutes of excitement had been some kind of free-form drama performance spontaneously inspired by the power of his and Q's art, joined them on the dancefloor.

'I don't really know what's happenin but I'm just so delighted that everyone's on board with the Sound Art. I've got really big plans. DJ Q is ecstatic.'

Andy winked at Gibby. 'Fuck off Tony. That stuff is utter shite. No way we're playin it.'

'Right! You leave me no option but to resign an seek out someone who appreciates my brilliance.'

'Hey Tony. Can you give me a lift? I'm going to the shops to spend my winnings.'

Tony stormed off with Cornelius in his wake. Gibby and Andy kissed each other's cheeks as they'd seen the Sopranos crime syndicate do and debated the gayness or otherwise of time and time again.

'Well, chief. I dunno how we could have played that any better. No protection payment required, we get to keep all the wedge we make from dealin, an all our limbs are intact. Fancy celebratin with the DVD extras at my place?'

Andy rubbed the week's growth he was sporting and yawned. 'Sorry Gibby. I've got to make things right with Michelle first. Everythin we've done today is for nothin if I don't have her by my side.'

THIRTY-FOUR

Unfortunately, making things right with Michelle proved more troublesome than Andy could have imagined. When he finally made it home, looking and smelling even more like a tramp than normal after five days AWOL, he expected recriminations, rather than Michelle shrieking and pouncing on him the second he walked into the living room.

'I was so worried,' she blurted between sobs. Andy was congratulating himself on letting Michelle's heart grow fonder in his absence when she added, 'Cornelius told me everythin that's been goin on.'

'Really? I'm pretty sure he doesn't know himsel.'

'An when I heard you really were bein threatened by gangsters an I couldn't find you anywhere I was so worried. So I called the police.'

Up to this point Andy's eyes had been shut tight as he enjoyed the first human touch provided by someone other than a flatulent spiv for the first time in days. Now he opened them to find two plain-clothes policemen sitting on his sofa and drinking tea.

'Police?' he whimpered, pushing her away. 'Michelle, what've you done?'

Michelle wiped her eyes and bristled at Andy's ingratitude. 'I've not done anythin. They just went to the club yesterday an wired the place up with cameras an microphones. They've come to discuss somethin they seen today…'

"Luckily" for Andy, the policemen turned out to be well-known faces on the club scene and were willing to turn a blind eye to the violation of laws regarding narcotics, bribery of public officials and the wellbeing of Betterware agents in return for 10 guestlist places each weekend and a cut of money earned through drug dealing.

The last offence was news to Michelle and, after a tirade of abuse equal to Emma + Clive x the Pistols on Grundy2, Andy was unceremoniously and officially evicted from his pre-marital home. His first instinct was to head for Emma and Cornelius' place but the prospect of sharing a house with his eight-and-half-months pregnant sister was bad enough without her finding out his relationship had broken down due to his entanglement with hypothetical drug deals and corrupt members of the local constabulary.

With no other family or close friends to rely on for succour in desperate times, Andy's options were therefore reduced to one, which just so happened to be the cause of his reduced circumstances. What had he been thinking? A once-in-a-lifetime pull that somehow turned into one lifetime together, and he had somehow managed to fuck it up. His Dad, pondering how someone so lazy and devoid of prospects had managed to snare Michelle, had told him that relationships were something you could never take for granted. He had just laughed and made a joke about endless love being a tennis match between Stevie Wonder and Ray Charles.

He was every bit as fucking hopeless as his Dad believed him to be. Andy could always forgive his own lack of academic, practical and economic prowess because he had a beautiful woman on his arm and the certainty of one day doing something in music that would make the naysayers sit up and take notice. He had his chance and he blew it, losing control of his nightclub within weeks, letting his partners run riot so they became a figure of ridicule in the local press. Perhaps it was the lack of sleep making him paranoid but Andy was sure people were pointing and sniggering at him as he walked out of his cul-de-sac in despair. Finally master DIY and run into a local crime syndicate. Get over that and end up bribing police and being dumped. Absolutely incapable of achieving anything, in music or any other sphere. Even The Go-Ahead Seagulls would probably turn out to be shite if he listened to them now.

Fate was not finished subjecting him to cruel twists, however, and his penury meant he was unable to afford transport to his temporary accommodation. He trudged from Lochee to the city centre with the few possessions he'd managed to gather in his backpack. They weighed far less than the misery which made every step as arduous as an hour in the company of Bono and Chris Martin.

The quickest route meant passing the house which, until a few months ago, had belonged to his father. But seeing his childhood home settled into by new owners with new hopes and dreams just as his were crushed was more than he could bear. Andy had barely begun the circuitous path to his place of refuge when the heavens opened. Heavy drops splashed across his face as he looked towards the sky for any kind of silver lining amongst the angry, black clouds and remembered that at least where he was going he could play records. Then he remembered that, in his haste, he had forgotten to pack Screamadelica and very quickly realised that he didn't care.

'What a fuckin hovel,' he spat as he looked across the road to the Quantum Club/Club Quantum from the same spot that he and Michelle had viewed it little more than three months ago. They still hadn't got round to replacing the 'STOR' sign, largely because they still hadn't officially got round to deciding on a name.

'What the fuck were you thinkin?' Andy shouted aloud to the bemusement of the downtrodden homeless denizens of this particularly regeneration-hungry part of town before answering their quizzical looks with 'I'm a stupid prick, alright?' He crossed the road and clumsily worked the succession of locks free, looking like an escaped resident of Carstairs who'd found the keys to a dilapidated nightclub on the guard he'd koshed.

'Might as well finish off the drink,' Andy muttered as he dragged his backpack towards the bar. He climbed under the serving hatch, grabbed a bottle of beer and attempted to open it with his teeth. A second later and with his molars, already unbrushed for almost a week, distressed, he resorted to a metal bottle opener and gulped down the warm, flat contents in one go. He shivered, wiped his mouth and burped before setting off under the bar in search of more bounty.

'Harder stuff this time,' Andy told himself, relieved to be engaging in a conversation that for once didn't involve lying, bribing, blackmailing or otherwise scheming. He grabbed the first bottle from the spirit box he could find, which, on inspection, turned out to be vodka. Andy reached into his backpack and produced a half-finished pack of Marlboro Lights and a disposable lighter. Gripping the bottle tight, he propped a fag in his mouth and went to light it when he realised the answer to all his problems was literally in his own hands.

Andy spat the cigarette onto the bar and held the bottle and light out in front of him. 'BOOM!' he said to himself, breaking into a demented half-cackle that very quickly brought on a severe coughing fit leading him to deposit the contents of his lungs on the floor.

He checked the bar area for further quantities of spirits, cleaning products and other highly flammable materials and kicked his bag all the way to the middle of the dancefloor. Without surrendering his grip on the lighter, Andy rummaged through the backpack for a suitable rag. He found only his beloved New Order t-shirt, which he suddenly had a great deal of contempt for. Kneeling on an important wooden historical artefact, he ripped the sleeves off his t-shirt and began piping them down the neck of the bottle, combustible liquid spilling over the sides and on to his hands as he did so.

Satisfied that he had a plausably incendiary device on his hands, Andy rose to face the axe-wounded bar. He closed his eyes, accessed the reserves of courage needed and pulled his arm back as he prepared to ensure that the Molotov was the only cocktail ever served at Club Quantum or whatever the fuck it was called.

Music had filled Andy's head from childhood, largely obscuring reality. But all he could hear now was the noise of the past four months – Emma phoning to say their Dad had died, Cornelius' revelation about Storm, Gibby farting, Tony's obnoxiousness, Lionel's insanity, and the sound of Michelle crying from behind the door as he stood on the step trying to make sense of what had just happened. Andy tensed his biceps, such as they were, and inched his shoulder joint forward to allow for better leverage.

'Better to burn out than fade away,' he said as he prepared for what he was now sure would be his final act.

'Mibbe so, but a burn-out has to be unanimously agreed by all partners,' the voice seemed so otherworldly to Andy that he wondered whether he had already thrown the bottle and through some sort of spacetime echo it was appearing from beyond the grave.

'Protocol, chief, protocol.'

*   *   *

Andy supped the sweet tea that Gibby had made him, with the words, 'that'll make you feel better an likely dislodge a colon boulder an all' ringing in his ears. He was still shaking but had at least stopped screaming and nuzzling into Gibby's chest for support.

'Cheers,' he said, unable to meet his gaze yet. 'What you doin here at this time anyway?'

'Well, after I left here I took my Angie to the tapas place in town an…'

'Frittata's?'

'Exactly. No way I was takin the consequences out on my pan so I nipped down here. Just as well I did.'

'You won't…you won't tell anyone about this will you?' Tower of strength as he'd been in the half hour since Andy had nearly killed himself in an ill-fated arson attempt, Gibby still wasn't someone you wouldn't trust to treat such information differently to Lionel's over-subscribed scrotum.

'Course no, chief,' Gibby pulled up a stool next to Andy at the bar. 'But speak to me. Why would a man with everythin goin for him do somethin so stupid?'

He held a fag out to Andy but he declined the offer and sighed. 'I've got nothin goin for me Gibby. My Dad died, I spunked his money away on a stupid dream cos I was depressed about my job an feelin I was goin to die without achievin anythin.'

Gibby lit his fag, considered Andy's claim and countered it. 'Haven't achieved anythin? How many people have ever podged a burd as tidy as yours? No many that aren't payin for it.'

'Yeah well, that's gone Pete Tong as well.'

'Aye?' Gibby was unable to stop his voice rising several octaves as concern and optimism fought an internal battle for supremacy. 'What happened?'

Andy told Gibby of the pressures his relationship had come under in recent months – the financial strain, the lies, the breakdown of communication and how buying off policemen in order to facilitate drug-dealing was the final straw. The only details he left out related to the time he had spent outside the big bed and the lack of action in it.

Gibby listened intently to the tale, instinctively wondering what it meant in terms of Michelle's gagging-for-it-ness, and waited until he was sure Andy was finished before stubbing out his smoke and dispensing his advice.

'The way I see it, chief, is that you've got three options – two if we're discountin the whole suicide-bid deal. We are discountin that aren't we?'

Andy nodded.

'Right, you can either call it quits, write off thousands of pounds, go back to workin in a call centre an beg Michelle for forgiveness that might no be forthcomin given the way you've neglected her sexually or…'

'I haven't neglected her sexually! Who said that?'

Gibby held a hand up to silence Andy. 'I haven't finished yet. Or you can accept the fact that from now on a small portion of your income,' Gibby held his thumb and index finger around an inch apart, 'comes from corruption an get back to tryin to make this a happenin joint.'

Stirring as Gibby's speech was, Andy's face remained set to miserable bastard mode. 'Yeah, but Michelle…'

'Look, chief. The followin is a truth universally known – women are far more likely to forgive sexually disappointin men if they've got a few quid in their back hipper.'

'I keep tellin you, it isn't about the sex.'

'What's it about then?'

'I told you, money an lies, mainly.'

Gibby smirked. 'So this is a clean slate, chief. She knows all there is to be known an can either accept it or no. What d'you say we go back to the way we were before you went off on that pyromania tangent?'

Andy performed a quick calculation as to the most likely way to win back Michelle and drug money + success + told-you-so did seem more appealing than far less money than he started with + humiliating return to insurance monkeydom. One thing still didn't seem to stack up, however.

'But you said yoursel that places like this aren't able to survive in the long term.'

Gibby guffawed. 'Aye, but what do I know? I'm surprised you've kept listenin to me thus far. You're very suggestible, chief. Very suggestible.'

Andy stared at him, unable to believe what he was hearing. 'But you've been my consigliore.'

'I know, it's unbelievable. You would've done far better to just sack me months ago. I told you to start smokin again so I could sell you stolen baccy. That's how trustworthy my advice is.'

Andy was speechless.

'Honestly, chief, there are only three things I've ever said to you worth remembering: don't kill yoursel, start drug dealin, an salts keep you regular. The rest is nonsense.'

It was some time before either man spoke. Eventually Andy experienced a moment of clarity and everything Gibby had said suddenly made sense.

'You're right, Gibby. I shouldn't listen to you an I won't. Thanks for everythin. I'm goin through to the office for some shut-eye then I'll work out how to leave this to the four of you. I'm no cut out for the nightclub caper. I can see that now.'

With a sad, knowing smile emerging at the corner of his mouth, Andy slipped off the stool. He yawned, stretched his aching muscles, slapped his soon-to-be-former partner on the back and trudged off in the direction of his soon-to-be-former office. Andy was so exhausted he didn't know if he'd make it without falling asleep. He felt his legs buckle beneath him and was vaguely aware of Gibby's voice fading in and out as the need to sleep overwhelmed him.

'Thing is…glamour…owners…hole…even…doesn't forgive you…opportunities…Chelsea…Tony…freak…Lionel…pervert…Cornelius…married…straight shootout between me an you, I reckon, chief.'

It was as if someone had thrown a bucket of icy water over him. He spun round, adrenaline coursing into every cell and synapses firing.

'Chelsea?' he gasped as he realised the opportunities that being single for the first time in a decade opened up. 'Really?'

'Undoubtedly, chief,' said Gibby with a wink. 'Undoubtedly.'

THIRTY-FIVE

Whilst Andy's spirits surged in the days that followed his breakdown, those of his brother-in-law plumbed new depths. Firstly, there was the matter of Emma lobbying him to publicly renounce all ties with Andy and declare his sympathy for Michelle. This he could handle on its own but there was the added complication that, whenever he attempted to talk to his brother-in-law about his estranged fiancée, a strange look came over his face and he talked about 'a sudden sense of liberty', 'ever strange the lives we lead' and other pearls of wisdom that Cornelius recognised as New Order lyrics.

Most worrying of all was the fact that the opening night had been pushed back so much it was scheduled to fall within the final month of his wife's pregnancy. Emma had insisted there would be a period of prohibition for him to ensure he was able to drive her to hospital and generally deal with his responsibilities in a cogent and lucid manner. It would just be his luck for his first-born's arrival to ruin the biggest night of his life.

He pondered the grave situation slumped in the big chair as Andy and Gibby danced around a flip-chart brainstorming ideas for the opening night. Although possession of the marker pen had changed hands several times, "VIBES" was the only word to have made it on to the paper so far.

'I knew this deaf lassie an she would go to...'

Gibby nodded. 'I know her. The rumours're true. Ironically, she's a screamer.'

Andy screwed his face up and grabbed the pen off Gibby in an attempt to regain control of his anecdote. 'What? No, I think this is a different one. I didn't know her as such. I know of her. She used to go to nightclubs.'

'So did mine.'

'Yeah but this one, I seen her on telly, she was talkin about how vibrations from the club drew her in an even though she couldn't hear the melodies or anything, the bass an the rhythm spoke to her an she would dance in front of the speakers all night.'

'So it doesn't matter if our DJ's pish, so long as we attract enough deaf people the night'll be a success?'

Andy held off Gibby's attempt to retake the pen. 'No, no, you're missin the point.'

'We don't want deaf people standin in front of the speakers all night. Also, I foresee problems.'

'Gibby, you're no...what sort of problems?'

'Well, you know how it's hard to speak to anyone in a nightclub?' asked a pen-possessing Gibby. 'Imagine tryin to tell somebody deaf to move from in front of the speakers, chief. Even more difficult.' He tousled his beard as he considered the implications of his scenario further. 'You'd have to indulge in some kind of elaborate mime. An over-elaborate mimes are somethin you want to avoid with the deaf, chief. It's just insultin.'

Cornelius sighed loudly enough to draw the attention of the other two. They looked at him as he delivered a dry, monotone translation.

'What he's trying to say is that Quantum'll bring people together, the music will draw them in and humanity will come together in one heaving, transcendental mass.'

'If the drugs are right,' agreed Gibby, ignoring the fact his partner was only half-heartedly participating in the discussion.

'It's all about the music, no the drugs,' said Andy. 'With that in mind, I was thinkin the openin night should have a Northern Soul feel.

'Oooooft! That's askin for bother, that is.'

'Why?'

'Soulies are a nightmare, chief. The scene split years ago an everyone's got their own idea about who's carryin the torch.

214

Locally you've got the Dundee Soul Club, the Dundee Northern Soul Club, the Soul Club of Dundee, the Northern Soul Club of Dundee an the Dundee People's Soul Club, although I've heard they're on the verge of another schism. Can't have them in the same room or they'll be slashin each other to pieces with broken 45s.'

Andy was not prepared to give up. 'Aye, but think about the dancefloor. Surely they'll come together to dance on a bit of Wigan.'

Gibby sucked his teeth and looked apologetic. 'Thing is, chief. That dancefloor's history can't be authenticated. For legal reasons, you understand.'

'So we don't even know if the blocks of wood we paid £5000 for actually came from the Wigan Casino or no?'

'Oh they definitely did, chief. I'm about 50% sure about that. My man, he's a bit dodgy though, so I wouldn't be shoutin about it cos there's probly people still lookin for them.'

Andy shook his head at Gibby, who he noted had invested in a new pair of shoes since going off to pay his associate, but decided there were more pressing issues to deal with.

'What's next on the checklist?'

Cornelius picked up a clipboard from the desk and sighed as he ran his finger down the list until he found the next item requiring attention.

'Red carpet.'

'It's a carpet, chief. An it's red. Well, rusty orange really.'

Andy nodded his satisfaction and encouraged Cornelius to continue.

'Guestlist.'

Andy winced as Gibby rattled off a list of 97 family, friends, journalists, council officials, policemen, suppliers of black market services and assorted hangers-on. Andy scratched his substantial head for a minute as he waited for Gibby to add more names that never came.

'An?'

'An?'

'An who else?'

'An who else what?'

Andy grabbed the pen off Gibby, but succeeded only in pulling off the lid. They looked at their respective spoils, and Gibby quickly wished for a threesome with Michelle and Chelsea in case marker pens were imbued with the same magical properties as wishbones and Christmas crackers. Andy felt that re-appropriating the lid was a victory of sorts and pledged to keep hold of his territory even if it meant the tip drying out and having to buy a new one.

'Who's openin the club? Who's cuttin the ribbon?'

'I've no idea.'

'Does anyone know?'

'You said you'd take care of it,' interjected Cornelius, unhelpfully in the opinion of his brother-in-law.

'Did I?'

Cornelius didn't look up from his doodle of a striking man, some would say reminiscent of a young Otis Redding, facing the gallows, but nodded. 'It was during that argument about celebrity culture. You said you didn't want Quantum becoming a celebrity hangout but it was just after Lionel was teasing Girls Aloud with the testicular trio so you eventually agreed we needed all the good publicity we could get. Then you said to leave it to you so we ended up with someone with musical credibility rather than someone from reality TV.'

Andy flopped in the chair and gently rocked back and forth as Gibby stared at him expectantly. He handed him the pen lid and instructed him to call a Code Red meeting of the partners.

THIRTY-SIX

Cornelius held the plastic birth canal in his hands and shuddered to think what Gibby might do to it. The model vagina came in two parts, which Cornelius clapped together, satisfied that the resulting sound would prove powerful backing for the neo-proto-funk sound he'd been working on his head for a while now. If he was ever to step back in the studio he would definitely go in armed with a fake fanny.

'Cornelius! Put that fuckin thing down. Dr Dorsey'll be here any minute.' Emma was slumped in the chair by her gynaecologists desk, awaiting his arrival. Every few seconds she would shift uncomfortably in an attempt to provide some relief for her back and hips, which had borne the brunt of the pregnancy. Emma ached all over and hadn't slept properly for weeks. She desperately wanted this to be over. And the hang-dog faced irritant who posed as her husband to sit the fuck down.

'Cornelius!' she snapped. 'I told you to put that away.'

'I did, baby, this is a new one.' He held up another moulding to show that he had indeed moved on to a model of a more advanced stage of childbirth. This one showed a decapitated baby's head stretching vaginal walls as it prepared to take to the great stage that is life. He returned to his seat next to Emma, shuddering to think what Gibby would do with the model given the chance, and at a conversation the two of them had about children a few weeks ago.

'Fair play to you, chief. Bein a proper, biological father – it's just no for me.'

'Honestly, man, everyone says that at your age. I can't wait to see my baby come out my baby.'

Gibby turned up his nose at the suggestion. 'It's that bit though, where the baby comes out. As far as I'm concerned that's an entry point an no an exit. You don't want to be rattlin around a gypsy's earring for the rest of your days, do you?'

Cornelius felt Gibby was missing the point. 'But, the miracle of life and all that. This is what it's all about.'

'No, sex is what it's all about. If you ask me, childbirth is just what some bible bashers invented to keep dudes away from each others bums.'

'I'm just saying that when you reach a certain point in your life you start to want a family.'

Gibby conceded the point. 'Okay, I get that, I do. At some point your mortality kicks in an you start to think, "I've achieved nothin" so going in bareback becomes more than just a way of injectin a bit of risk into loveplay, herpes roulette, if you will. But still, how no adopt? That way you can do a Woody Allen if they turn out to be tidy.'

Cornelius was aghast and was trying to ascertain if this conversation was really happening before attempting to counter the clear flaws in Gibby's argument.

'Tony told me all about it,' said Gibby, lighting a fag. 'Made some very interestin points about how character flaws shouldn't detract from reverence of genius. Then he asked how many dreams did he shatter an how many did he make, but I think he was on about Savile again.'

Cornelius had continued to blink at Gibby.

'I'm no sayin I agree with him, chief. Just that it was something that got me thinkin.'

As Cornelius was confirming that his moral code remained unaligned with Gibby's, he felt a sharp tug at his sleeve followed by his skin being nipped.

'Ow!'

'Cornelius! Dr Dorsey asked you a question.' Cornelius looked at the doctor, who was sat across from him at the desk. He couldn't remember him coming in.

'I asked you how you were feeling about becoming a father.'

Cornelius looked at the doctor then his scowling wife and decided an effusive response was expected.

'Err…yeah. Chuffed, man.' he said with as much enthusiasm as he could muster. The look from Emma suggested that his display had failed to hit the mark so he blew her a kiss and repeated the gesture for Dr Dorsey.

Emma seethed. Her husband's day-dreaming usually took place with undisguised cheerfulness so when she was unable to make contact with Planet Cornelius at least someone was enjoying the basslines and beats in his head. The past couple of weeks had seen him become incommunicative through a haze of darkness. She hoped this was down to his concern for her idiotic brother's plight or that doomed nightclub rather than any second thoughts about parenthood. She would kill him if it was.

'…so Emma,' said Dr Dorsey after he recovered from Cornelius' advance. 'How're you in general?'

Emma rattled off a litany of mental and physical difficulties she was experiencing, leaving nothing out except the profanities that would have otherwise peppered her prose. This took several minutes before she finished by adding "I just want this f…thing out of me.'

'She wasn't sayin that during the conception, chief.' Cornelius clamped his hand to his mouth, shocked he hadn't been able to supress his inner-Gibby, as Emma's jaw tightened to the point that he felt sure her teeth would surrender under the strain.

With two decades of experience defusing potentially difficult consultations behind him, Dr Dorsey recognised the need to move the conversation on and glanced at Emma's notes. 'Well, it's maybe not what you want to hear, Emma, but if I was a betting man I'd say you're most likely to go full term.'

Emma shrugged and considered another three weeks of this torture before turning to see how Cornelius was taking the news. Though silent, his lips were moving up and down, a sure sign he was counting. Suddenly his face lit up.

'Full term? So that means…'

'That your daughter will most probably be born on the due date.'

'Which is?'

'Three weeks tomorrow.'

'YAAAAAAASSSSSSSSSSSSSS!' In Cornelius' mind it was as if Kenny Jackett had scored a last-minute winner against Luton then run to the Rookery with his top off in celebration as Soul Finger played over the tannoy. That was three days clear of the grand opening. Even better, it fell on the first of Tony's Sound Art nights they'd consented to in an attempt to keep up the Art Happening charade that Cornelius still didn't fully understand.

'Thank you, Dr Dorsey, thank you.' He was leaning over the desk and vigorously shaking the gynaecologist's hand before hoisting Emma out her chair with a fervour that would have been unwelcome even if she wasn't nine months pregnant.

'Cornelius! If this is about that fuckin nightclub I will fuckin kill you.' Emma was unable to stop herself swearing as she was whisked to the door by her husband as he whistled the aforementioned proto-funk classic by the Bar-Kays.

THIRTY-SEVEN

Though Dundee had much to recommend it, a stubbornly high teenage pregnancy rate was something the city fathers were unlikely to boast of to visiting dignitaries. That his contemporaries collected sexual partners like Morrissey collected grudges while his own adolescence was as sexless as a fortnight in Fife with Ann Widdecombe had always seemed particularly unjust in Andy's eyes.

He matriculated at university before dropping out months later because of his unrequited love for a girl called Lucy, to whom he lost his virginity during Freshers' Week. Insurance-Insurance.com brought with it a few embarrassing daliances with co-workers but it was only after Michelle walked into the office that he became familiar with the twin wonders of love and regular coitus.

He thought about Michelle almost constantly but fought the urge to call her because, in addition to her almost certainly wanting him to keep his distance, he needed to work out how he felt about her. Michelle was a wonderful woman and he would always be grateful for everything she had done for him but New Order never sung about gratitude being the only thing worth living for. Also, he would be stupid not to take advantage of the 'single' status on his Facebook page.

Through counselling sessions with Gibby, Andy had come to suspect that his behaviour over the past four months was at least in part driven by his unsown wild oats. Maybe I just need to be with someone else, he thought. A proper go now I know what I'm doing. Just once. Then I'd know.

Furthermore, Gibby hypothesised that insecurity rather than any mental or physical defects on Andy's part had caused his delayed entrance to the world of sex. He was sparing no effort to boost his colleague's confidence and prepare him for single life by providing advice about what people got up to these days that both excited and terrified Andy.

It was an article in one of the lifestyle magazines Gibby had gifted him that made up Andy's mind about one such feature of modern life that he had been agonising over for a while. Now was the time.

*   *   *

Cornelius had it all planned out. He was going to tell Andy that everything was going to be okay and that love will conquer all but he had to be a man about it. He was going to give him a lift home and not let him leave until he'd emptied the contents of his heart to Michelle. They were going to have the best opening night in history then he was going to become a father for the first time and call his daughter Estelle, after the co-founder of Stax.

What he hadn't counted on when, in his determination, he forgot to knock for the first time in 17 years, was finding Andy draping his genitals over the office desk and hacking away at them with a pair of scissors.

'ANDY! NOOOOOOOOOOOOOO!' he cried and leapt towards his brother-in-law, who reacted to the intrusion by jumping at a very delicate stage in proceedings.

'AAAAAAAAAAAAAAARGH! I'VE CUT MY COCK! I'VE CUT MY COCK!'

Cornelius held Andy on the ground and attempted to wrestle the scissors out of his grasp. 'I know, I know. But you might need it again someday. Just cos things are tricky with Michelle doesn't mean you should go eunuch. Love will conquer all, Andy, but you need to be a man and your junk helps in that regard.'

'What the fuck're you talkin about? Owwwwww! It hurts. You stupid bastard. I was trimmin my pubes.'

Cornelius was by now lying on top of Andy pinning his hands to the floor. He lifted his head off his shoulder and looked him in the eyes.

'Trimming your pubes?'

'Yeah,' winced Andy. 'I thought it was about time.'

'But I thought you were proud of your thicket. You said public grooming was emasculating.'

'No as fuckin emasculatin as you causin me to nearly slice my dick off then mount me like I was Kenny Jackett.'

Three things were going through Cornelius' mind: if Andy could trim his pubes then so could he; when he did, a razor would surely be more effective; and they really needed to get a lock fitted on that door.

'What's going on…oh my…'

Getting caught in a compromising position with an inflatable girl group was one thing, Lionel thought as he surveyed the scene, but being found with your trousers down, brother-in-law between your legs was quite another.

'What's all the shoutin about?' said Gibby as he rushed to the scene. His legs nearly buckled as he joined Lionel in the doorway 'Chief? Chiefs?'

'Awww, you guys are so cute together,' said Chelsea tilting her head round Gibby to get a view of proceedings. 'I love gays. I've got, like, five gay BFFs and we go shopping together all the time. You can, like, totes come with us now that you're out. For realsies.'

'We're no out,' said Andy struggling under Cornelius' weight and desperate to inspect the damage to his groin. 'We're…I was…it's a man thing.'

'Indeed it is, Andrew. The love that dare not speak its name.'

'Shut up, Lionel. Chelsea, can you give us a minute? We'll see you though at the bar.'

She left and Andy pushed Cornelius off him. He clambered on to the big chair and looked down at wee Andy. He had trimmed either side of his thatch before Cornelius burst in, meaning he'd been left with a blood-smeared pubic Mohican. He moved the spike to one side and, whimpering, looked at what appeared to be a fairly superficial wound.

'You penis appears to be haemorrhaging, Andrew.'

'Thanks very much for that astute observation. I was trimmin my pubes when this tool burst in an made me nearly Bobbit myself.'

'I thought he was cutting it off cos him and Michelle have split up.'

Lionel nodded his understanding, but Gibby wasn't having any of that.

'C'mon now. Behave. Why would a big…' he looked down at the crime scene, '…approachin average-sized stud do somethin like that? He's back on the market an he's gonna be puttin it about like Led Zep in the 70s. Provided it doesn't need stitches, that is.'

This was a spanner in Cornelius' brainworks and he protested. 'No, look. It'll be okay. Love will conquer all. That's what I came to say. Michelle and Andy can sort this out. He just needs to make the first move.'

Gibby reached above the cupboard in the corner of the room and produced, somewhat improbably, a first-aid kit. Neither Cornelius or his brother-in-law had known that Quantum possessed such a thing before but, as Gibby blew dust off it, Andy was mighty glad it did.

Gibby kneeled by his traumatised colleague's side. 'That ship's sailed, isn't that right, chief? My offer to go round an check on her for you still stands, though.'

'No but…' Cornelius tried to protest further, but the withering look Andy gave him suggested he was not currently best disposed to listen to his advice. Lionel told him they didn't need to be present for what happened next and Gibby's inimitable bedside matter could be heard as the door closed behind them.

'As the club's resident first-aider I'll have that walloper of yours right as rain for the inevitable sex lock-in after Quantum's debut. Won't just be a nightclub openin that night if you get my drift. Before we start, d'you have AIDS or any other blood-borne viruses? No? I won't bother with the gloves then. I'll warn you, this might smart a little bit.'

The door was closed by the time Gibby applied his magic

lotion but the resulting scream was heard not just by Lionel and Cornelius at the other side of it but in the rattling bones of substance-dependent residents of the homeless shelter.

*   *   *

It was half an hour later before Andy and Gibby joined the rest for the Code Red planning meeting. His brand-new fitted jeans were heavily blood-stained and the way he lowered himself on to a bar stool suggested he was still feeling the effects of his near-castration.

'How's your penis?'

'Errrm, fine, thanks Chelsea, an thanks to whoever told her.'

'You are most welcome, Andrew.' Lionel stood by the door staring straight ahead and nodded his head while Andy shook his and changed the subject.

'Right, thanks for comin in. The preparations are goin well for next week's openin, except it's been brought to my attention that we don't have a special guest to cut the ribbon.'

'That's cos you said you'd do it,' said Tony, who had only just stopped chuckling at the story he'd been made privy to.

'Aye, well I forgot, what with dealin with gangsters, gettin kicked out my home an...'

'Shavin your pubs to make your toby look bigger.'

'It was about hygiene, actually,' Andy awkwardly looked at Chelsea worried that she might believe Tony. 'So, does anyone know anyone famous?'

The question was primarily directed at Chelsea, who Andy reasoned was more likely to have a foot in the world of celebrity than any of the rest of the assembled pack, but she remained as impassive.

'Somebody must know someone,' Andy pleaded. 'How many footballers live in this city?'

All eyes turned to Chelsea, except those belonging to Lionel – they remained fixed on the wall.

'Don't look at me!' she cried. 'I don't go around sleeping

with footballers, you know,' she added, less than truthfully, and wrinkled her nose. Andy had come to realise that the gesture was not the cutest thing he's ever seen but something that teenage girls did to take advantage of slavering older men stupid enough to think they had a chance.

Andy had always prided himself in not judging a person based on their appearance, age, occupation or intelligence, preferring instead to concentrate on more important categories such as musical taste. Despite the fact they would always have Grease, the more time he spent with her the blonde, 18-year-old gym instructor, the more Andy felt that blonde, 18-year-old gym instructors weren't for him after all.

'I've got it!' cried Cornelius, interrupting Andy's thoughts. 'Bernard Manning!'

He beamed at an audience who now looked as bemused as Chelsea had for much of the conversation.

'He opened the Hacienda,' he continued, expecting whoops, cheers and "way to go Cornelius's" rather than the frosty silence he actually received.

'He'd be brilliant. He could tell racist jokes about his mother-in-law and pull in the punters and...'

'He's dead, Cornelius.'

'What?'

'Has been since 2007. Kidneys.'

The buzzer announcing a visitor at the door perforated Cornelius' deep disappointment and Chelsea announced her intention to answer it.

'It's a letter for the owners,' she said when she returned and handed a bright green envelope to Andy. 'It was couriered over.'

Andy ripped the envelope open and pulled out what appeared to be a greeting card.

'Aw, look, a good luck card. Wonder who it's from?' He opened the envelope. 'Oh…'

'You alright?' Chelsea asked. 'What does it say?'

Andy closed the card and re-read the front. 'It says Good

Luck,' he opened it once more and revealed the message inside. 'In court. I, acting on behalf of DJ QUANTUM inform you that the name DJ QUANTUM and all derivatives eg DJ QUANTUM2000, The Quantifer, Quantum DJ Esq, have been trademarked since 1999. Any infringement of these trademarks will be pursued through the courts. We demand you cease and desist using these trademarks immediately, yours faithfully etc etc etc."'

Gibby shook his head with grudging respect. 'That DJ Quantum is one tricky bugger.'

THIRTY-EIGHT

As tended to be the way with the club, the meeting broke up without any solution being found to the cease and desist order that DJ Q had slapped on them. Tony promised to check out the validity of the claim and, in addition, offered to find a special guest for the opening night. As this meant the others could absolve themselves of responsibility for two potentially make-or-break decisions, the suggestion was met with enthusiasm.

For Andy this meant returning to the house he still owned half the debt on. Cornelius' badgering had little impact but the fact all the pants Andy had managed to flee with had been worn twice, inside and out, forced the issue.

His finger lingered over the doorbell for a few seconds before pressing it. He tried to check his appearance in the frosted glass window pane but the warped reflection did little to boost his confidence. After what seemed longer than a Pink Floyd track but was really less than a minute, he saw familiar curly hair bouncing towards the pane.

'Hi,' she greeted him with an uncomfortable smile.

'Hi. Didn't know whether to use my key or no. I...'

'I know. I'm the same. Dunno what to...I mean...well... Come in.'

Andy followed his ex-fiancee into a house that suddenly seemed foreign to him. I hope she doesn't want that ex sex Gibby was telling me about, he thought. My cock's still a day or two away from passing a fitness test.

Half an hour later they sat at opposite ends of the room, small talk punctuating extended periods of silence as they avoided discussing their feelings, finances or anything else of substance. There was something different about Andy, Michelle thought. Had his head grown or...

'Have you lost weight?' she asked finally.

'Yeah,' said Andy, delighted she'd noticed and fearing amorous attention now she had. 'Been cuttin back on the beer an crisps.' This was true. In addition, Andy had been going out jogging every morning since the ill-fated attempt on his and Quantum's lives a fortnight ago. He found it kept his mind from the fact he was currently the only non-rodent resident of a damp, heavily beige and fiscally ruinous nightclub. He had read somewhere that exercise improved mood by releasing endorphins, but Andy's enhanced happiness was more likely down to Gibby's insistence that the 5lbs he'd shifted would have Quantum's female clientele "drippin" come opening night.

'You look nice,' she smiled at him. Andy returned the compliment but with less sincerity – Michelle looked frankly awful in her jogging bottoms and baggy jumper, her hair unkempt and eyes puffy. Maybe word of his dramatic weight loss had already filtered through via Cornelius and she'd been lying awake each night beating her pillow in anguish at what she'd thrown away. Or maybe she'd finally checked the joint account. Either way it was best to leave this one nebulous.

'How's err...Quantum?' Michelle had been trying to build up the guts to discuss the source of all her anguish since Andy arrived. He looked thoughtfully for a second before answering.

'D'you mean the DJ or club?'

'Both.'

'Well, the DJ is a fuckin little cunt,' he caught Michelle's expression. '...but things are goin well with the club. Kinda. You know how it is. Two steps forward, one step back.'

Michelle nodded at Andy's overly optimistic version of progress. From what Emma had told her there was another legal wrangle going on and some talk of a séance so Bernard Manning could tell a few one-liners at the opening. Still, at least it looked like they'd make it that far now.

'You must be excited.'

'Oh, aye,' Andy enthused. 'It's gonna be...I mean, Tony's DJin, so it'll only be alright, but it'll finally be, you know, my own club. Kinda.'

When she started working with Andy, Michelle had been instantly glad of her posting next to his, and not just because the outlandish size of his head proved a handy landmark as she sought to locate her place among the dozens of identical cubicles each morning. Despite being a bit of a prick about music, he was kind, funny and, in his own way, romantic. They had barely exchanged a cross word and she felt she could trust him implicitly. They were happy. Until he bought that fucking club and started lying about everything.

Michelle fought back tears and smiled at Andy, who recognised her efforts by rambling on.

'Yeah, I mean. It'll be great. You should...err...I mean, we should meet up again after that's out of the way. Talk things over properly.' Just a few weeks ago, Andy would have been desperate for Michelle to be at the opening of his club, everyone seeing the beautiful brunette on his arm as he went about wise-cracking and back-slapping all and sundry. He still wanted her there but he was also a free man shedding weight at a rate Gibby assured him had people whispering words like "anorexia" and "cancer" when he wasn't around. The place would be full of ladies, inhibitions lowered by drink and drugs, and he would be the top dog. It would be stupid for a red-blooded male not to explore his options at this juncture of his life.

'Yeah, that'd be good,' she agreed while looking away to wipe away a solitary tear that had battled through her defences and ran for freedom down her cheek. Andy was conflicted. The world that Gibby promised was a club owner's for the taking sounded like the type of deal Jihadists got on buses and blew themselves up for. But he never wanted to leave this earthly paradise in Lochee either.

They talked about Emma and Cornelius' impending arrival for a while before Andy announced he had to leave as his driving instructor was picking him up outside.

'You're takin drivin lessons?' After more than a decade of hearing excuses ranging from selective environmentalism to the alleged effects of driving on a keyboardist/songwriter's soul, Michelle was as surprised as if Andy had just announced that Cornelius was to appear on the Krypton Factor.

'Err...yeah,' Andy nodded, fully realising the extent to his hypocrisy. The heavily discounted lessons came courtesy of a mate of Gibby after Andy's co-owner had shown him a formula proving how much a man's chances of sexual relations increased with a car. 'Emma won't let Cornelius drive me around anymore an with us...well, I can't just... You know what I mean.'

The estranged couple looked awkwardly at each other then, after several false starts caused by them moving in the same direction, hugged. It was only when the door shut behind him 30 seconds later that Andy's heart sunk to the pyromaniacal levels of the other week once more.

THIRTY-NINE

With just a few days until the grand opening, Cornelius was deliberating over his outfit like a starlet about to walk the red carpet on Oscars night. This, after all, was the return to clubland of a former DJ whose name was known by literally dozens of proto-funk enthusiasts from as far away as Kirkcaldy and Stonehaven. He had to look the part.

The electric blue tux had been repaired at significant expense only to be discarded due to the incompatibility of its cut and his bulk. The cane-and-overcoat number was ruled out in case Adrian managed to score a fake ID and recognised the owner of Dundee's newest and hippest joint as his visually challenged tormenter. In the depths of his wardrobe he re-discovered an old mustard polo-neck that inspired him to pay over the odds for a black, large-lapelled imitation leather jacket in a vintage shop. Combining the two items for the first time, Cornelius declared himself satisfied with the look. Blowing the mirror a kiss, he walked into the living room where Emma fidgeted for comfort on the sofa.

'Check me out. Who's the black private dick that's a sex machine to all the chicks?'

With no little difficulty Emma craned her head round to take him in. 'No you, that's for sure.'

Cornelius was not rattled, however. 'Imagine there's some wah-wah guitar playing, cool as you like, and take another look.'

'There is wah-wah guitar. You've been playin the Theme from Shaft on repeat for the past two hours.'

'Can you dig it?'

Emma stretched her arm towards the coffee table and picked up a remote control, which she used to call time on Cornelius' Isaac Hayes session.

'No really, no. EastEnders is on, so Shaft can shaft off.'

Cornelius looked crestfallen for a few seconds before inspiration hit him. He picked up the house phone and stretched the cord to the far end of the room to ensure he was in Emma's eyeline. She did her best to ignore him as he tapped numbers into it and held the handset to his ear. A look of confusion fell across his face as he heard ringing, moving on to utter disbelief as a voice on the other end answered.

'Err...sorry, wrong number.' He said before hanging up, taking a scrap of paper from the pocket of his flared jeans and trying again.

'Cornelius! Will you just shut the fuck up? Bianca an Ricky are gettin back together here.'

Cornelius was too busy concentrating on the task at hand to hear what Emma was saying and his efforts were rewarded – in his mind anyway – a few seconds later, when a familiar hi-hat pattern made itself heard, followed by a classic 70s funk guitar riff. Despite the substantial amount of time it had spent ringing around his head of late, Cornelius had underestimated the length of the intro and Emma was snapping at him to shut the fuck up long before the vocals kicked in. Eventually he was forced to spring his surprise early and produced a glossy new mobile phone from his pocket. This did pique Emma's interest.

'But I thought mobile phones were a ploy by the man,' she used her swollen fingers to indicate quotation marks around the last two words, 'to give brain damage to righteous dudes like yoursel.'

'Well, yeah, they are baby. But I figured that it wouldn't do me any harm to get down with new technology for a few months so you can contact me anytime, anyplace. Except lifts and subterranean environments.'

Emma's face displayed both her physical pain and suspicion. 'This better no have anythin to with that slapper from the gym.'

'Course not, baby.'

'An you're sure that she won't be anywhere near the club in future?'

'Andy's on the case,' Cornelius lied.

'Hmmmm...you can actually be quite sweet when you want to be. Just one more thing, Cornelius.'

'Anything, baby.'

'Turn fuckin Shaft off. I'm tryin to watch TV here.'

Acknowledging that he had let his phone ring for more than two minutes now and Isaac was halfway through the first chorus, Cornelius hung up the landline, only for his mobile to ring again almost immediately, drawing a deep sigh from Emma.

'Oh, hey Tony. You're outside? Why don't you come in? Come on, she's not that bad.' Cornelius rolled his eyes at Emma, whose recent warm feelings for her husband were fading fast. 'Ok, I'll come out.'

He hung up and turned to his wife. 'That was Tony. I'll need to see him outside cos he says you're the worst human being he's ever met. Won't be a minute.'

He bent down to kiss Emma, but she turned away so she could watch the action on screen, leaving her husband to headbutt the sofa's armrest. 'If you could be 23 minutes at the bare minimum I'd be eternally grateful.'

*   *   *

After several caustic comments about Cornelius' latest sartorial direction, Tony got down to business: he could bring Bernard Manning back to life.

'No literally though, but we could get an impersonator in, do a few of his jokes, cut the ribbon an that.'

Cornelius had briefly thought that Tony had been working with DJ Q on his long-vaunted project to master reincarnation by fusing light and sound to cause ructions in the time-space continuum. Whilst slightly disappointed with the more prosaic reality, he was far from against the plan.

'And you've found a guy who fits the bill?'

'Yup.'

'So why didn't you just book him?'

'Well,' Tony exhaled and looked away. 'I'm no authorised to make executive decisions am I? My unilateral privileges are still suspended. I need a second partner to give approval.'

Cornelius saluted his visitor with a double thumbs-up and had a piece of paper thrust into his face.

'Here, follow all the instructions on this. Best get it locked down tonight.'

'Err...okay.' Cornelius scanned the sheet and rang the Multi-Decade Entertainer Impersonator Agency on his new phone.

'Hey man, I'm needing an impersonator for the opening of my nightclub. Yeah, Friday night. And you'll do jokes? Racist ones? Brilliant. How much? Is that all? You've not been in demand much lately? Why's that?'

Tony grabbed the phone off him. 'I'll take it from here, Cornelius. Great to have you on board with this.'

Tony wasn't such a bad guy, Cornelius thought. Terrible DJ, but a decent enough bloke once you got to know him. Should we do a whole resurrection theme and pretend it's the real Bernard Manning come back to reprise his star role in the Hacienda story, he wondered? He would go in and ask his wife, he decided. She would definitely be interested in this latest development.

FORTY

The first thing that Cornelius noticed about Emma was the bulbs. It was the same the night after she made it clear that he would never again get near her bulbs, or any other erogenous part of her anatomy, if he didn't shut the fuck up about the miraculous resurrection of Bernard Manning and leave her in peace to watch her soaps.

He stared at the club's exterior wall for half an hour before basic motor functions restarted again and he was able to approach the source of his wonder. STOR was no more, the four letters now abandoned on the pavement below dozens of lightbulbs that spelled 'QUANTUM'. A hole in the wall had been drilled and seven exposed wires snaked through it and under each of the letters. Masking tape held the whole display together and the lettering may as well have spelled out 'DANGEROUSLY AMATEURISH', 'DEATHTRAP' or 'WHERE THERE'S BLAME, THERE'S A CLAIM'. Cornelius cried with happiness and ran inside expecting to find his colleagues in a similar state of rapture. Instead, four heads were bowed around a table in an atmosphere as depressing as Ian Curtis' living room.

'What's wrong? Why aren't we celebrating the sign? It's like Times Square out there!'

'Yeah, guy who owed me a favour sorted us out this afternoon, chief. But events have overtaken us since then.'

'What events? What's going on, Andy?'

His brother-in-law gulped from his can of SlimFast and looked up. 'Tony advised us to ignore DJ Q's demands but he's escalatin his campaign against us.'

Tony slid a series of postcards over to Cornelius, telling him he'd received them last night. He inspected the design of each in turn. All seemed to be a variation on the first 'Good Luck'.

'This is terrible,' he said, shaking his head.

'You haven't even read them yet, Cornelius.'

'Oh, right. I was meaning it's horrible when an artist's output becomes derivative of their earlier work. Like Oasis after What's the Story?'

Against the backdrop of universal sighing and head-shaking, Cornelius finally got round to reading DJ Q's correspondence. 'What's Quantum Aftershave?'

'We'd never heard of it either,' said Andy. 'But we're apparently breachin its copyright.'

'So what does this mean?'

'Keep readin.'

Cornelius moved to the next communique, which had an American postmark. 'We're being sued by NBC?'

Tony spoke up for the first time, looking up from the copy of The Idiots Guide to Intellectual Property that he'd borrowed from Lionel to do so. 'Apparently they made Quantum Leap.'

'Oh boy...' Cornelius was a big Scott Bakula fan and thought the reference would lighten the atmosphere, but it was clear he had misjudged the mood of his partners. He pulled up a seat beside them at the table and joined in the silence, which he actually found quite relaxing after a morning of Emma screaming at him every time he tried to tell Bernard Manning jokes.

He drifted into one of his favourite daydreams, in which he was on stage with the latter incarnation of the Bar-Kays, belting out anthems written especially for him by Isaac Hayes and David Porter and generally being the coolest cat ever to cut an album for Stax. He felt bad about not missing the original band more, especially as they died in the same plane crash that claimed Otis Redding, but it was the new version that had been pivotal in bridging the gap between soul and funk. Also, if Otis hadn't died then Al Bell might not have taken a chance on him. Sure, Memphis in 1967 would be a harder place for a black guy to fit in than Dundee in 2014, but he was sure he could talk some of the Klan round after they heard his voice, which had been transformed into something other-worldly...

'Cornelius!' He was awakened by Andy's abrupt plea for

his attention. 'I asked you what DJ Q's up to these days. How come he can do all this writin if his hand's still fucked?'

'Oh, he's all better now. Reckons he'll be DJing again soon. If only he'd stop encouraging the whole world to sue us…'

Gibby and Andy were sat either side of Tony, whose head was jammed in the book once again. Andy leaned back in his chair to ensure Tony couldn't see him raise his eyes at Gibby and tilt his head in the direction of the DJ. Gibby nodded and turned to try to draw Lionel in to their conspiracy with similar gestures. Lionel continued to stare at the table, eventually Gibby tugged at his sleeve only to find his colleague lacking the subtlety required to pull off such a silent assassination.

'If you wish to converse, Gibby, please address me directly. I don't care for your furtive glances and sweaty digits upon my person.'

'It won't work, anyway.' Everyone turned to Tony, who was doodling on the book rather than studying it for means of countenancing DJ Q's legal assaults.

'What you talkin about, chief?'

'You an Andy tryin to sack me an get DJ Q back in my place.' He leaned back in his chair and looked at his betrayers. 'Mind we agreed that 80% of partners had to be in agreement before the other 20% could be binned?'

Gibby and Andy looked embarrassed that their plan had been rumbled. Tony went on. 'Even with tri-ball, you still wouldn't get the required percentage.'

'Oh no?' smirked Andy. 'Cornelius is DJ Q's biggest champion. Pretty sure he'd be up for getting him behind the decks here.'

Tony nodded. 'Ordinarily I would agree with you, which is why – after receivin these postcards last night an guessin that you two back-stabbin bastards would pull somethin like this – I paid a visit to Cornelius. Didn't I, mate?'

All eyes turned to Cornelius, who was nodding enthusiastically. 'Tony's fixed it for Bernard Manning to do the opening!'

'I told you, Bernard Manning's dead.'

'No, not the original Bernard Manning, the impersonator-Bernard Manning-Bernard Manning.'

Andy grunted his frustration. 'Cornelius, what's more important to the future of this club, the pioneerin DJ Q or some fat bastard pretendin to be a racist an sexist comedian?'

'I know, chief. This is a chance to put the past few months behind us an power on. Lionel, what d'you think?'

The bouncer stared straight ahead for several seconds. Gibby was just about to check whether his drug and violence-damaged brain had even registered the question when Lionel finally delivered his verdict. 'Whilst, I'm not overly keen on mounting bellum omnium in omnes, it would make sense given the current problems we face and DJ Q's vastly superior turntable skills. Gibby is Gassius, Andy, Octavius. If you, Cornelius, are Cicero, then I shall be your Brutus.'

'Eh?'

'If you're up for it, then so am I.'

'Oh right,' Cornelius shrugged his shoulders. 'Sorry guys, but when I got into the nightclub game it was for three reasons – the music, the world's biggest mirrorball, and Bernard Manning appearing on the opening night. You took my mirrorball away and you can't do the same with my Bernard Manning.'

Tony patted Cornelius on the arm.

Andy spat his syllables through gritted teeth. 'But. What. About. All. The. Quant. Um. Cunts. Try. In. To. Sue. Us?'

'Wouldn't sweat it, man, something'll turn up. And, besides, now Tony's promised me an hour on the decks every night, how can we go wrong?'

Tony, who until now was delighting in out-manoeuvring his partners and congratulating himself on always being one step ahead of them, dropped his head into his hands. Cornelius winked to all present before patting Tony on the arm and enthusiastically turning the conversation to more important matters – the 75% of the playlist he would select, even when not DJing, in recognition of his role as kingmaker.

FORTY-ONE

Andy was down on his knees before Cornelius, hands clasped in front of him. Even in a lifetime of degrading moments, the scene that was unfolding in the club office was easily a new entry in the Top 10.

'Cornelius, look at me, please. I'm beggin, please reconsider. We can get rid of Tony once an for all, we can keep our arses out of court, we can make a go of this.'

Cornelius regarded him with a sympathy that approached condescension. 'I hear you, but this isn't what we got into this game for. Getting a shot on the decks, looking cool, having a laugh, that's what this was meant to be about.'

Realising the futility of his efforts, Andy would have risen at this point but his knees appeared to have seized up completely. 'Come on, mibbe DJ Q will let you have a go every so often.'

Cornelius' face changed. 'And what about a mirrorball?'

'We've been through this...'

'Then it's Tony, Bernard and Cornelius – the three amigos.'

Change tactics, Andy told himself. This is the world's softest man. Appeal to his better nature. 'An what about your best amigo? This place's already claimed my relationship. At least if we can get it open I'll share in the fanny bonanza with Gibby.'

'But it hasn't claimed your relationship!' Cornelius cried. 'I told you, you just need to be honest with each other and talk about what's happened.'

'We tried. There's no point.' Andy turned away from Cornelius, who lowered himself onto his haunches.

'Please, Andy. Don't give up on Michelle.'

Andy remained silent. He hadn't given up on her but before he could even consider asking for forgiveness he owed it to Michelle to make sure he wouldn't hurt her again. In the meantime, there was the aforementioned festival of flange to look forward to if Cornelius would just throw Tony under a bus. Literally, if he liked.

Cornelius kneeled opposite him, hands clasped. 'Please.'

His proximity forced Andy to turn back and face his brother-in-law. 'My knees are fuckin killin me, Cornelius. Can you help me up?' Cornelius obliged and helped Andy over to the desk, which he leaned against, rubbing his kneecaps.

'Cheers. What about I try to make things right with Michelle if you ditch Tony an get on board with us?'

Cornelius shook his head. 'I'm asking you to do something for you, you're asking me to do something for you. The two don't cancel each other out.'

Andy was sure it used to be easier to fool his friend. 'So what're we gonna do about the DJ Q situation?'

Cornelius shrugged. 'I don't know. Like I said, something'll turn up.'

'But what? As things stand, we're no openin tonight, we're gonna have to beg for our old jobs back an spend the rest of our workin lives payin off the debts on this place.'

Cornelius pulled at the lapels of his faux-leather jacket. 'We're opening up tonight, Andy. I didn't get dressed up for nothing you know.'

Andy had been wondering what Cornelius' get-up was all about but was wary of another PVC-related diversion as, for once in the history of Quantum (both claims having been formally dropped in favour of a still-litigious compromise), the issue had to be dealt with head-on.

'Okay Cornelius,' he said. 'We've three hours til a club, officially Art Happenin, we've practically staked our lives on is meant to open. If, in three hours time, we don't have a solution to the whole DJ-encouragin-the-world-to-sue-us-from-his-mum's situation, what d'we do?'

Cornelius turned his head to the side and appeared to be looking into the middle distance. He scratched his head and shrugged. 'I dunno. Open anyway?'

Andy clenched his fist, his knuckles whitening. 'Cornelius. I'll say this very slowly. DJ Quantum is tryin to sue us for tradin on his name.'

Cornelius shrugged again. 'Yeah, what's the worst that can happen? Quantum's been in hiding for years, nobody knows his name so how can we trade on it?'

'An what about Quantum aftershave?'

'Who's ever heard of that?' Cornelius arced his middle finger towards his face and snapped it upright as something occurred to him. 'Did we ever check whether it was an actual thing?'

'Well, no...'

'Then let's ask the Internet,' said pointing to the laptop behind Andy.

Half-an-hour later, and after many failed attempts and a lengthy conversation with a Bangladeshi call centre operative at 56p per minute, Andy and Cornelius had finally succeeded in making the Google search engine appear on the screen. A minute later and they had their answer. DJ Q, it appeared, had invented Quantum aftershave in an attempt to intimidate the partners.

'And as for the other one...' began Cornelius.

'Quantum Leap.'

'Yeah. Scott Bakula. He's way too cool to let them sue us.

Andy considered the fact that the only thing standing between him and a fully opened, barely functioning nightclub was a nerd with mummy issues.

'Know what?' he said finally as a look of triumph came over his face. 'I'm puttin the sign on.'

'YAAAAAASSSSSSSSSS! Way to go man. Let's do it together then go outside to look.'

They turned to the wall and placed a finger each on the switch that would, through some Newtonian miracle, announce to the world, or at least south-east-central Dundee, that Quantum was finally and irrevocably open for business. Andy counted 'One, two...' and on a silently mouthed three the chemical brothers-in-law flicked the switch. The magnitude of the moment shocked the both of them and they stepped back to marvel at the deep electric hum that filled the air.

After a second the noise stopped and Cornelius, who was nearest the door, stepped aside and indicated that Andy should lead the triumphant and defiant march into the cold, Scottish air.

They were just about to stride out into the street when they were sent sprawling by an explosion outside. Screaming, they scrambled for cover behind the bar.

'It sounded like a gun!' said Andy, hugging Cornelius tight to his chest. 'Maybe Clive's back.'

'It wasn't a gun.'

'An how'd you know?'

'You don't think I witnessed my fair share of gun crime growing up on the mean streets of North London?'

'Shut up, Cornelius. You grew up in Hertfordshire. Welwyn Garden City. Your Dad an Nick Faldo's Dad were members of the same golf club.'

'But...'

'It most definitely was not a gun. I can confirm that.' Lionel had appeared by the serving hatch, looking towards the far end of the club.

'How d'you know?'

'What you heard was several high wattage lightbulbs blowing at once. The sound of substandard electrics, one might say, if electricity had a sound.'

Andy pulled himself to his feet, holding his hand out for Cornelius to use for leverage as he did likewise. 'An you witnessed this, did you?'

Lionel nodded. 'Indeed. I was standing outside practising for tonight when the explosion occurred. It was just after the courier left.'

'Courier?' A horribly foreboding sense of déjà vu swept over Andy.

'Yes. I had to sign for a postcard and a CD.' From a pocket

inside his bomber jacket, Lionel produced the aforementioned items and handed them to Andy.

'Who's it from?'

Andy closed his eyes. 'Who d'you think it's from, Cornelius? Who else sends us postcards?'

'DJ Q. Brilliant! What's the CD? Is it a white label?'

'"DJ Quantum presents the Mardi Gras Megamix 2004,"' read Andy. 'The postcard says, "Just in case you thought I didn't have a name to trade on".'

'Shit.'

Andy opened his eyes as wide as they would go before blowing a dejected raspberry. 'Will we go see what what's left of the sign looks like before we switch it off for good?'

He trudged to the street like a condemned man who, having exhausted his delaying tactics, now just wanted to let the firing squad go home for their tea. Cornelius paused, expecting Lionel to follow, but after a few seconds of watching him stare straight ahead, arms crossed, it became clear this was to be a two-man mission.

He followed Andy, his gait far bouncier than his friend's, and drew up next to him on the street. The two looked silently up at the flickering sign, which no longer featured a 'U' as all the bulbs charged with picking out that particular letter had blown. Cornelius placed an arm round his brother-in-law's shoulder and waited for divine intervention to plot a course out of the predicament they found themselves in.

Their guardian angel arrived dressed in knee-high fuck-me boots and a fur coat that stopped an inch beyond the hem of her sequined shorts. No matter how much her youth and stupidity grated on Andy, he couldn't keep his lascivious thoughts about Chelsea at bay. If only she was a bit older, he thought. And funnier. And cleverer. Maybe with darker hair. Curlier darker hair.

'So, like, we're not called Quantum anymore?' she asked.

Andy spoke without turning to face her, 'I don't think we're called anythin. Might as well go home. This Art Happenin ain't happenin.'

Chelsea screwed her face up, assuming Andy's defeatism to be solely down to the unfortunate timing of this latest electrical outage.

'Why not make it, like, shorthand?'

'Shorthand?'

'Yeah, I learned it for my Fitness Centre Management BTEC. You take out all the vowels.'

Such was the power of her words, Andy turned to Chelsea and instantly retracted his previous criticism of her intelligence. 'Take out the vowels?'

Chelsea was becoming concerned by Andy's frenzied look and feared she might be doing secretaries and journalists the world over a disservice by diminishing the role of shorthand. 'I mean there's more to it than that. It's highly sought-after in certain sectors.'

Cornelius was beginning to understand the concept. 'So you take out the vowels and make it a new word. But it's really the same word. Like text speak?'

Andy pumped his fists skyward. 'Exactly. So we break more bulbs an call it QNTM. Which everyone will know means Quantum, but technically, legally, it won't.'

Cornelius gasped. Chelsea didn't know what was happening but they both seemed happy and she was always glad to see couples getting on so joined them in the three-person huddle that was suddenly jumping up and down on the pavement.

FORTY-TWO

Though technically he didn't actually own a nightclub but an art happening, and only a 20% stake in one at that, Andy nevertheless felt his chest swell with pride at the sight of people queuing to get inside whatever it was he shared however much in.

He and Cornelius greeted the revellers as they arrived with two free glasses of champagne to help them celebrate this momentous occasion. The fizz was, as predicted, cheap, bulk-bought wine with bubbles added later but, since Trading Standard's top man locally had, equally predictably, been bought off with guestlist passes, this was of little concern.

Lionel, an old hand at this game, was better placed than the brothers-in-law to estimate the crowd gathered on the freezing, rain-splattered pavement. He counted 12, and the queue was entirely down to Chelsea's difficulties with simple arithmetic creating an unnecessary bottleneck as she worked the front desk. This was not such a problem for male punters, who were happy for her to keep the change, but was less acceptable to females. Cornelius immediately leapt to her defence, pointing out that odd and even numbers were a tricky concept for some people to get their head around and pleading for her to be cut a little slack.

Andy had never seen Lionel at work before, and he was impressed by his stern professionalism and very definite threat of violence as he glared down the queue attempting to identify potential troublemakers. He had already turned away six would-be paying customers for no discernable reason, making clear that a good bouncer must set arbitrary standards subject to change depending on shifting whims from the off.

In his right hand a counter clicker kept track of how many people entered the club while another in his left recorded the number that subsequently exited. This way, he explained to Andy, he would not let the crowd rise to much more than a hundred beyond capacity. Even the fact he punched out the superfluous A and U bulbs with his weaker hand so the good one remained usable if things kicked off later was a touch of class in Andy's eyes.

'This is amazin, isn't it?' Andy enthused to Cornelius as some of the shards Gibby had failed to clear up crunched under his foot. 'I can't believe we're doin so well.'

'It's a triumph, man. How many have come in now?'

Lionel lifted the rope to allow two out-of-shape women in ill-fitting clothes through and consulted his right clicker. 'Twenty. Although we should probably lower capacity due to the size of the last pair.'

Andy punched the air. 'Amazin! An it's only 11.30. An look at this lot out here. If it continues at this rate there'll be at least 40 by midnight.'

'Not quite, Andrew.'

'What d'you mean?'

Lionel consulted his left clicker. 'Four have left already.'

'They've left already?' Cornelius was dumbstruck. 'Why?'

'They obtained entry via one of those guestlist passes that have been going round Dundee like Chlamydia, downed their free fizzy wine and headed off to a decent nightclub.'

'For fuck's sake,' Andy shook his head. 'How many've paid?'

'I can't be sure,' pondered Lionel as another two guests left to withering looks from Cornelius and Andy. 'But judging by the time Chelsea's taken to process their payments and take coats, factoring in about a minute of gawping by each male patron, I'd say eight.'

Cornelius nodded at what he felt was a positive piece of news, so Andy explained to him what this meant in terms of QNTM's balance sheet.

'Oh,' he said as the penny dropped only to be instantly swallowed up by one of Quantum's growing list of creditors. 'Ah well, we've got to see tonight as a loss-leader, Andy. Once people lose themselves in the vibe then they'll be paying over the odds to come back. Won't they?'

Andy bit his lip before answering the question with one of his own as Lionel let in another half-dozen guestlistees. 'How can't I hear any music? I mean, normally outside a club all you can hear is a distant thud, like the Zulus comin over the hill.'

'Tony's probably just warming them up. Quietly, you know.'

*   *   *

At that precise moment, Tony was not warming the crowd up but was, as he had been since doors opened at 10.30pm, searching through his carry box for the perfect first track to announce QNTM's arrival on the club scene. He'd removed several 12" sleeves from the case before deciding they weren't the killer tune that the two dozen or so customers, trying to work out if the silence was something to do with the Art Happening rumour, would remember for the rest of their lives.

Finally, Tony's sleeve flipping ceased when he chanced upon Essential Blaxploitation. He pulled it out the box, gently slipped the vinyl out the sleeve, blew on it for good luck and eased it onto the turntable, which started rotating as he inched the needle to the groove.

*   *   *

'That's more like it!' cried Cornelius to Andy and, to a lesser extent, Lionel. He began grooving on the spot. 'That is one stone-cold classic man, I'm glad we stuck with Tony.'

'Cornelius, that funk's comin from you.'

'It's like the posters used to say when I was DJing "Cornelius Morgan is the proto-funkiest."'

'I mean the noise.'

'Oh shit…my phone. Yeah.' He searched in every crevice of his Shaft jacket before finally locating it in the back pocket of his jeans. 'It must be an emergency. Shit. How d'you answer? Andy!' He threw the phone to Andy. 'Make it work, man.'

With some difficulty, Andy made the ringing stop and he held the phone to his ear.

'Alright...oh, it's you, is it? Nice to hear from you too. No, he's no drunk...an neither am I...same to you.' With a shake of his head, Andy passed the phone to Cornelius. 'Emma.'

'Hey baby, what a night. Let me tell you all...'

'It's happenin, Cornelius! It's happenin!'

'You're damn straight baby. This is the most happening joint around.'

'I MEAN THE FUCKIN PERSON TRYIN TO ESCAPE MY WOMB, CORNELIUS. THAT'S WHAT'S HAP-PENIN.'

Cornelius' eyes widened. Think, man, think, he said to himself. 'But...but...Dr Dorsey said you had weeks to go yet.'

'Yeah, well he's wrong. My waters broke.'

'Where? It wasn't near my decks was it?'

'CORNELIUS!'

Andy's face was tense as he tried to make sense of Cornelius' ramblings and the shouting from the other end of the line. He mouthed the word 'go' to him. Cornelius nodded.

'Okay, baby. Andy says I need to go but I'll be home in a couple of hours. Just wait til we've closed. I'll see if I can get away before we clean up?' Cornelius looked to Andy in an attempt to determine whether that dereliction of duty would be acceptable but the screaming in his ear brought his atten-tion back to the present before he noticed Andy shaking his head.

'OOOOOOOOOOWWWWW! I need you here now Cornelius. Pleeeeease.'

Cornelius couldn't remember many occasions when Emma had said please before, so he knew the situation was serious. 'Okay baby, I'll be back as soon as my turn on the decks is finished, no matter what Andy says.'

Andy grabbed the phone off Cornelius. 'Emma? He's leavin now an I'll be at the hospital as soon as I can. Take care, big sis. I err...I...I love you.'

'I love you too. Hold on I'm coming!' Cornelius shouted into the phone. Andy hung up. Cornelius prowled about on the spot.

'I can't believe it! I'm about to become a Dad! This is amazing! Wow! He settled back alongside Andy and nodded in approval as Across 110th Street announced the arrival of Quantum from inside.

'What the fuck're you doing?'

'What? I like Bobby Womack. Great song.'

'No, I mean, what're you still doin here? Get goin, Emma needs you.'

Cornelius' face fell. 'I thought I'd maybe catch five minutes of Bernard Manning first.'

Andy had never reminded Cornelius so much of Emma as he did during the ensuing verbal assault during which he was reminded of his responsibilities as father to his niece and husband to his sister and briefed that childbirth wasn't something that could be easily programmed.

'Holy shit. I'd better go now then, hadn't I?'

Lionel, who had performed his rope-lifting, wide-o-identifying duties with diligence throughout the drama, nodded.

'Right,' Cornelius bounced on the spot, checking his multitude of pockets for car keys that he finally located. 'Right, I'm off.'

Andy hugged him tightly and told him not to worry about the club. 'Phone as soon as there's any news. I'll see you both as soon as I can.'

'Thanks, man,' said Cornelius as he spun towards the nearby car park and past a shelter resident pleading for change. 'Just make sure it's a good night, okay?'

FORTY-THREE

The rest of the night was something of a blur for Andy. The numbers waiting patiently to be a part of musical history, in this corner of north-east Scotland at least, continued to snake down the pavement. Given that Chelsea had now mastered basic sums, this was a good sign. Old friends were warmly met while adversaries who had enjoyed the demise of The Go-Ahead Seagulls were met with 'I told you so' handshakes and superior smiles.

Tony had finally begun to string something resembling a set together, although any time he threatened to get momentum going and dancers on the floor he – free from the threats posed by DJ Q or even Cornelius – would sabotage the mood with some off-putting selections. Alerted to this development by the increasing number of absconders once their "champers" was downed, Andy invited Lionel to write a note reminding Tony that he had a financial stake in this venture and what would happen to happen to him if he didn't start to play the game. Dance-friendly and not-too-challenging soul, ska and indie numbers followed. Floor-fillers you might have called them if the total attendance hadn't remained significantly below the number potentially accommodated by the small square of Wigan.

Still, Andy reasoned, people were continuing to make their way from the pubs after last orders. The next hour would be critical to the success of QNTM's opening night, especially as the percentage of non-paying guests remained worryingly high. He excused himself from meet and greet duty and passed Chelsea, who smiled at him as she leant forward at the desk pushing her cleavage towards the approaching customers, who, happily, were male.

The beat got louder and louder as he walked down the

corridor towards the club itself. He gulped before pushing open the double doors. A half-dozen overweight women were dancing round their handbags to Gloria Jones' Tainted Love as Tony screamed from the booth that the Soft Cell version was infinitely superior. Maybe another 50 patrons were seated at tables around the dancefloor, while a group of 10 lairy looking lads clad in Stone Island, who Lionel had grilled for a good 10 minutes before permitting them entry, stood at the bar demanding to know where gear could be found and why Kasabian, The Prodigy or, at a push, the Stone Roses, weren't being played. Chelsea's under-dressed and possible under-aged pals yawned, played on their phones, and pretended to be shocked by the lewd comments the lads were chucking their way.

Andy ducked under the serving hatch and sidled up next to Gibby, who was staring into the palm of one of Chelsea's mahogany cohorts and trying to convince her that the lines indicated she was in for a good stiffing from a slightly older owner of a nightclub-cum-Art Happening.

'Part-owner,' Andy interjected.

'Scuse me love, one of my staff needs help.' He pulled Andy over to the far end of the bar. 'This better be good, chief. That lassie's the most gullible tart I've ever come across. Reckon if I told her the scabs on Gibby junior are cos I'm part tiger she'd believe me.'

Ignoring him, Andy asked, 'How're sales goin?'

'Gear-wise, brilliant. The young casuals are hooverin up the stuff I've been floggin them like it's goin out of fashion.'

Now that he was no longer just a hypothetical participant in the trade of illicit intoxicants, Andy hoped for better news on the stuff they were legally allowed to sell. 'Drinks-wise?'

'Drinks-wise, we've sold hardly anything. It's the...'

'Free champagne, I know. How would you gauge the night, with your years of experience of this caper.'

'Beyond my wildest, chief. No seen it this packed for many a year.'

Andy looked back across the club, which now boasted a

deserted dancefloor. The Type 2 diabetes candidates had not fancied Tony's follow-up, an obscure techno number that had Brian, now reconciled with his musical hero, nodding enthusiastically whilst remaining rooted in his seat.

Andy thought of another demographic which didn't appear to be represented yet. 'What about your mates?'

'What about them?'

'Well, you know loads of people. Any of them comin?'

'Why would they come?'

'Well, it's openin night. This is a big thing.'

'I don't go to their work an pester them on the job. Why would they come here?'

Andy's attempt at an answer was cut off by the buzzer behind the bar indicating that Lionel required assistance outside.

'Shite. It's all kickin off. Fuck, we're a man down without Cornelius too.'

'True, would've been handy havin a big geezer from North London here at the minute.'

'He's from the Home Counties. He...never mind.'

Andy scuttled off down the corridor, passing several new arrivals on the way and squeezing past more party-goers in the doorway before being hit with an icy blast as he left the building. Lionel was restraining a troublemaker with his bandaged hand as he waved in punter after punter with the other. A familiar face was being held at arm's length.

'Andy! Congratulations! I honestly didn't think you'd get this far.'

'Alright Ben. What can we do for you?'

Andy stood by the bouncer's side and cocked his head at the partisan journalist. 'Don't be like that. I was only doing my job. All I said to Lionel was that I didn't recognise him with his clothes on and he started getting all aggressive.'

'I am actually enjoying a zen-like state. If I got aggressive you would know about it.'

'Threatening a member of the fourth estate is a dangerous business. I might have recording equipment on me, and your doorman licence must be looking fairly shaky anyway with what went on in the Betterware wars.'

'Just fuck off, Ben. This isn't your kind of place. We don't like you, you don't like us.'

'Look,' Ben said stepping back and appealing to Andy. 'I was genuinely interested when I heard about this Art Happening thing and the name change. QNTM. I like it. Postmodern.'

Andy's face remained unflinching, so he turned to Lionel. 'And big man, honestly, your video attracted more comments than any other on our website. Obviously we had to edit a lot because we're a family newspaper, but if you were to see your way to let me in then I'm sure I can dig out email addresses for your many, many, female admirers.'

Andy turned away in disgust at the weak attempt to trick Lionel, only to find him waving Ben through the door when he looked back. He followed Ben to the desk where he did a double take at Chelsea.

'Hiya. What'll it be?'

Speechless, Ben produced a guestlist pass from his pocket, only for Andy to grab it off him and rip it up. 'I'm afraid that's no longer valid, Ben. £7 please.'

Feeling pleased with himself he walked outside, where Lionel had recommenced his routine of staring, growling, threatening, waving through and clicking.

'How many now, Lionel?'

'78...79...77 again,' Andy scowled at the Burberry-clad teenager walking arm-in-arm with the reputedly naïve former object of Gibby's attention who may not have believed his tiger tale after all.

'78...hold it there a minute. Right on you go. 79...80...' He closed his eyes and looked like a member of the Skywalker trying to feel the force. 'Large group of females making their way toward here. Picking up pace now.'

Andy was astounded to see a sizeable pack of women, as described by Lionel, round the corner and clack their way to them in high-heels.

'That's amazin,' he said to Lionel who was staring silently ahead trying to gauge where the next set of revellers would arrive from.

'Years of training,' said Lionel. 'A good bouncer must possess a sixth sense so he knows how to prevent the queue swelling to levels where inebriates are likely to become impatient and aggressive. That same ability allows him to smell danger a mile away. Entertainment arrived when you were inside by the way.'

'Oh for fuck's sake. D'you think we can get away with can-cellin that Bernard fuckin Manning tribute act now Cornelius isn't here?'

'He said he was paid in advance so we may be as well let-ting him get on it. Tony had given him full briefing over the phone so I just waved him through and told him he could get changed in the office. 81...82...83...Hold it there a min-ute.' The flock that Lionel had foreseen were now upon them. 'Thing is, was Bernard Manning not a fat man?'

'Absolutely. Bigger than my Dad was.'

'Strange. This guy was skinny. And old. You four may pro-ceed...84...85...86...87...Oh, hello Michelle. I didn't see you there.'

Andy spun on his heel and the imbalance of that manoeu-vre, allied to the vision that awaited him, nearly knocked him to the ground. There stood Michelle, her hair tied up but for rings that hung down either side of her face. His eyes darted across her body, not able to fully take in one part before another grabbed his attention, the jeans that appeared to have been ironed on, the boots that raised her a good four inches off the ground and made her appear even slimmer and more elegant than ever. The top that was just dressy enough not to be formal in a place like QNTM, her lips, picked out in deep red lipstick that remained just on the right side of tarty, the cut of the top that showed enough but promised more. Her long, beautiful neck. Andy had a bricker. Out in the street and on the biggest night of his life he had a raging hard-on.

'Wow,' he said to her as he attempted to conceal his bulge. 'You came...'

'Course I came, it's your big night.'

'An you look...Wow...'

'Thanks.'

'An you brought a crowd,' he said nodding over his shoulder to the ongoing procession of girls making their way in.

'Figured we had to try to get that joint account replenished somehow.' The way Michelle tilted her head to the side like a Latino hoodrat warning off a rival indicated she'd had more than a few drinks tonight.

Andy coughed. 'Ah...ahem...yeah. An you heard about Emma?'

'Yup. Headin up there after here.'

'Great. Mibbe we could go up together?'

'Mibbe. I'm still really, really fuckin angry at you.'

'Probly justified.'

'Definitely.'

'Definitely justified.'

'I'll see you inside. We need to talk.' She reached into him and Andy puckered up in expectation of a kiss that never came. 'You do know you've got a bricker don't you?' she whispered before heading in with a smile on her face.

Andy stood there, heart and penis seeming to throb in time to the beat coming from inside QNTM. It was several seconds before he realised that Lionel was still speaking to him.

'...I wouldn't have let him in, ordinarily, the way he was dressed...Cease you four. Proceed. 98...99...100...101...hold it there you three...A multi-coloured shell-suit...And I thought he was blind to start with, not just because of the clothes but because of the dark glasses...on you go...102...103...104...I know I already mentioned it, but Bernard Manning didn't have long, straggly blonde hair, did he? Two of you can go in...105...106...rest of you wait a minute...and was he not from Lancashire? I am no expert in sociolinguistics but I definitely detected a Yorkshire twang. Don't worry though, I told him to finish the cigar before he went in...107...108...'

Andy returned to flaccidity like a space shuttle re-entering the earth's atmosphere. His heart now tried to thump its way out his ribcage because of rising panic rather than love. He heard the music stop inside followed by some good-natured booing. The microphone-amplified voice of Tony was muffled, but Andy was able to make out some choice phrases.

'Ladie an gentleman...special guest...huge role to play in the history of clubbing...reputation ruined by the media...want a great night? He'll fix it for you, an you an you...'

'FUUUUUUUUUUUUUUUUUUUUUUUUUUUUUUUU UUUUUUUUUUCK!!!'

FORTY-FOUR

'Thing is, apart from the Jimmy Savile stuff, it was actually a great night.'

Andy nodded his agreement. He and Michelle sat on hard plastic chairs next to each other in the maternity waiting room at 4.30am. Emma still hadn't given birth yet, but QNTM had most definitely emerged fully formed, kicking and screaming into the world.

'To be fair to Tony, how was he meant to know one of Savile's victims would be in the crowd?'

'Andy, you could walk down any street in this country, chuck a brick an the chances are you'd hit one of his victims.'

He conceded the point. Reactions to Tony introducing the impersonator had fallen into three camps; those who cheered the sick spectacle, those who were neither impressed nor aggressively offended, and the victim, who jumped up on stage and smashed a bottle over the fake Savile's head before trying to smash Tony's skull with a stiletto. Lionel eventually managed to drag her away as Andy grabbed the mic and tried to reassure the audience that the spontaneous piece of anti-paedophile drama was the type of performance to be expected at a pioneering Art Happening and that a percentage of all admission money that night would be donated to a charity for victims of sexual abuse. He felt very, very guilty when the victim later apologised for misunderstanding their intentions and offered them a tenner from her purse for the fund.

'Did you sort that prick from the Tele out?' I seen him filmin the whole thing on his phone.'

'No me,' grinned Andy. 'But Lionel did once I'd gotten hold of Washie an had him explain to Lionel that half the negative posts about his dance had been posted by Ben under a variety of aliases. He didn't take it well. That phone presently works about as well as Ben's nose.'

Michelle giggled. 'He had it comin. What if he reports it to the police though?'

'Ah, you see. This is the really clever part. Lionel shoved a gram of coke so far up Ben's arse that unless Gibby's been cuttin it with salts again, he'll be in possession for days yet an goin nowhere near a police station.'

The adrenaline rush from the Jimmy Savile incident sparked an alertness in Andy that he hadn't previously known he possessed. Instead of walking around playing the big man and revelling in the glory, he pulled pints with Gibby at the bar, fetched change from the office, mopped up sick and spilled drinks, provided relief whenever one of his colleagues needed a break, located lost property, dealt with customer queries and generally directed operations to ensure everyone had a great night. He even unquestioningly dealt with a minor blockage in the ladies toilets and suffered only a minimal amount of turd-related torment. He had loved every minute.

'It was a great night though, Mich. An it really wouldn't have been the same without you. You made it. At least for me.'

Her knee slipped off to the side, brushing Andy's. They looked eye-to-eye for a moment and Andy thought about moving in for a kiss before Michelle turned away. After a few seconds, she raised her eyes at him, the black coffees she'd almost emptied the vending machine of having failed to lower her intoxication levels any. 'I thought havin that wee hussy at the desk would've made your night.'

'Michelle McKimmie, are you jealous?' he asked, puffing his chest out.

'You wish.'

Andy smiled. He had realised two hours ago the folly of listening to one part of your anatomy to the exclusion of all others. It was a long time since he'd seen Michelle dance, and had forgotten what a glorious, libido-lifting sight it was. Seeing her swing away to Loaded, which Tony finally consented to play after Andy threatened to reveal to Cornelius his duplicity over the Bernard Manning affair, was like having cataracts removed and remembering what the world used to look like. He decided to use his new phone for the first time to record this inspiring moment for posterity. And for Cornelius. As he did so he decided to check how QNTM was being received on Twitter. Among the generally positive reviews and the odd comment questioning the wisdom of hiring a Jimmy Savile impersonator was a tweet from Chelsea, which read, 'In QNTM. Song abt freedom & loaded hurtin my eers!!! Where's Rihannaxxxxxxlol'

'So how did tonight rate financially in the end?'

Andy produced a draft balance sheet from his pocket and showed it to Michelle. She drew in closer to squint at it. 'As you can see, followin on from the charitable donation we now have to make, the staff costs, imitation Jimmy Savile, free drink, four million guestlist passes an all the rest of the overheads, the losses are, surprisinly, in the low hundreds.'

'Impressive. An only 20% of that loss has to be borne by yoursel.'

'I know, thanks. An sorry for everythin. My Dad an...'

'Save that for another time. For now, let's just hope everythin's okay with Emma an the baby. An that Gibby's a good dealer.' Andy turned to face her, shocked. 'The Art Happenin needs money. Once that's done then things need to straighten out. An then we talk about what happens between us.'

Andy couldn't help but break into a huge grin.

'I'm serious,' Michelle chided him.

'I know, it's just I can't help be confident about Gibby's drug dealin. You know how all they casuals started givin him shite about his coke bein cut? Well, he'd ground up a load of E's an cut it with that. Coke buzz lasted no time at all but they were soon loved up an tellin everyone it was the best night of their lives.'

'I seen that. They all had their tops off dancing with gay guys to Pet Shop Boys.'

'Mental eh?'

Michelle licked her lips and turned back to Andy. 'He's still a little bastard though. You know what he said in front of all my pals?' Andy shook his head. 'He bounded over to us and was like "alright, sweetheart. On the pull now you're single, eh? How's the thrush?"'

'What did you say?'

'I said that my tongue was still a little inflamed but on the whole it was much better.'

Andy sniggered. Michelle, finally realising the power of the silent W, covered her mouth, before punching Andy on the arm.

Andy looked up to the clock on the waiting room wall. 'Jesus. Why's it takin so long?'

'I don't think there's a set time for this sort of thing.'

'My sister's been around, though. You wouldn't think there'd be that much resistance, if you know what I mean.'

'Aye, but the poor wee lassie's probly got your family head. That thing'd get stuck in the Channel Tunnel.' Andy tried to think of a response but his brain was too tired. With every blink it became harder to open his eyes and ...

*   *   *

Michelle was snoring in his ear, that much Andy knew. There were others around him as well. People. The opening. Hospital. The baby.

'Cornelius!' he cried, waking Michelle up with a jolt.

'What, urrgh,' she managed to snort before snapping the string of drool that hung between her mouth and Andy's ear.

'It's not Cornelius, Andrew, it's us.'

Andy forced his eyes open and saw three faces beam at him, those of Lionel, Tony and the Jimmy Savile impersonator.

'The three wise men have arrived! We bear gifts of gold, frankincense and myrrh. Or at least what we were able to procure at the 24-hour bakery. Better make sure this macaroni pie isn't too hot when you give it to the baby.'

'Err, thanks,' said Andy as he pulled himself up on his chair as Michelle stretched and yawned next to him. 'It's nice youse're here.'

'Hi,' Michelle said to the septuagenarian with blood-matted blonde hair. 'We've no been introduced.'

'Ay oop love. Nigel's thee name. 'Ow be the parents?'

'Still waitin to find out. Err...I'm no sure how to say this without seemin ungrateful, but I'm not sure a notorious child abuser is what first-time parents want to see havin just brought their bundle of joy to the world.'

The presence of a Savile look-a-like in a hospital was indeed generally regarded as being as welcome as a large doner at Morrissey's breakfast table but Tony stepped forward and placed his arm around his shellsuited new compadre. 'Ah, but you see, Nigel's actually the anti-Savile, aren't you?'

'Aye,' he nodded. 'Bottom fell out t'game when the allegations started. So I thought, 'ow can thee mak money from loorkin like Jimmy Savile these days? So I started doing this act, see. I goes round t'schools warning kids about the dangers of t'kiddy fiddlers. I thought that's what I were t'be doing t'night.'

Tony nodded. 'We had a long talk after we finally managed to stem the blood. Nigel's been teachin me why what Savile did was wrong. I've renounced him as my DJ hero an realise that great music isn't the most important thing in the world.'

Michelle felt Andy rub her back at this point, although he seemed to be unaware he was doing it.

'Yup from now on, John Peel's the man for me. Someone that never faced any allegations of impropriety with underage girls.'

Andy closed his eyes and counted to 10. When he emerged, he decided to address the issue of the vicious attack at his club.

'So, err...sorry Nigel. About you gettin bottled, I mean.'

'Water off t'duck's back, lad. Happens all t'time.'

'But that's shite man, it takes a lot of guts to make the most of a tragedy to reinvent yoursel. Look at Joy Division becomin New Order.'

Michelle yawned loudly. Andy took the hint.

'Anyway,' continued Nigel. 'Tony says it's a little lass your sister's 'avin. Brought her a little gift.'

He handed Andy a baby girl doll, dressed in a pink dress and looking cute as a button.

'That's really nice, Nigel. I'm sure they'll all love it.'

'Aye, sorry it's not new. Usually use it for t'little kiddies I work with to point out all t'areas it's not okay for adults t'touch them.'

Andy handed the doll back to Nigel. 'Right, like I was sayin. Brave to change careers like you did.'

Nigel cuddled the doll and asked if anyone needed anything from the vending machine. When they answered in the negative he went off on his own, drawing uncomplimentary looks from all he passed on the way.

Andy shook his head and turned to his partners. 'Gibby no with youse?'

'He is still at the club. When we left it was just him, what looked to be the female cast of Hollyoaks and that casual who came out when Tony played I Am What I Am as the penultimate track.'

'I don't even want to think about how many free drinks he's givin away to get them to give him favours in return.' He looked up to the clock. 5.30am. What's going on? Please let them be okay, he thought, and tried to remember how to pray.

'WHO'S THE BLEEDIN' DADDY?' Cornelius burst through the doors that led to the delivery suite. He wore a gown, hair net and face mask, which had slipped down to his neck. He was covered in a considerable amount of blood.

Andy and Michelle stood up, holding each other's hand without even realising they had done so.

'Is everythin okay?'

'Yeah man. Emma and I have a daughter. She's...beautiful.' He burst into tears but managed to compose himself and add, 'I want to call her Estelle, after the co-founder of Stax. Emma likes Sophie and called me a stupid fucking prick.'

Michelle ran over to Cornelius and, ignoring the afterbirth smeared over his apron, hugged him.

Andy strode over and tried to avoid falling into the same

trap, what with him having his good Charlatans t-shirt on, but once Cornelius had put Michelle down there was no escaping his tractor beam. 'How's Emma? How's my sister?' Andy gasped as Cornelius hugged him with rib-cracking intensity.

'Well, exhausted. And threatening to kill me if I ever go near her again but yeah, she's good.'

Hands, congratulations and a macaroni pie were offered by Tony and Lionel and warmly received by Cornelius.

'How come you're not at the club?' he asked through a mouthful of pasta and pastry, a combination that would have moved his carb-addicted father-in-law to tears even if the birth of his granddaughter and his son's triumph had not.

'It's way past closin time,' answered Tony. 'The place was jumpin, Cornelius.'

'And Bernard? How was Bernard.'

'Look,' said Andy getting between Cornelius and the other two. 'The club's no really important right now I mean...'

He trailed off as he saw a bike courier, crash helmet on, looking around the waiting room. Eventually he spotted the likely recipients and came over to hand them a postcard.

'What's he sayin now?' sighed Andy as Cornelius held it up to eye level.

'JESUS WAS A DJ,' he read. 'I FORGIVE YOU MY FRIENDS. CONGRATULATIONS.'

'Umm,' mumbled the courier as he backed away. 'Congratulations on the baby. I'm sure you'll be great Dads.'

He left the five of them in peace. Eventually, Cornelius held his palms together and thanked them all from the bottom of his heart for coming. 'But if you don't mind, I'm gonna check on my family. I don't know if Emma's up for visitors yet.'

One by one, they embraced him again and instructed him to pass on their best wishes to Emma and Sophie. Cornelius turned to face his family and friends, feeling like the richest man in the world and eager to get back and gape in wonder at his two favourite girls. He saluted the QNTM crew and turned on his heel, straight into what appeared to be the blood-stained reincarnation of Jimmy Savile, holding a child's doll in one hand and a cup of steaming hot coffee in the other.

'Eee-oop lad. Congratulations. Now, would your little gurl like something to play with?'

The resulting scream outdid anything Emma had managed during childbirth in both volume and pitch.

FORTY-FIVE

Early morning light filtered in through the gunshot wounds in the club's roof. Andy barely had the strength to push the doors open but was pleasantly surprised when he did. The chairs had been neatly stacked while the tables sat face down on upholstered booths to allow access for the rigorous vacuuming and mopping that Gibby had subjected the floor to. Hearing the closeted cleaner hard at work behind the bar, he turned to find he was gazing on a less pleasing sight. Over the weeks and months since he'd first decided to squander his father's legacy, he'd grown used to seeing Gibby wander around semi-naked. What he could never understand is why it was always the top half that was covered.

'I wish you wouldn't do that you know.'

'Mornin, chief. Everythin okay?'

'Apart from your ballsack rubbin on the glasses, everythin's good.'

'I don't want cleanin products ruinin my threads. That a crime now?' He winked. 'Glad Cornelius is sound. He missed an epic night.'

'Didn't he just? Where're the Hollyoaks burds?'

Gibby smiled at him. 'You're no gonna believe this, but there I was in a lock-in with Chelsea, seven of her pals and that homo with the Stone Island tattoo, an I thought, you know what? If they want drink they can pay for it! I'm no gonna to let them use me for free drink on the off-chance one of them opens their legs for me.'

'Really?'

'Absolutely. I very politely asked them to leave an decided to get a headstart on the cleanin.'

Andy was speechless.

'Plus, I don't like bein around gay dudes when I get the comedown horn. If the chicks hadn't been up for it an he was, well...I can't say I wouldn't have gone Ronnie Kray just cos the bone needed buried.'

Andy remained silent.

'Really should Facebook Clive an apologise. Don't worry chief, I've cracked a few out since then so you're safe now.'

'That a relief.'

'Actually thinkin about turnin over a new leaf. Reckon things have run their course with my Angie an that's the reason for all the philanderin an drug-induced bi-curiosity. Tell you what, chief. She's a right tidy piece. If you want to give it a blast you've got my blessin.'

'You're okay, Gibby.'

'Honestly, me an you, we've become big mates over the past few months an that's the type of relationship we have where our exes are...'

'Gibby?'

'Chief?'

'Stop tryin to shag my burd.'

'Fair enough. Can't blame a man for tryin.'

Andy looked around, wishing Gibby hadn't done such a proficient job an there was was more evidence that the past few months had achieved something.

As if reading his mind, Gibby said, 'We totally smashed it here tonight. Well, you really, chief. Busiest I've ever seen it. Let me cover up my WMD and we'll toast our success.'

Andy averted his eyes as Gibby scampered across the dancefloor. The phone by the bar rung and he answered it.

'Hello?...Yeah it's fine...No good...no there aren't any Hollyoaks lassies...I think he's had an epiphany...no you don't need to come down...we're just gonna lock up...go an get some rest...look, Cornelius just cos you've got a mobile doesn't mean you need to use it...okay...I'll let you know...bye.'

Andy hung up just as Gibby sauntered back across the dancefloor. Three things struck Andy about this vision – the bottle of champagne in one hand, the giant spliff in the other, and the boxer shorts that appeared to have been designed for a midget during a time of cotton rationing.

Gibby held the cork between his teeth and twisted the bottle until it popped. He spat the cork out, poured two glasses and sparked the doobie up.

'To QNTM!' he said, raising his glass.

'To family,' said Andy chinking his off Gibby's.

Gibby pulled icy blue smoke deep into his lungs and spoke while exhaling, 'What a night, chief. What a night."

'Except the losin money part.'

'I wouldn't say that.' Andy stared at him and Gibby passed him the spliff. Andy held it in his hands, well away from his mouth as Gibby reached into the back of his boxers.

'There, proceeds of the black economy.' He held out a hefty roll of bank notes for Andy, who indicated it should be left on the bar top and passed him back the joint.

'Much?'

'Enough to cover the shortfall an a good bit more split five-ways. It's a shame we didn't know an accountant who can squirrel this out of the eyes of the taxman for us.'

The phone rang again.

'I'll get it, chief...Hello...My man! Who's the daddy?...Aye... no he wasn't lyin it was great...no, nobody complained about the lack of mirrorball...I don't see how a mirrorball app on your phone would help...yeah I'll tell him...catch you later, chief. Give my best to the missus an the nipper.'

Gibby sat back down, took the last few drags on the joint and stubbed it out on the bar. He looked around the club he thought he had known so well but as it turned out had barely begun to appreciate.

'Know what?' he asked after a few moments' contemplation.

'What?'

'I think he's right. This place does need a mirrorball.'

ACKNOWLEDGEMENTS

Thanks first of all to Vicki Birmingham, my wife, biggest supporter and harshest critic. There isn't enough paper in the world to list all the things my Mum and Dad have done for me so I'll just say thanks for everything. Cheers also to my sister, Nicola, brother-in-law Gordon, nephews Sam and Alex, parents-in-law Harry and Shirley and all the rest of my family.

Big up Stefan Morkis, who is responsible for a goodly chunk of Clubbed to Death, and Barry Phillips for sage advice and letting me ride the crest of his wave.

This book wouldn't have been possible without ongoing support from Linda Isles, Chris Collins, Anna Day, Bob McDevitt, Ross Cargill, Roddy Isles, Chris Brookmyre, Ryan Law, Craig "Scoop" McGregor, Neil Forsyth, Stephen Flynn, Ranald Henderson, Simon Donald, Alan Wilson and Frank Marra.

A shout-out to Luke Ivins for allowing us to hold the old Teckle nights at the City Function Suite and taking us into the inner sanctum of CFS, which in no way inspired this book. Big love to Lindsay and Ian with whom I shared those nights as we inflicted our musical prejudices on an unsuspecting public.

Finally, from the bottom of my heart I would like to express my undying gratitude to Kyle Letheren for the save that won the league.